THE
SEAT

TYLER G. IRWIN

The Seat
Copyright © 2020 by Tyler G. Irwin

For more information, or to contact the author, go to www.TylerIrwinAuthor.com

Digital Marketing by: Bent Liquid LLC
Cover design by: COLONFILM
Interior design by: Gray Dog Press, Spokane, WA
D.Wible poem from: Terre Haute Fairgrounds Action Track Program,
    August 11th, 1963

Softcover ISBN: 978-1-7355510-0-5
eBook ISBN: 978-1-7355510-1-2

Printed in The United States of America

Dedication

For my wife, daughter, and family
who have always helped me realize the meaning and importance of
The Seats I have had.

"Only be thou strong and very courageous . . . "
Joshua 1:7

THE SEAT

CHAPTER 1

Duck Blind

A COLD MORNING. A chalk line of heat surrounding his body under the covers. Remington rolled over and suddenly he was lying on a sheet of ice.

Across the frozen abyss, Remington's alarm clock went off, spurring a chilly journey to stop the clanging of an oaky country song.

"Who listens to this?" Remington mumbled as he slid across the bed to find the snooze button. He sat in a frozen stupor at 4:30 a.m. the last day of the duck-hunting season and a rare opportunity to spend time with his father.

Remington stumbled to his suitcase and rummaged through his belongings until he found his long johns. He slipped them on before deciding a hot cup of coffee would make the laborious process of preparing for a cold morning in a duck blind more manageable. He could already hear the bubbling and hissing of the coffee and his father cracking eggs on the cast iron skillet that had been around as long as he could remember. Light from the old wood stove danced at his feet underneath the bedroom door. He could smell the pinewood as it popped and burned.

Remington slowly opened the door that framed his father's figure working away over the kitchen counter. His father cracked a final egg and started in on frying the sausage he pulled dripping from a bath of maple syrup, Remington's favorite as a child. While much of his father's labor of love remained unchanged, Remington noticed he moved a little slower as he shuffled through the kitchen in his chest-waders and plaid shirt.

"Morning, Dad," Remington said rubbing his hands together over the wood-burning stove.

"Good morning, Rem." Lionel embraced his son, the whiskers of his white stubble clinging to Remington's shirt. "You ready to go bag a limit of ducks today?"

"You know it. It's been way too long since I made some feathers fly."

"Me too. I don't get out nearly enough. Especially with all that has been going on this year."

"I know Pop. This is long overdue for both of us. How about some of that breakfast?" Remington nodded at the sizzling sausage.

"It's ready," Lionel said as he limped back to the kitchen. Remington sipped his cup of black coffee and slid out a chair at the Amish oak table his family had shared so many meals and stories around. While he was excited for the day, there was also a corner of his heart that ached for his father. It was hard to see him getting older. His delicate saunter through their family kitchen nearly brought tears to Remington's eyes.

"Let's eat so we can get to the blind," Lionel said as he set the plates down. They were both halfway through a patty of sausage when Lionel suddenly looked up.

"I darn near forgot to bless this food. I think God will forgive us half a sausage." Lionel chuckled, then cleared his throat. "God, I am so grateful I get to spend this day with my son. You know I cherish these moments and I'm just thankful he is here with me now. Please bless this food to our bodies and, Father, we particularly ask that out of your gracious mercy, you would send some ducks our way. Amen."

A hard chill hung in the morning air as Remington threw a set of decoys over his shoulder and whistled for Pepper, their Labrador retriever. "You all set?" Remington asked.

Lionel stuffed extra hand warmers into his gloves and chest waders. "I'm ready," he said as he grabbed his shotgun. "I'm not as quick as I used to be Rem. Sorry you have to wait on your Old Man."

"You know I don't mind, Dad," Remington said. "I'm going to be the one who regrets not stuffing more of those warmers in my own clothes. Although, with as many as you put in your waders, I'll only need to be in the same blind as you to stay warm."

The first hint of light silhouetted the Mission Mountains and exposed the rafts of mallards, pintail, and teal that had made camp for the night. Pepper whimpered with excitement, sensing the prey even before his masters could see them spread out on the marsh. The waterfowler's heartbeats quickened with the rising sun, and for a moment, they stood in awe of how fortunate they were to be in this special place, and above all, how fortunate they were to simply be together.

Time had assigned new roles to the members of the hunting party. Remington fondly recalled his father bundling him up in oversized hunting gear, putting a hot thermos of cocoa in his gloved hands, and setting him atop a pile of decoys in their inflatable fishing pontoon. He would tie a rope around his waist and tow Remington and all of the gear through the frigid, knee-deep water, to their blind on the end of the point. The vegetation was too thick to brave an on-land journey. Pepper would bound ahead, dashing in and out of the marsh and into the dark forest, causing a mass evacuation of the roosting fowl.

Watching all the easy targets leave the marsh was frustrating for Remington. The concept of shooting hours and fair chase were not as easily embraced as the thrill of blasting away at the unsuspecting game. Lionel would settle him down by having him watch where the ducks landed on the lake so they would know where they'd come from when the pounding of the wind and waves became too great and safe harbor beckoned once again.

This time, Remington carried much of the same gear that served as his seat when he was young, but now it rested on his shoulders. The fishing pontoon had long since been decimated by mice in their garage, but Remington was no longer a boy and could easily carry the gear along the same path they had traveled many times.

"Let me take your gun for you, and you can focus on all those roots that have sprung up under the water," Remington said as he waded in.

"I'm fine. There may be a lot of things I can't do anymore, but I will always carry my own gun."

"You give me the same answer every time," Rem said. "I just want you to be safe."

Remington finished setting the decoys while Lionel organized the blind and positioned himself to hit the tough passing shots this location offered. Very few ducks cupped their wings in commitment to the decoys, but they'd make one or two exploratory passes and then fly toward the calmer toe of the bay, setting the stage for the tricky shooting. The main body of water was to the east, toward the mountains. Lionel and Pepper situated themselves to the bay side of the blind, leaving the first shots to his son.

As much as Lionel lived and breathed to hunt, he experienced no greater joy than watching his son shoulder his Beretta and bring a mallard spiraling to the slough in front of them. Pepper shared the same excitement, the splashdown of a fowl his call to action. When they didn't fall, Pepper gave a scowling look of annoyance as if to ask why they wasted a perfectly good shot shell. Even if the snow was the only thing that tumbled from the sky, the day was already a success: the three of them were together again.

"What do you think?" Remington whispered as he took his seat in the blind. "Is this cold, calm weather going to keep them from flying?"

"I've got a good feeling, Rem. This snow and that wind starting to blow down from the mountains is going to get them moving. See the whitecaps forming on the lake?" Remington grabbed the same Thermos that warmed his hot cocoa and his hands as a kid and poured a cup of black coffee. The Thermos's camouflage coating had long since given way to the shiny metal underneath. Green duct tape served in its place.

"I think you might be right. Coffee? I hope this will be the only chance you have to drink any."

Lionel took the cup from his son's hand as he followed a deer in the sprawling field across from the marsh. He watched until it gracefully vanished into the fortress of ponderosa pines guarding the base of the mountains. Remington holstered the coffee and ensured his shotgun was loaded with three, cherry-red Winchester number twos. It was then he noticed the longing look in his father's eyes. He knew the reason.

"I miss her too, Dad."

Remington watched as a wave of anguish furled his father's brow, driving a tear from his eye. He quickly tried to hide it. Lionel was a man of rare emotion. Neurosurgeons cannot become puppets to feelings when someone's brain is exposed on an operating table. It's an innate gift of great doctors and Lionel Mason was one of the best. But losing your wife to cancer is something no amount of medical training or resolute grit can pull you through. Lionel felt he were on the operating table, a part of his body ripped away, no longer in control, unsure of his prognosis. He had his share of friends, but loneliness wasted no time making camp in his heart and home.

"She was my best friend. We could not have asked for a more lovely woman in our lives. I miss her. To be honest, if it weren't for God in my life, I don't know what I would do. I'd probably still be self-prescribing the Maker's Mark I allowed myself after she passed." Lionel shook his head and quickly gathered his emotions. "Let's not talk about this. Not a moment that goes by that I don't think of her, but this morning belongs to you and me and good old Pepper, just like it used to be."

Remington anxiously snapped the head off a cattail blocking his view from the blind. "I'm glad the God thing is working for you." His face now matched the troubled countenance of his father. "I'm sure it is much healthier than the bourbon but damn it, I just can't forgive Him. I know you were both getting older, but she was so healthy and vibrant." Steam billowed from Remington's lungs as he exhaled. "It just wasn't her time to go. I don't understand why He took her. Do you know how much I worry about you alone in the cabin?"

"You don't need to worry about your old man. I have plenty of friends to help me out if I ever need it."

"You are missing the point, Dad." Remington's tone sharpened as he broke from the whispers of the blind. "I am having a really hard time focusing on all I have going on while you are all the way across the country chopping firewood in the middle of winter."

"Shhhhh." Lionel put his finger to his lips and pointed to the sky. Remington slowly turned his head to locate the flock of ducks whose dark bodies were almost invisible against the mountainous backdrop.

"They're heading this way." Lionel reached for his duck call and began belting out a welcome cackle, interwoven with the subtle staccato garble of the duck's version of an invitation to dine. He continued to call as Remington eyed the birds with his finger on the safety, but the flock of mallards maintained altitude with other dining plans in mind.

Remington shook his head. "Dad, you need to hear me out. I worry about you. Without Mom to help around the cabin, I just don't think it's safe for you to stay here. Montana winters can last the better part of a year. I came up to spend time with you, but I also wanted to ask you to move in with me. I think it would be good for both of us and I wouldn't have to worry about you living like a mountain man up here. At least think it over."

Lionel surveyed the frozen landscape through a thickening curtain of snow. The wind had stopped and all he could hear was the snow gracefully settling on the reeds around their blind, and the occasional sigh from Pepper as he licked snow from his black nose. The silence was comforting.

Lionel softly broke the quietude. "This duck blind has always been an important place for me. I sit on this point, and life — it somehow just makes sense. The everyday worries melt away back there at the cattle guard. Even now that your mom is gone, as I sit here today, I know it is going to be all right." Remington listened intently, hoping Lionel would accept his invitation. "As beautiful as this all is, Rem, I know I am going to see my bride again one day in a place that is even more beautiful than this, as hard as that is to fathom. And I want you to hear me out. I know you are mad at God right now, and you're worried about me, but don't turn your back on Him. The Bible says our thoughts are not His thoughts and that our ways aren't His ways. I'm probably not getting that quite right, but just try to believe that God knows what He is doing. Even though it may not seem like it to us, His plan is perfect. Just trust Him in your own life and trust that He takes care of your old man too, okay?"

After a long pause, Remington collected his thoughts and took his eyes off the horizon. "Look, I appreciate that you and Mom raised me in the church. I just don't feel real spiritual these days. So is that your way of saying you're not going to take me up on my offer?"

A soft smile emerged from under Lionel's frozen mustache. "This is my home, Rem."

CHAPTER 2

Biscayne

THE SOUTH FLORIDA HEAT DRIPPED off Remington. His head spun and his ringing ears told him it was time for a break. His mind reeled as he stepped onto the balcony overlooking Biscayne Bay. He collapsed on the nearest beach chair.

"Rem, come on!" Jax said as he located his best friend. The breeze off the bay was only somewhat comforting, like a paper fan in a sauna.

"Give me a minute, man," Remington mumbled as Jax tried to pull him from the chair. "We've been going hard all day. I need to relax for a few."

"Fine," Jax griped. "Ten more minutes and we're meeting you by the bar, getting you a Red Bull, minus the vodka this time, and heading to the front for the finale. You don't want to miss this. Not to mention, that cute blonde you were talking to? She was asking where you went. Lots of reasons to head back down, man."

"Wouldn't miss it for the world, Jax." Remington took a deep breath and watched the palm fronds sway above him. He tried to relax but the tiny, pulsing, vein of guilt tarnished his heart once again. He laughed it off as he imagined trying to describe EDM music to his father. And the girls — never mind that. Remington wouldn't even venture there.

It was hard to believe how much life had changed over the last four years — how much *he* had changed. At his core, he was the same person he had always been, but he had become a more worldly, educated version of himself. He still acknowledged the spiritual principles his parents had instilled in him, but he was simply at a stage in life and in a city that evoked a sense of adventure he had never experienced before.

Remington closed his eyes and squeezed the bridge of his nose as he sat up. "I deserve this. I deserve to relax. This is my night."

"Look who decided to show up." Jax tossed a Red Bull to Remington.

"I told you ten minutes." Remington smirked and gave Jax a playful punch. "Here I am. Let's do this!" The group of friends parted the sea of spectators and moved to the front of the massive amphitheater. Their Miami Ultra Music Festival VIP seats were cordoned off by a red velvet rope, access granted only after flashing their expensive credentials. Cost was not a concern. They had plenty of reason to celebrate. It was their spring break as college seniors, the real world now imminent. It would be jobs for some, graduate school for others, each going their separate ways.

As the stagehands completed their final sound checks, Jax cupped his hand and yelled to Remington over the clamoring crowd. "You remember how we met, Rem?"

"How could I forget kicking your ass in that kart race? Of course I remember!" Remington puffed up his chest.

"The race you won by punting me into the tire barrier on the last lap?" Jax put his fists up as if he were ready to fight. "I still owe you for that."

They both laughed as the blonde woman who had been talking to Remington earlier broke up the harmless fight by dancing her way between them.

"No, in all seriousness Remington, I wouldn't trade these past four years for anything. Miami, getting our college degrees, working on becoming professional racing drivers." Jax scanned the expansive crowd behind them. "I don't think it gets any better. Still sucks you had to wreck me so we could become friends. Did I ever tell you I saw stars for a week when I closed my eyes after that wreck? Still wouldn't trade it though." Jax raised his beer. "To us, man. One of us USAC boys needs to make it to the big leagues and show 'em how it's done."

Every time Remington walked into the room, he paused to bask in the nostalgia. The subjects surrounding him tugged at every fiber of his being, a catalyst for the passion he so readily pursued.

Foyt – Hurtubise – Wheldon – Vukovich – Clark – Sachs – Kenyon – Andretti.

The walls read like a who's who in motorsports history, highlighting triumph and defeat, passion and tragedy. Every time Remington flipped the light switch, he could almost feel these pillars of open wheel racing looking down upon him. A few of his own trophies and pictures hung on the wall, and Remington was determined to follow in the footsteps of those who claimed their stake in the upper echelons of motorsport, all of whom sacrificed, some with their lives. Remington was willing to do the same to inhale the shared, elusive air as his heroes.

Jax strutted through the race shop door, startling Remington. "I swear man, every time I walk in here I find you staring at these walls. Maybe if you did a little more work on your car you might have a few more trophies up there yourself." They both laughed as the rest of their small team filtered into the shop and began final preparations for the day. It was their first car race of the new season, and their college graduation. While racing professionally was the dream, getting their college degrees was a crucial step to navigating modern motorsports. No longer was racing merely about driving cars as fast as your courage permitted. The world of motorsport had evolved into a multibillion-dollar marketing machine where business savvy and financial backing were just as important as driving ability. Without them, drivers got swallowed in an abyss of one-season wonders, with shattered dreams and flat wallets.

Young drivers, often with more money than talent, predominated in motorsports. The day where a hometown kid raced his way to the top with sheer determination, not reaching the pinnacle of his career until 30 or even older, had been replaced by virtually unknown drivers filling out entire starting fields. A few of these "kids" went on to become staples in their sport, but the days of rooting your small-town hero to victory through the course of a blossoming career had sadly been buried under the mounds of dollars it took to race successfully at any level. Remington knew he had to have financial backing to race, but he was determined to avoid the list of forgotten drivers. He wanted to do it his way, the old-school way, like his heroes on the wall.

One of Remington's racing heroes, Bill Vukovich, was a testament to the older, rockier road to racing glory. One of eight children, Vuky grew up on a California farm owned by his parents, immigrants from Yugoslovia. Vuky's father committed suicide on his fourteenth birthday and he and his brother were forced to drop out of high school to support the family. Vuky discovered in the early 1930s that he could actually get paid to drive race cars and not long after that, unearthed his first opportunity to get behind the wheel. Car owner, Fred Gerhardt, gave him the seat. Vuky would soon win races for Gerhardt while developing a lifelong friendship and emerged as a Southern California hometown hero. Racing was in Vuky's blood.

Vuky settled for repairing trucks and Jeeps during World War II after being sidelined from the war with a racing injury. He saved $750 to buy his own midget racing car, and he became a California Midget racing champion in 1945 and 1946.

Vuky's first attempt at qualifying for the Indianapolis 500, the pinnacle of motorsports achievement, was in 1950 at the age of 31, a stark contrast to the 19 and 20 year olds making their first attempts at 500 glory today. Vuky failed to qualify in 1950, but in 1952 he finished his first Indianapolis 500 after leading nearly the entire race until mechanical failure slowed him with just eight laps remaining. Vuky qualified his Fuel Injection Special on the pole position in 1953 and won his first Indianapolis 500. Vuky returned to Indianapolis a legend and fan favorite in 1954 to win the race for a second time.

With a coveted third Indianapolis 500 victory in sight, Vukey returned to the Speedway in 1955. Fate had other plans. Early in the race, his Lindsey Hopkins Special went careening over the outside wall and ultimately ruptured into flames.

Bill Vukovich had a legendary career and had amassed a loyal group of fans and admirers. But like so many of his contemporaries, his life was cut tragically short by the ruthless sport he loved so much. The very same grit that inhabited Bill Vukovich's blood, also poured through Remington's veins. While his father had helped support his racing, he was not one of the new-age drivers buying his way to the top. Remington was cut from the same cloth as his heroes and was determined to prove it.

CHAPTER 3

Mortarboard

"THANKS POP. I really wish you could be here." Remington wedged his cell phone between his shoulder and ear as he and Jax took one more look at their Beast Midget chassis before their teams pushed them into their haulers. Occasionally, a final eyeballing of the car caught a critical oversight that could have been disastrous on the track, or cause the car to cross the razor-thin line between victory and defeat.

"I wish I could be there too. I am so proud of you," Lionel said. "You've worked hard to get to this point. I know your mother would have been proud, too. She worried so much about you, Rem. I think it was more about you living in Miami than strapping into the race car every weekend. I know she would give anything to see you graduate today."

"I know, Dad. I miss her. I owe so much to both of you. All the time and money you invested in my racing and in me." Remington signaled to his crew to close the hauler door. "I think about all the tracks we traveled to when I was racing quarter midgets, and how you and Mom did your best to make our trips about more than just racing. You made them about learning and family. I appreciate you two making that effort. That's probably why I'm getting my college diploma today."

As the haulers pulled away from the shop to head to the racetrack, Jax tapped his watch to let Remington know it was time to leave for campus. Remington nodded and disappeared into the shop lounge to grab his gown, tassel, and mortarboard.

"I have to get going, Dad," Remington said. He threw his helmet in his race bag and slung it over his shoulder along with his graduation garb.

"All right, but don't forget to give me a call after your race. I can't relax until I hear your voice."

"I know. I'll call you as soon as I get back to my pit stall. I might have to make a quick stop in victory lane first. I love you, Pop."

"I love you too, Rem."

Lionel hung up the phone as he walked into his library. He sat in his leather chair, tracing the edge of a framed picture of him and Remington, taken after his son's first victory. He asked God to guide his boy into whatever new endeavors lay ahead. While the thought of Rem racing professionally scared him, Lionel knew how much it meant to his son and he pleaded with God to make his dream come true. After all, it had become their dream.

With a flurry of hats streaking across the sky, and the shouts of a few thousand college students, it was over. Remington was a college graduate. He stood beaming in the midst of the chaos, proud of his accomplishment. A defining period in his life had come to a close, but Remington looked to the future with hope. A new race season was upon them and with his head now freed from the endless pages of textbooks, he could put what he'd learned to practice trying to land a sponsor to usher him to the next level of his racing career.

"Can you believe this, Jax? We are done! We are college graduates." Jax gave a loud holler as Remington approached him and his family. In essence, they had adopted Remington as a second son over the past four years.

"So proud of you buddy." Jax embraced Remington. His family followed suit.

"Congratulations, Rem," said Jax's father. "It has been fun having you around. Thanks for taking such good care of our son."

Rem said, "Lord knows he needed it." Jax's younger sister twirled her gum on her index finger and adamantly agreed. "No, in all seriousness, I could not have asked for a better friend. And thank you guys for everything you have done for me as well. By the way, Dad wanted me to say hello."

"How is he doing, Rem?" asked Jax's mother. "It broke our hearts when Jax called and told us your mother had passed. He said you were taking it pretty tough."

"Dad is getting by all right I guess. He always talks about his faith pulling him through and it seems to work for him. I just keep focused on racing. Honestly, I worry more about him being alone up there in Montana than anything."

"I am sure you do, Rem. I know how close you two are." Jax's mother flashed him a warm smile as she squeezed the back of his arm. "If there is anything we can do, please don't hesitate to ask."

"Thanks. You ready to ditch this party and go have some real fun? We are already missing practice time and we all know Jax needs as much help as he can get. Let's head to the track. Race season is on!"

As they approached the track, the floral aromas of early spring mingled with the burnt methanol still hanging in the air from the earlier practice sessions, an intoxicating elixir for a race driver, signaling the dawn of a new season. The excitement, the nerves, the anticipation, the focus: the culmination sent Remington's heart soaring and boulders tumbling through his stomach. To once again feel the vibration of the steering wheel in his hands delivering minute messages from the racing surface; to feel the car rocket forward as he squeezed the throttle in response to those messages: it was magical. For Remington, going to the track was like coming home. Amidst the danger, the noise, the fierce competition and the screaming fans was a place of solitude, a place where Remington was most himself.

As Jax's father pulled his Escalade up to the track, the stadium lights were just warming up and the sun lazily fading behind the turn two grandstands. The bleachers were already crawling with fans excited for the start of a new season and the party that goes with it. Beers slid into their koozies as the announcer excitedly proclaimed the action about to unfold, and trophy girls waved as they completed parade laps sitting on the back of rumbling muscle cars. It was a scene played out on short-track stages around the country as the curtain raised every Friday and Saturday night, and Remington thrived at the epicenter of it all.

"Good luck," said Jax's mom as they swung the Escalade parallel to the pit gate. "We'll be cheering you on from turn four. Go get 'em, boys!" Both young men flashed their credentials to the attendant at the pit gate who waved them through, wishing them both good luck. With nods and waves from their fellow racers, they headed straight to their team haulers and slipped into their driving suits. They had already missed the practice sessions and were in jeopardy of not posting qualifying times without a dose of hustle.

"How's the car look?" Remington asked his mechanic, Mark, as he came out of the hauler with his helmet and his head and neck support, or HANS device.

"I think we are good to qualify, Rem." They discussed the setup in detail as Remington organized the belts in his driver's seat. "Tire pressures are set, the engine is up to temp and based on our notes from last season, I think we have the right shock and spring combination for this track. You were fast here last year, and we have the same setup on the car."

Remington circled the car as Mark continued to give him the rundown on the preparation done prior to his arrival. Rem checked every nut and bolt, gave the drive shaft a quick twist to ensure it was free, and used his thumb to spit-shine any blemish obscuring his sponsor's bright logo.

"Drivers to your cars, drivers to your cars," the pit announcer said over the loud speakers. "Drivers to your cars for qualifying."

"All right," Remington said with a nod. He put on his fire-proof head sock, slipped his HANS device over his shoulders and fastened it to the locks on the side of his helmet. "Let's go try to put old number seven on the pole!"

Remington climbed through the top of his open-wheel race car that was equally built for speed and safety: a high-horsepower front engine, a fuel cell inside a tail cone, and a cockpit sandwiched between the two. It was like strapping yourself to a rocket wrapped in a chromoly tubing chassis, meticulously fabricated to shield the driver during high impacts. The advanced engineering of the cars fused with the daring skill of the men and women who piloted them made for some of the most exciting racing in the world.

Remington settled into his race seat as Mark began latching the harnesses and straps designed to keep Remington and his limbs inside the roll cage. Midget and sprint car wrecks can be spectacularly violent, cars often catapulting through the air and bouncing like pinballs off concrete walls and other cars. Remington was eternally grateful to Mark and the engineers who worked to keep him safe.

Mark cinched Remington's lap belt with a crescent wrench. "Too tight, Rem?"

"Just right," Remington said as he pulled on his gloves and took a deep breath. "Let's go do this!"

"All right bud, be smooth out there. We didn't get any practice laps in, so let's just take the first couple laps easy, give everything a little shake-down, and then see what we can get from there." Out of superstitious habit, Mark patted the nose of the car then pushed Rem into the qualifying line. Remington did not hear a word he said. Even if he had, there was no going easy in time trials: a good qualifying run could make or break an entire race day.

Jax's family yelled as static gave way to the race announcer over the loud speaker. "And coming to the track is the number seven machine of Remington Mason. Folks, get on your feet and cheer last year's runner-up to the national champion as he gets on the throttle going down the backstretch."

Mark fidgeted the stopwatch in his hand as he fumbled to press the lap timer. "First race jitters, just breathe," he said to himself.

Mark had been a racing mechanic his entire life and knew most of the other drivers and mechanics in the pits, but Remington Mason had carved out a special place in his heart. In his seventies, Mark had lived through the earlier days of racing where safety was slipshod and human life considered expendable in pursuit of championships. He had lost a number of friends to the sport and vowed to never get close to another driver. But the bond he built with Remington had given life to his ailing bones as he approached one of his last seasons as a mechanic.

"Folks, he is really on it now. Inches from the wall out of turn number four — and there's the green flag! Three laps is all he has, all he has to get the quickest time of the night. Looking good through one and two and rocketing down the backstretch. Turns three and four get ready: coming right at ya. Oh! A little loose through the corner but great recovery. This kid is phenomenal! Can he pull it off? Get on your feet and bring him home. White flag and four more turns to go."

Mark watched the timing and scoring board, still unable to get his trembling hands to start his own stopwatch. "A little slow through turns one and two. Too loose. Too loose. Come on Rem. The motor sounds good. Let's go. Run a little higher line through three and four. Come on." Mark paced nervously in and out of the other mechanics gathered on the front row of the pit grandstands.

The loud speaker boomed once again, startling Mark as the tenths of seconds continued to accumulate on the timing board. "The checkered flag is waving and here comes Remington Mason to the finish line. 15.17 seconds! Not a bad run at all. I'm sure it's not what the seven team was hoping for, but that should put them solidly near the top for tonight's main event."

Mark was already back at the pit stall laying out tools and a brand new set of sticker tires when Remington brought his car to a stop. The methanol fumes burned Remington's eyes as he turned off the fuel, causing the motor to roar as it starved itself out. Mark hurried to his side to help him out of the car.

"Not bad, Rem. Especially with no practice. You ran a 15.17. We should be looking at fifth place. Only two more cars to qualify, neither top-tier teams. I have a few changes I think will help us out." Mark scurried into the hauler as Remington climbed from the car, then came shuffling back down the ramp with a mound of shocks and springs balanced in his arms.

Remington laughed as he approached. "Just a few changes, huh? We'll be just fine, Mark. It was a little loose through three and four but it should tighten up now that the sun is down and the track is cooling."

"Trust me on this one Rem. A couple of tweaks to the shocks and springs and you will be on rails tonight." Mark put the car up on jack stands and began to work.

CHAPTER 4

Green, Green, Green!

REMINGTON FLIPPED THE FUEL SWITCH to the on position, unleashing potent methanol to rage through the veins of his machine. The back of his helmet bounced on his seat as the push truck hurled him forward, bringing a 400-horsepower metallic heart to life with a guttural growl and a surge of energy. Remington waved-off the truck and began veering his car back and forth to warm his tires.

The tension heightened with each new car that roared to life, the field of competitors eagerly awaiting the final push trucks to exit the track. The drivers quickly jabbed their throttles, depositing fresh layers of Hoosier Tire rubber on a track that had been washed clean by the spring rains. It was a temporary cure for the fix they had craved all winter, to be racing once again.

There were no lines at the restrooms and mustaches were wiped clean after sipping a fresh head of foam off a second beer. Parents placed earmuffs on their excited children, pointing at the field of cars as they rumbled by. The flagman waved a dual set of checkered flags as the cars came out of the final turn and onto the main straightaway, lined up in perfect formation as a salute to the swarm of cheering spectators. Fans raised their hats in acknowledgment to the waving gloved hands of their favorite warriors about to enter battle, and the drivers' girlfriends, wives, and families sat silently, asking God to protect their loved ones.

Three more laps and the nerves would be gone. Remington never understood the phenomenon. Maybe adrenaline overwhelmed his nerves or maybe it was the unwavering focus it took to drive fast laps. After the first green-flag lap, the tight fists in Remington's stomach and the pulse of his heart pounding in his temples would be replaced with an icy determination and focus. One lap to reform after the grand salute, one final warm-up lap and the new season would be in full swing. The flagman presented a rolled up green flag, signaling the field that the next time they crossed the start/finish line it would be at 150 miles per hour.

Remington gave his racing harness a final tug to ensure it was tight and cracked his visor open to clear the condensation that had collected on it from his heavy breathing.

"Okay, this is what you live for," Remington said, coaching himself through the final pace lap. "It's who you are. Now make it count." He slapped his visor shut and squeezed the steering wheel like a stress ball. The importance of this season weighed heavily upon Remington. Good finishes were imperative to attract sponsors. Without them, there was no guarantee of making it to the next level, or even the next race.

The field of cars built momentum going down the backstretch as they entered turn number three. The pole sitter determined the pace of the start, and with first-race-jitters running high, Remington could sense the field quickening at the leader's anxious command. The cars were nearly full throttle at the apex of the turn. Remington would typically hold back to get a jump on the car in front of him, but he dared not even breathe his throttle at this pace. Slowing his car would spell certain disaster, an avalanche of trailing cars ready to swallow him.

A fraction of a second later, the first green flag of the season waved in the warm spring breeze setting free an ocean of pent-up nerves as right feet found floorboards. The field morphed into a blurred mural of neon colors as the cars careened into turn one. Remington backed off the throttle and gently squeezed the brakes as he closed on the rear bumper of the second-place car. G-forces lunged from the apex of the corner, pinning him to his seat. Before they could relinquish their grip, he was back on the throttle. The sudden acceleration snapped the back of his car toward the outside wall as he and the second place car blew by the pole-sitter going down the backstretch.

Remington repeated the same process going into turn three, inches away from what was now the lead car. Any lingering nerves vacated his stomach as he focused on his driving routine, one he had rehearsed his entire career. Every driver had their own style. Remington had mastered a perfect concoction of a calm, smooth precision topped with an occasional dash of timely aggression. His record spoke to its effectiveness.

The fifty-lap feature event was quickly approaching the crossed white and green flags, signaling the midway point of the race. Remington began lap twenty-six still tied to the lead car's bumper, unable to make a pass.

Compared to Remington's relatively static race, Jax had entered the picture after overcoming a bad qualifying run to find himself running fourth.

"C'mon boys! C'mon," Jax's father yelled. Neither of his drivers were able to take the point. "They have to make a move," he said to his wife, who was only slightly better at controlling her nerves.

"It's okay sweetie." She smiled and patted his leg. "Rem is right there and has plenty of time. He'll make a move when the time is right. He's going to force the leader into a mistake. I'm calling it now. Your boy is doing just fine too. He's already made up eight spots."

The flagman bowed to the field, waving five fingers at the cars roaring down the front stretch beneath him. Upon his cue, gaps between cars instantly closed and tires chattered for mercy as they slid through the turns. The last five laps of a short-track midget race are a wild skirmish to the finish line as drivers madly siphon every ounce of speed from their machines. Every position counted and every driver knew it.

Jax made a bold move to the outside going through turn two to take over third position. Remington's number seven car was next in line. Jax pushed hard to reel him in. Like many times before, the race was shaping up as a showdown between friends.

With three laps remaining, Remington pressured the first-place driver to make a mistake so he could attempt a move for the lead. With Jax now breathing down his neck, it was time to strike or be struck. Sweat burned Remington's eyes as the back straightaway melted away once again. His arms felt heavy as fatigue set in, a result of the G-forces repeatedly punishing him lap after lap, trying to rip his helmet from his head. He pushed harder. There was no time to let anything derail him. All the hours in the gym during the off season were paying off, allowing his mind to forget the pain and focus on hunting his first win of the year.

And then, it happened. Remington noticed the first place car enter turn three a few inches lower than it had the rest of the race. This subtle clue tripped his reflexes to action and he drove his car into turn three a few inches higher than usual. The principles of loose and tight were at play. When a race car is loose, the back end of the car begins to slide toward the outside of the track during cornering. When tight, a driver steers through a corner and the car does not turn, instead pushing to the outside of the track toward the wall.

No one in the stands could have noticed the lead driver shifting his line by inches, but minor calculations by drivers could pay major dividends, or spell disaster. Remington knew that by entering the turn lower, the centrifugal force of the lead car would push it to the outside wall more quickly than on previous laps, scrubbing off speed and maybe even causing the driver to back off the throttle to avoid contact. By entering the corner higher, Remington could get on the throttle and make his car loose, unlocking the ability to dive under the lead car as it drifted toward the front stretch wall. It had worked before.

The phone startled Lionel as he removed his reading glasses and set them on the cluttered table where he was adding the red feathers to a Royal Wulff fishing fly. He never tied his best work while his son was at a race, but it kept his nerves in check until he heard Remington's voice on the other end of the line. The occasional confused cutthroat trout would bite the gluey mess of ruffled feathers, but that was not the point of his work on race nights.

Lionel picked up the telephone and heard the familiar buzz of post-race commotion.

"Hey Pop," Remington said, "how are you?" Remington paced in his hauler while Mark readied the car to be loaded and fans lined up near his pit stall with hopes of snagging an autograph.

"I'm good. How did it go?" Lionel asked.

"It was good," Remington said. "Good outcome, but a tough race. I ran second most of the night with Jax knocking on the door behind me. I made a move for the lead with three laps to go. I thought I had it dialed in, but the car pushed coming out of the corner and I had to let off the throttle to keep from hitting the leader. Ended up second."

"That's great, Rem," Lionel said. "I would consider that a success."

"I don't think we had the car set up quite right. It would have been nice to at least run a few practice laps. Glad I only have to graduate once."

Lionel chuckled alone in his library.

"All right, Dad." Remington waved to the group of fans from the back of the hauler. "I've got a line of people out here wanting an autograph and some kids hoping to sit in the car and snag a picture. Looks like there may even be a couple of cute girls in the line."

Lionel laughed again. "Sounds good, son. Keep those fans happy. I love you."

"I love you too. Talk to you soon."

Remington posed for a final picture as the remaining race haulers exited the pits. While Mark double-checked all the tie downs in the trailer, Remington dismissed himself and slid onto the first row of metal bleachers overlooking turn 4. The seats were void of life except for the hatches of curious bugs swirling around the stadium lights. Remington could still feel the steering wheel fighting his hands and the horsepower of the cars reverberating through his body. He pushed the events of the day aside and took a moment to quiet his mind. As the stadium lights began shutting off with a click, Remington couldn't help but feel grateful. Grateful for the day and excited for a new season of life.

CHAPTER 5

Summer Night

A WARM BREEZE blew off the ocean as Remington kicked back in his beach chair. He clicked on his iPad and began scrolling through pages of race results and performance data compiled during the first half of the season. The can spiraling carelessly through the air was the only other thing to capture his attention. Remington looked up just in time to catch the airborne beverage.

"Are you kidding me?" Jax yelled as Remington cracked open the beer. "I was trying to gun-down that iPad so you'll come chill with your friends. Seriously, it's our mid-season break and you are studying sector times. Get a life, bro!"

Remington took a swig of the suds, toasted Jax in spite, and threw the iPad in his bag. In a swift motion, Remington sprang from his chair, stole an inner tube from a brunette woman standing next to him, and sprinted into the surf. A water fight erupted as he was promptly pursued by his friends.

The salt water stung Remington's eyes, and before he could see to fire back, he found himself under siege from the woman whose tube he had taken, playfully attempting to steal back what was hers. Her skin was warm on his back as she tried to wrestle him from the tube and Remington could smell the coconut sunscreen she had rubbed on before they jumped in. "You are going to need to tell me your name if you want this tube back," Remington said, running into deeper water as she clung tighter to him.

"You think so, huh?" she said, grabbing Remington's muscular shoulders and dunking him under the water with two hands. She screamed as he grabbed her ankle and pulled her under with him. They splashed their way to the surface laughing and out of breath, the inner tube their only reprieve. "Fine, I guess I'll be the one to keep us both from drowning. I'm Jersey. Jersey Antonelli." She smiled and stuck out her hand as a peace offering.

"Remington Mason. Nice to meet you, Jersey," Remington said as he grasped her hand. "I guess this tube is big enough for both of us. Not to mention, we may need it to get back to shore." Remington nodded toward the beach where the rest of their friends had already started in on another round of drinks. "Jump on, I'll swim us back."

Jersey climbed on top of Remington and put her arms around his neck. She could feel his strong arms and back working underneath her as he began paddling them to shore. She did not care that her friends were already back on the beach. She was in no hurry to join them.

Remington squeezed another lime into his drink and continued a flirtatious conversation with his new friend. Jax was right — he needed to lighten up and enjoy his time off. It felt good to cut loose a little. But racing was never far from his thoughts and often spilled over into his conversations. To keep rising through the ranks, he'd have to minimize any distractions, including the beautiful blue eyes, white smile, and red lips on the face of the woman sitting at the end of his beach chair.

As the sun made its final plunge over the horizon, water was dumped from empty coolers and sand shaken from beach towels. Having pretended it was full all afternoon, Remington threw away only his second beer of the day. He hugged his friends goodbye and offered to drive anyone home who needed a lift.

As Remington was unlocking his truck, he felt a hand gently grab his shoulder. His heart pounded with anticipation, knowing whose it was. He had selfishly avoided telling Jersey goodbye to make it easier on himself, to avoid having to tell her he was too in love with racing to ask for her number, to tell her she was a distraction. He turned around to her piercing blue eyes and long black hair. The moonlit sky made her hot orange bikini glow on top of her tan, toned body. His heart sank.

"Oh, hey Jersey," Remington said. "There you are. I was trying to find you to say goodbye."

"Really? You walked right by me on the beach."

"Are you kidding?" Remington mumbled, feeling bad for lying and already regretting what he knew he had to tell her. He had been staring at her all day, including when he walked by her on the way to his truck. She was stunning and there was something more to her. Whatever it was, Remington had never seen it in any girl before, especially in Miami. She had the look, but somehow just didn't fit in. She moved with a sense of peace, confidence, and wholeness.

After an awkward pause, Remington finally tripped through some hastily chosen words. "I really enjoyed spending time with you today, Jersey, but I'm really not . . . " He paused, words abandoning him as Jersey looked into his eyes. Their lips drew close. Jersey grabbed the back of his arm. Remington turned away. "I'm sorry, I can't."

"What makes you think I was going to let you?" Jersey asked in a matter-of-fact voice.

Remington was caught off guard by her response. "I am so sorry. I just . . . never mind. I feel like an idiot," Remington said.

After letting him twist in the wind for a few seconds, Jersey laughed. "Don't. I was actually just going to ask you for a ride home since you offered. The girls I came with are hitting the clubs."

"You don't want to go with them?" Remington asked.

"Not really my thing to be honest with you. I don't drink at all and that seems to pretty much be what they do there. I noticed you didn't drink much today yourself. Not quite like your friend Jax in that regard. What holds you back?"

Temporarily freed from the clutches of the awkward moment, Remington nodded in the direction of his truck and opened the door for Jersey. "Jump in. I'll tell you." He offered her his hand as she climbed in the passenger seat. "Pretty simple really. It's a stumbling block between me and what I want out of life and I'm not willing to let any distractions get in the way. Especially as our mid-season break wraps up over the next couple of weeks and we get back to racing full time. That's it. Not that I haven't had crazy nights, just not during the season."

"Jax told me you were a phenomenal race car driver. He said if anyone was going to make it straight from the midgets to IndyCar, it would be you." She smiled at him.

"Well, that is kind of him, but that's a big jump to make. Most guys spend a couple of years in the Indy Lights feeder series first, but he's right, it would be nice. Jax is a great driver himself. We just see things a little differently off the track." Remington put his truck in gear, rolled down the windows, and pulled off the beach. "So what do you do, Jersey?"

"Marketing for a retail chain right now, but I actually just applied for a job with Sebring International. I've always wanted to work in motorsports."

Jersey was cut off by Remington's cell phone vibrating in the center console. "I'm so sorry. I have to take this. It's Jax. Probably still drunk on the beach wondering where everyone went." Remington winked at Jersey and answered his phone.

"Hello?"

"Buddy!" Jax yelled in a slow, drawn-out voice. "You aren't fooling me man!"

"What are you talking about?" Remington looked puzzled.

"I saw you and Jersey take off together! You know exactly what I mean. Don't try and hide this from your bro," Jax slurred. "You two are hooking up!"

Remington whispered Jersey an apology as he lowered the phone from his ear, shaking his head while Jax rambled on in the background. She had to have heard him.

"Hey, listen bud, not at all what's going on," Remington said.

"Don't *even* tell me that. Dude, she is so hot."

"Jax, stop! Yes, she is gorgeous but she's cool, man. She's different. Plus, I am married to racing right now with no plans to cheat on it. It wouldn't be fair to either of us to pursue a relationship. So, you should probably go sober up so you can get your facts straight. You have a ride home?"

After an uncomfortable pause, Jax's voice came back through the phone. "So, why is she in your truck then?"

"Jax, I'm taking her home because her friends are as drunk as you!" Jersey was laughing in the passenger seat. "Okay buddy. I'm hanging up. You be safe tonight."

"Yeah, yeah, always the responsible one. So annoying!" Remington shook his head. "I'm just pulling your chain, Rem. You're a good guy. I had fun today. Night man."

"Ditto, buddy. Thanks for keeping things exciting." Remington hung up.

"Wow," he said as he merged onto the interstate. "Sorry about that. Jax is a great guy but he does love to party. I hope that didn't embarrass you?"

"Are you kidding me?" Jersey said. "That was great entertainment. Please do not apologize." They continued to laugh and talk until Remington parked his truck in front of Jersey's Art Deco townhouse.

"Well, this is me, here. Thank you for the ride home, Rem."

Remington hesitated putting his truck in park, knowing it would do the same to their conversation. His unwavering dedication to racing was his shield, but the unabating darts of romance that had pelted his mind all day had temporarily rendered it useless. All he could think about was how cute Jersey looked wrapped in her little blue hoodie, the beach towel unable to cover her long legs, and the smell of strawberries permeating the cab as she applied a fresh layer of lip gloss. It had to be intentional; she wasn't making this easy.

"Your truck okay?" Jersey asked. Her question jarred him from thought.

"Yeah, it's fine. Sometimes park gets a little sticky," Remington said in a fraudulent attempt to cover for his momentary disappearance. "As much as I wish it wouldn't go into park and we could keep driving, I'm sure you are probably tired." Remington easily slipped the truck into park, further exposing his phony alibi.

"Oh, looks like you got it!" Jersey said, playing along.

"I guess I did," Remington said reluctantly as Jersey cracked open the door. "It was really a pleasure to meet you today, Jersey."

"It was a pleasure to meet you as well, Rem. Can I call you that?" Jersey asked as she rummaged through her bag.

"Of course you can."

"Here's my business card. It has my cell on it. Give me a call sometime. I would love to come watch you race." Jersey smiled as she hopped out of the truck and waved goodbye with her fingers. "Thanks for the lift. Have a good night, Rem."

Remington pulled away from Jersey's house and once out of sight around the block, mashed the accelerator in frustration. As much as he loved racing, Remington felt he had missed an opportunity. That he had let an amazing woman slip away. Maybe a relationship with someone of Jersey's caliber would have been good for his career, a positive distraction. It was a moot point, he would probably never see her again and whatever spark may have been was extinguished with the closing of his passenger door.

Remington sat in his truck at home, unable to shake Jersey from his mind. He slid her business card through his fingers before tapping it nervously on his dashboard. It was one in the morning, and sleep was the last thing on his mind.

Remington laced his running shoes as a song pumped heavy guitar riffs through his headphones. He locked the front door behind him and took to the street with a mission.

CHAPTER 6

Boardroom

REMINGTON SHOVED A DOLLAR BILL into the plastic container beside the cash register and moved to the end of the counter to wait for his iced Americano. It was only 6:30 a.m., but there was already a lively buzz in the cafe as a warm breeze filtered in.

"Iced hazelnut Americano for Rem?" the barista said.

Remington grabbed his drink and meandered to a quiet corner of the patio. A stand of sabal palms moved in step with the smooth jazz that pumped life into the bustling shop. The first sips of caffeine filtered through him as he took a moment to watch the horizon bow down to the first rays of sunshine coming over the ocean. His Oakley sunglasses were already in place. Remington was rarely unprepared, especially this morning.

Remington snapped open his laptop, not wasting another second. Two more hours and he would be presenting his proposal to one of the hottest companies in Miami. Above all, presenting himself. He had pored over the data hundreds of times: the benefits of sponsorship; the potential costs; the race schedule; the TV and radio broadcasts; business-to-business marketing opportunities; promotional appearances; even a professionally rendered mockup design of his car and hauler with the company's logo. It was all there. Didn't matter. Remington's compulsiveness drove him to review it once more before he reached across the boardroom table to grasp hands with the CEO of Flux Energy Liquor. Remington knew he could deliver on the track. He had his entire life. Now, it was time to wow the suits.

Remington tucked a lock of hair behind his ear as he looked at his reflection in the truck window. He took a gamble on the peach tie, the primary color of the vibrant Flux logo. It offset his gray suit and black shirt and perfectly matched his neatly folded pocket square. No detail was spared. Remington felt so close he could taste it. His future tasted like Flux Energy Liquor.

Chet Buckner, the CEO and founder of Flux Energy Liquor, could construct the bridge that would deliver Remington to the next level, and he was close to meeting the potential architect. Four more floors to be exact. The elevator came to a halt just shy of the roof in one of the most beautiful high rises in Miami. The silent opening of the elevator door was the green flag and he prepared his mind and nerves just as he did in the race car. He stepped off the elevator with steely determination. At the end of a long hallway proudly displaying beautifully lit bottles of Flux products, he was warmly greeted by a receptionist wearing a short black cocktail dress. Quiet dance music echoed through the hallway. Remington felt more like he had just entered the VIP section of a club than a multi-million dollar company.

"You must be Mr. Mason, here to see Mr. Buckner?" the receptionist asked in a soothing voice.

"Yes ma'am." Remington nodded politely as she slid from behind her desk.

"Follow me, please. Before I take you in to see Mr. Buckner, he asked that I first escort you to the Flux Ice Room." The woman took him to a black door just down the hall, pushed it open, and motioned for Remington to follow. He stepped into a vibrant lounge and was immediately greeted by another woman wearing the same dress as the receptionist.

"Mr. Mason, this is Jessica. She will be taking care of you and I will be back in ten minutes. Enjoy!"

Jessica appeared excited to show off the lavish room. "Mr. Mason, welcome to the Flux Ice Room. Please feel free to take a look around." Jessica continued to talk while Remington took in the impressive display of Flux products. "You may have seen this room before. This is where we filmed our 'Flux, Paint the Town' commercial that is currently airing. We have also hosted numerous celebrities here and even filmed music videos. The room is getting quite a little reputation around Miami." Ice boxes built into the wall around the room housed individual bottles of Flux. Each chamber contained a unique flavor of the drink and black lights drew out the neon colors of the packaging. The dark liquid inside glowed too. On the wall above the ice caves were the words: "Flux: the flow of fluid, particles, or energy. The rate at which light flows." Below the description were the words, "Let the light flow through you!"

Jessica momentarily disappeared behind the bar and came back with a frosted glass.

"Mr. Mason, please pick out a bottle of Flux." Jessica gestured toward the wall of caverns.

"Oh, no." Remington smiled. "You don't have to do that."

"Mr. Buckner insists. We treat all our guests at Flux as VIPs. Try as many as you like," Jessica said as she gently touched Remington's arm. He opened the ice cave containing the original Flux Peach.

"Excellent choice, Mr. Mason." Jessica gave a smile of approval as she placed the bottle on a tray with the chilled glass. "I will have this delivered to the boardroom for you." Remington thanked Jessica kindly, hoping that Mr. Buckner could picture the beautiful peach color splashed on the side of a race car as well as he could.

The receptionist returned to escort Remington to meet Mr. Buckner. She guided Remington through a door that opened to an expansive floor of futuristic-looking see-through cubicles. The entire tier of the building was wrapped in glass, with a panoramic view spanning the Miami skyline and Atlantic Ocean. Neatly tied to the outer edge of the room, a staircase led to an upper floor overlooking the offices below.

The receptionist led Remington past the smiling faces sitting in the cubes, who appeared to be enjoying whatever work they were doing. They climbed the staircase to the penthouse level of executive suites where he was ushered past a row of plush offices toward a boardroom where members of Mr. Buckner's executive team were gathering. His heartbeat quickened. Just a few more steps and Remington would be on the threshold of making his dreams come true. One important presentation was all that divided the two.

"Hey! There he is! There's the man we all came to see, or should I say, came to see us," said Chet Buckner as he walked around the boardroom table to greet Remington. "Hell, you do look like a movie star. Didn't I tell you folks?" Mr.

Buckner displayed Remington to his executive team as if he were his show-and-tell item. "This could be the face of Flux Energy Liquor. Please, call me Chet and have a seat. I'm going to pour you a frosty glass of the elixir of life my receptionist brought up for you. Classic peach. I like the way you think, son."

Mr. Buckner did not exactly strike Remington as a successful businessman with a liquor product that pumped life into the uber rich Miami club scene. He was about a hundred pounds overweight, forehead sweating grease, and a cigar protruded from the corner of his mouth. He wore an ill-fitting taupe suit with a sweat-stained cowboy hat. His bolo tie pulled it all together. But his country ways immediately put Remington at ease.

Remington plugged his laptop into the docking station on the boardroom table and pulled up his presentation as Chet continued to chat with his executive team.

"Did I ever tell you how I found this kid?" Chet asked as he knocked the ash off the end of his cigar. Most of the executive team nodded that he had already told them. "No! Well let me tell you!" Chet repeated the tale of how he and a couple buddies went to a local USAC Midget race Remington won. Chet was so impressed with Remington's victory speech that he came down to the pits after the race. He watched Remington from a distance interacting with fans and his crew. "And that's when it hit me. We need this guy to sell our drinks on the side of a race car!"

That stroke of luck now had the two of them sitting across from each other in the same room: the unpolished businessman and the up-and-coming racing star. An unlikely pair at first glance, but maybe, just maybe Remington could nurture this moment, this relationship, into a full-time ride in the IndyCar Series.

Remington breathed a sigh of relief as he jumped back on the elevator. Two days. That was it. Two days and his phone would ring with a call from Chet Buckner, Miami business mogul and nightlife connoisseur, letting him know the board's decision. The anticipation ought to be dulled by the bottle of Flux in Remington's hand, but the camera in the corner of the elevator ceiling probably went right to Mr. Buckner's personal assistant. "Chet would probably love it if he caught me polishing off a bottle of Flux in his elevator." Remington laughed to himself. A robotic voice stated, "lower level" and a beep signaled the opening of the elevator door. Remington stepped out. Two more days.

CHAPTER 7

Night Cap

REMINGTON AND JAX pushed their shifter karts into their shared trailer at a Miami kart racing track after a day of competition. Their midget racing midseason break was coming to a close and it was once again time to trade the quick left and right turns of the karting courses for the smooth arced left handers of the oval tracks.

The two friends had trained for years on karts when they weren't on the road with the USAC National Midget tour, and full time during the warm Florida offseason. They were joined by many of the nation's top drivers who came to wait out the winter behind the wheel of some type of racing machine until their home tracks thawed and the rest of the country roared to life in late April. Some true oval enthusiasts disdain road racers. But as Remington and Jax knew, modern IndyCar racing was a blend of street, road course, and oval races, and any aspiring open-wheel driver had to master them all to have any hope of a career in IndyCar.

Traditionally, IndyCar racing in the United States was dominated by oval tracks, but transitioned to include the street and road races in later years, putting a premium on any driver who could conquer the trifecta of courses. In the "roadster" IndyCar days, sanctioned by USAC, there was a clear path to achieving the badge of professional IndyCar pilot. Good drivers raced midgets, sprint cars, and finally moved up to the big cars as they were fondly called, all the while racing some of the most famous — and deadly — tracks in motorsports: Langhorn. Salem. Winchester. These tracks took the last breath of plenty of men and permanently maimed others in the pursuit of racing glory. The road to success wasn't paved all the way up; it consisted of asphalt, dirt, and even "board" tracks. Little towns rumbled to life to host these daredevil drivers, and although the racing surfaces they drove on varied, the crown they pursued never changed: Indianapolis.

In Remington and Jax's time, the path to becoming a professional IndyCar driver was much less cut and dried, with many open-wheel racers coming from the ranks of the European racing scene. It was rare to see a local USAC hero racing in the IndyCar series. Tony Stewart, Sarah Fisher, Ed Carpenter, and the late Bryan Clauson rounded out the list of notable midget and sprint car drivers to land an IndyCar ride in the modern era. Most of the starting field was made up of foreign names with their racing pedigrees forged on the world's road courses. But Remington and Jax were not about to let their spot in IndyCar be filled because of a few extra right-hand turns on some European road-course.

"Rem!" Jax slapped him on the back as they finished buckling their karts to the trailer walls and organizing the specialized tools strewn about the workbench. "Tomorrow is the big day. You ready for the news, man?"

"You have no idea, Jax." Remington wiped the sweat from his forehead and threw the cloth on top of his helmet. "Pretty sure I have never been more ready for something in my life. I thought our graduation day was a long time coming, but this is draining, standing on the edge of something I've worked for my entire life."

"I bet. No one deserves it more than you, Rem. You want me to go put a blown race tire in Chet Buckner's bed? You know, rough him up a little." Jax smirked, trying to give his best Vito Corleone impression.

"Great idea, Jax, the perfect way to single-handedly kill my dream. By the way, who were you impersonating? You sounded like a drunk Aussie trying to order a gourmet hot dog at a Boston food kart with a Brooklyn accent." They laughed as they closed the trailer door, ending another day at the track.

Remington knew Chet Buckner liked to add a little flair to everything he did. He would fully grasp just how much at 12:01 the next morning. The knock on Remington's townhouse door jarred him from his sleep.

"Who in the world?" Remington thought as he fumbled through his dark room, using his cellphone to check the time and light his way down the stairwell.

The street light cast a shadow on Remington's wall as he peeked around the still-chained door to see who had rattled him from his much-needed rest.

"Mr. Mason?" asked the voice.

"That's me," Remington murmured as he cleared his throat. "Can I help you?"

"Why, yes sir," the man said. He was dressed in a black suit, wearing a badge. Remington rubbed his eyes to try and get a better glimpse at the name tag.

"What can I do for you, Mr. Carlton?"

"Oh, please sir, call me Mack. Your ride is here." The man smiled and gestured toward a long black vehicle.

"My ride? I think you have the wrong address, Mack." Remington started to shut the door.

"You are indeed Mr. Mason, correct?"

"Yeah, but I'm not going anywhere other than back to bed. Sorry Mr. Mack. Night." Remington shut the door and turned to head back up the stairs. He had hardly turned around on the cold tile floor before a polite knock echoed through the hallway once again.

"Seriously, Mack. I need my rest. Can I just help you find who you're looking for?"

"Mr. Mason, please allow me." Mack pulled a letter with a wax seal from his pocket and handed it through the crack. Remington broke the seal on the envelope and pulled out the letter.

Dear Mr. Mason,

You are cordially invited to attend a celebration of the highest honor. A feast to honor those who dare. Who rise above. Those of whom Teddy Roosevelt spoke: "Who know what it is to live and whose faces are marred by dust and sweat and blood. Those, like you and me, who spend ourselves in a worthy cause; who at the best know in the end the triumph of high achievement, and who at the worse, if we fail, at least fail while daring greatly, so that our place shall never be with those cold and timid souls who neither know victory nor defeat."

Welcome to Team Flux, Mr. Mason.
Sincerely,
Chet Buckner
CEO, Flux Energy Liquor
P.S. Now get your ass in that limo kid!

Remington was beside himself. At 12:07 a.m. he fully understood Chet Buckner's flair for the dramatic. Remington felt as if he had slept for a year straight and would never need sleep again. He flung the chain off the door and embraced Mack in a hug that knocked the limo-driver cap right off his head.

"Mack, I can't believe it man — I'm going to be an IndyCar driver! The Indianapolis 500! Can you believe it?" Mack picked up his hat as Remington rushed back inside to get dressed. "Oh shoot, Mack, I'm sorry. Please, come in."

Mack chuckled as he dusted off his hat and stepped into the foyer of Remington's home. "No worries at all, Mr. Mason." Mack smiled. "Mr. Buckner warned me you might be rather excited."

It was nearly one in the morning as the limousine pulled up to the Sapphire Sands Nightclub. "Are you ready for this, Mr. Mason?" Mack asked with a tone of concern. "Your life is about to change in major ways. Mr. Buckner has every intention of making you one of the hottest celebrities in Miami — maybe in the country. I have worked for him for eight years now and everything he touches turns to gold. You seem like a fine young gentleman. Don't lose that."

"I appreciate the advice, Mack. I think I'll be all right. I guess I will be seeing you around then?"

"You most certainly will."

"Thanks for the lift." Remington shook Mack's hand and stepped out of the limo. He was immediately snagged by one of the Flux girls, who ushered him with VIP alacrity through a door just past the long line of club-goers anxiously awaiting their turn to hit the dance floor. The Flux girl flashed credentials to the two musclebound guards, who parted and granted them entrance. The pulsing bass reverberated through the small hallway as she escorted him to a back room equipped with stage lighting and two chairs. Behind the stage was a curtain that displayed a "Flux Energy Liquor Racing" logo.

"Mr. Mason! Welcome." A well-dressed woman quickly seated Remington facing the largest wall of vanity lighting he had ever seen. "Are you ready for your interview?"

"Interview?" asked Remington. Another woman began to powder his face with poofy little brushes.

"Yes, sir," said the woman. "Mr. Buckner has a taste for the unusual. It is part of what has made him so successful. He does things with . . . what's the word? Zeal! And with a rather large dose of it."

"I am beginning to catch on," Remington said. The makeup artist continued to poke and prod his face with all sorts of uncomfortable little gadgets and creams. "I thought I was a descent-looking guy until you sat me in this chair and started my surgery." The team of artists and producers laughed as they continued to bustle around. "I feel like my face is going to be stuck like this for good." As the makeup artist finished her work, another Flux girl approached him with a cup of coffee.

"Oh my, you have no idea how perfect this is." Remington held out the cup as she poured in some creamer.

"If there is anything else you need, Mr. Mason, please ask."

"We are on in five!" yelled a man with a clipboard and headset. "Please cue Mr. Buckner and Mr. Mason. We are on in five!"

While the coffee started to meander through Remington's veins, he still wasn't entirely convinced he was awake. The limo at his door, the club, the makeup, the service — he felt like he had become an A-list celebrity overnight. Remington was at a complete loss for words, not a good thing considering he was T-minus four and a half minutes from taking the stage for his first press conference as a professional driver. He downed his last drip of coffee and walked to the stage.

Remington was already seated when he heard a boisterous ruckus in the hallway. He did not have to see Chet Buckner's grin to know who it was.

"Remington Mason!" Chet yelled as he walked through the door, theatrically brushing his hands across the sky as if he were painting Remington's name on a billboard. "It's Remington Mason folks, driving for Flux Energy Liquor approaching turn number four and he's *on it!* Vrooooommmmm!" Chet bellowed in a surprisingly accurate impression of the legendary Indianapolis 500 broadcaster, Tom Carnegie. "One more turn to go — and it's a new track record!"

Remington clapped with approval as Chet leapt onto the stage, grasped Remington's hand, and gave it a vigorous shake. "Welcome to the team, kid. You ready to make some noise?"

"I could not possibly be more ready, Mr. Buckner. I've worked for this moment my entire life and I am truly grateful."

"I know you are, Rem. One of the many reasons I chose you to represent my brand. We are going to do some great stuff, you and me." Chet pulled a pen from his pocket as he received a stack of papers over his shoulder from his lawyer. "What do you say we make this thing official?"

"I think that sounds fine. The only thing missing now is my dad. I owe him so much of this and he can't be here to see it." Remington smiled as he stared at the stack of papers before him, thinking of how proud his father would be.

"See these cameras, kid? He's not going to miss one moment. This entire city, ESPN, the Indianapolis Motor Speedway Radio Network, the *Indy Star*, *Miami Herald*, the *Missoulian* . . . shoot, I might even get you in a darn comic strip. You catch my drift? No one is going to miss this moment, Rem." Chet slapped Remington's shoulder. "You ready? Let's make you famous."

The remainder of the night disappeared as quickly as a bottle of Flux. Remington was pretty sure he remembered signing a contract, doing a press conference, dancing with an assortment of good-looking women, and what was that last thing? Drinking a product-spokesman-worthy amount of Flux Energy Liquor.

The line between hungover and still dreaming was beautifully blurred as Remington attempted to reassure himself that last night had actually happened. Remington's phone vibrated in the pants he was still wearing. It was Jax.

"Hey bu — " Remington said before he was cut off.

"You freaking did it man! You did it!" Jax yelled. "I just saw your press conference on ESPN. I can't believe it, man. I am so happy for you."

Remington flipped open his laptop and pulled up ESPN. There it was. "Flux Energy Liquor to enter IndyCar Series as primary sponsor for USAC race driver, Remington Mason."

Remington sighed with relief. "So, last night was real. Could have been the flashing strobe lights, or the drinks, but I half expected to wake up this morning to find out I had made it all up. Jax, I can't believe it."

"No one deserves this more, Remington. So proud of you. I'm sure you've got a million calls to make. I'll let you get to it. Beers on me — soon!"

Remington slapped his laptop closed and threw it to the foot of his bed. He collapsed on a mound of pillows, thoughts of the future billowing in his mind. Speed, glory, victory, the Indianapolis 500 . . . he was an IndyCar driver.

CHAPTER 8

St. Pete

REMINGTON GLANCED OUT the terminal window. The snow continued to pile up on the runway. Lionel held Remington's shoulders, looking at his son as if it were the day he was born. "I will see you in St. Pete in two weeks. It will be a nice reprieve from the spring snows of Montana. What do they say? March snows bring — "

"March snows bring people to Florida, Dad." Lionel chuckled. Remington knew his father had enjoyed his offseason visit, and he obliged Lionel's attempts to maximize their remaining time together as the gate attendant began boarding his flight. It was after Remington said a final goodbye and turned to head toward the lengthening security line, that Lionel pulled out a folded copy of the upcoming IndyCar schedule.

"Okay, Rem," Lionel said as he slipped on his reading glasses and tapped the crinkled paper with his finger. "I will see you in St. Pete in two weeks. Then you are off to, let's see . . ." Lionel scrolled the handwritten schedule. "Phoenix, Long Beach, Barber. Oh, and then I'll see you in Indy for the entire month of May. My son racing in the Indy 500. Wow. I'll travel with you to Milwaukee. So glad to see them going back to Milwaukee this season. You know, when I was younger — "

"I know, they used to race a lot more of the classic ovals." Lionel smiled sheepishly. They had discussed the same topic over dinner many times.

"Anyway, it will be good to spend a month with you and stay on Mackinac Island. I haven't been to the Grand Hotel since I was a kid." Lionel paused in a moment of wistfulness before diving back into the schedule. Remington patiently listened while bags continued to stack up in the little gray bins on the back side of the X-ray machine. "Then on to Belle Isle, Texas, Road America, Iowa, Toronto, Mid-Ohio, Pocono, the new race on the streets of Las Vegas, Sonoma, and finally California Motor Speedway in October." Lionel re-folded the schedule and removed his spectacles. "I know I'm keeping you from your plane. You tell Mr. Buckner that I can't wait to meet him in a couple of weeks."

"I will, Dad. I better get in line. Don't want to miss practice — I'll need all I can get. You know, being a rookie and all." Remington grabbed his duffle bag, slung it over his shoulder, and jumped in line.

"Oh Rem, I almost forgot. Here, take this." Lionel handed his son an envelope with his name on the front. "Open it sometime before you race."

Remington gave his father a proud glance as he threw his bag on the conveyer belt. "Thanks Dad. See you in a couple weeks."

Remington settled into his first-class seat and peered out the window as the blizzard suddenly gave way to the peaks of the Mission Mountains floating in a blue backdrop. The sun was swallowed by ominous clouds, the final rays obliging the sky to the stars that could only be seen from 35,000 feet. Before Remington closed his eyes and woke up in Florida, he extracted his father's letter from his jacket and began to read:

"When engines stutter into life and the racers start to move. When you see that all are rolling and are heading for the groove. When the rows of rainbow colors flash their message to the sun, and they line abreast in grand salute before the race is run. When the great crowd rises as the field gets ready for the start, and the muted thunder from yon turn quickens every beating heart. When you see the pace car drop away and the engines start to roar, when the green flag falls upon them and opens up the door. When you see them straining for the turn, you cringe and hope and pray that somehow God will guide each wheel in safety on its way. God, speed these men who have to race, for racing is their skill. They love to race, they live to race, and men like this most always will.

You always loved this poem. It was on the back of an old racing program I gave you when you were five. You even did a school project about it. I know it's just a poem, but Mr. Wible's prayer is one I pray for you every day of each race season. So God, please guide my son in safety on his way. Speed this man who has to race, for racing is skill. He loves to race, he lives to race, and I know he always will. And I am blessed to call him my son. Amen"

The walls, the catch fences, the grandstands, the towering high rises of St. Petersburg, Florida, closed in on Remington like a pounding wave as he fought to maintain a regular pattern of breathing. The Lamaze techniques his trainer rehearsed with him during the offseason seemed useless as he blasted through the rough street course in the first round of qualifying in the new IndyCar season, Remington's first. His hands did the opposite of what he had trained them to do his entire career as they clenched the wheel, wringing sweat from his racing gloves. His mouth felt as if he were trying to swallow a fistful of sand and his head was pinned to the side of his cockpit by the G-Forces that exploded from the apex of each corner. The ten minutes of the first segment of qualifying would determine the rear of the field. To the rookie, it felt like an entire race.

Remington wrestled his clenched hand from the steering wheel and fumbled for his radio button, desperate to communicate with his new crew chief, Craig Doucet. "How much time left?" Remington panted as he hurled down the airport runway front stretch at nearly 200 miles per hour.

"You're almost there, Rem. Two more minutes. Keep focused. You're running some great times," Craig said. Remington came into the series with exceptional skill and physical ability, but the first time he was on the clock in IndyCar competition, his nerves drained his energy, leaving him reeling for breath and on the outer limits of his ability to focus. Craig coached his young driver through the qualifying session, keeping him as calm as possible so he could focus on driving and relaying crucial feedback on the car's handling. This communication and trust was the glue that linked a driver and his crew chief and was the key ingredient in both on and off track success. It was a bond forged at speed, and for speed.

Remington sat, still buckled in, swimming in his own sweat as his crew leapt over the wall and began attending to his car.

"How did I do?" Remington asked on the radio. He looked toward the top of the pit box where Craig sat reviewing the onboard telemetry from the qualifying session with his engineers. Each car was equipped with a sensor that communicated live mechanical and performance information to the crew. The constant feed of data was crucial to setting up a car and adjusting it throughout the course of a race. It also provided broadcast teams and fans with their favorite driver's running order, current speed, and live driver and crew communications.

"How did it feel?" Craig asked.

"Honestly, I couldn't tell. I was so focused on running my line I didn't even think of anything else. Don't even try asking me for feedback on the car."

Craig laughed as he jumped off the pit box and sat on the side pod of Remington's car. He leaned in to speak with his driver. "Keep your helmet on. You made it to session number two."

Remington was filled with a surge of energy, like Craig had injected him with liquid confidence. All it meant statistically was that he would be starting somewhere between the front and middle of the twenty-two-car field, but the added confidence certainly couldn't hurt.

"What are you thinking, Rem? Do you want to try a shorter run for round two and use a sticker set of reds?" Remington had long understood the concept of tire compounds, but unlike his days racing midgets, he would now be pitting multiple times during the course of a race and changing tires, which meant he had to have an intimate relationship with the various tire compounds and how they made his car handle. During an IndyCar race, drivers were required to use two tire compounds, one soft and another harder, for at least one lap of racing. The red-walled tires had a softer compound that was quick right out of the gate but degraded rapidly. The harder compound, or black-walled tires, lasted longer and ran some of their fastest times after they had been raced on for a few laps. Teams were only allowed a designated number of tire sets for every race weekend, and had to use those tires to qualify on as well. The further a driver went into the qualifying segments, the more tires were used and the fewer there would be available for the race, but the greater the chance of starting toward the front of the field.

With the second round of qualifying about to start, Remington told Craig to put on a sticker set of the softer red-walled tires. "I want to get out there fast and try and lock in a quick time on my second or third lap as the tires really come in." Remington felt like a different driver as he pulled his gloves back on: more confident and alert.

"Good choice," Craig said. His signal to the crew to put on the set of tires sent their air wrenches whirring. "You're going to have to really push hard on your out lap to get your tires warm, and then give it all you can for the next two to three laps. I'll call you in after that and we can see where we sit." Remington gave a thumbs up as the crew inserted the starter and the car ripped to life, idling at a higher RPM than most high-performance street cars reach on a spirited romp between stoplights.

"You are clear. Go, go, go!" Craig said as the flagman started the second round of qualifying. Remington popped the car in gear and slid out of his pit box in a trail of smoke, instantly building up heat in the red-walled tires. His heart still raced as he approached the exit of pit road, but his hands were relaxed. He was breathing in normal patterns, and his focus was razor-sharp. Remington squeezed the throttle as he crossed the pit exit and the car jumped to life as he quickly tapped his paddle shifters through the gears. He rocketed through the first couple of turns, the back of the car breaking loose as he pushed hard to further warm his tires.

As he brought the car up to racing speed, Remington calmly coached himself from behind his visor. "Okay, hard on the throttle out of turn three. Brake early and get down to second gear for the sharp right hander in turn number four. Easy on the throttle through five, six, and seven. Quick acceleration and back to third gear in the short chute between seven and eight."

As Remington coached himself through the first lap, he began to feel a rhythm he hadn't experienced in the first session. "Chalk that first one up to the crew preparing a good car," he thought. This time was different. He didn't notice his breathing or even the G-forces, just the subtle rhythmic movements slingshotting him through the race course, almost as if he and the car had become one fluid machine.

"Pit this lap; pit this lap." Craig's voice jolted Remington from his concentration. Had he already cranked out five laps? He took the dive into pit lane as he came out of turn fourteen and slid to a halt in his pit box. He jumped on the radio to ask Craig how he did.

"Another great run, Rem," Craig said, scanning the lap times of the rest of the drivers. "You ran a one minute, one-second lap. I say we hold on that and see how the rest of the field lines up. I haven't seen anybody beat your time so far."

Lionel clapped from behind the pit wall as Remington unbuckled and climbed out of the car. Remington gave him a hug before stuffing his helmet and gloves into their slot on the back of the pit cart. "Seventh place, Rem," Lionel said. "What a way to kick off your IndyCar career."

Lionel looked on as Craig jumped down from the pit box to debrief with his driver. "I agree with your Dad, Rem, what a way to kick-off a career."

"You think he did all right then, Craig?" Lionel asked.

"Did all right? I have been wrenching on IndyCars since the early sixties and I have not seen a driver put together a rookie qualifying run quite like that," Craig said.

"Well, I have been watching IndyCar since the early sixties myself and I can tell you I have never been so nervous," Lionel said with a laugh.

"Rem reminds me a lot of the drivers we old-timers watched back in that era. It's refreshing to finally see a driver emerge in IndyCar because of his skill and determination in the USAC ranks. It is rare and I am enjoying the nostalgia. Helps recall why I fell in love with this sport to begin with." Lionel relished Craig's word. "Who knows, maybe we have the next Foyt, Unser, or Hurtubise here."

The driver's names Craig listed roared with lived authority in Lionel's bank of early racing memories. To hear Remington mentioned in relation to some of the most legendary names to ever wheel an IndyCar, validated the sacrifice he and his son made to race. Sure, Remington was raw and untested, but so far, the draft of his legendary predecessors was just ahead, and Lionel could sense it pulling his son toward greatness.

CHAPTER *9*

Down to Business

BY THE TIME REMINGTON FINISHED his debrief with Craig, the team had already taken his car to the garage and were closing up the pit box. Remington unzipped his race suit in search of some reprieve from the Florida heat before waving Lionel onto the back of the moped he used to navigate the expansive infield. As he popped up the kickstand and pulled away from his pit stall, a hand gently touched his shoulder.

"Remington," said a female voice. Remington rolled to a stop and pulled a Sharpie out of his pocket, ready to sign another autograph. Before he had a chance to turn around, the woman continued speaking.

"Remington, my name is Jersey Antonelli."

Remington dropped the Sharpie as he turned around on the scooter. "Jersey?" he said, stunned. "Jersey from the beach?"

"Surprise!" Jersey smiled at Remington and gave him a wink. Even though it felt like yesterday, it had been almost a year since they met, and while he had not seen her since, her image had often floated into his mind. He jumped off the scooter and gave her a hug.

"It's great to see you, Jersey. You said you were a race fan. I'm glad you were able to make it out for the race."

"Actually — "

"I'm so sorry. This is my dad, Lionel, by the way. Dad, this is Jersey as I presume you gathered."

"Pleasure to meet you, Jersey," Lionel said.

"I was going to sign you an autograph, but I guess that would be a little weird given we know each other and all."

"Actually Remington, I'm glad you mentioned autographs. Signing them will get you a long way in this business. You know, taking time for the fans.

It will make your public relations person happy too, make their job a little easier."

"It's funny you say that. I actually don't have a PR person yet. My team owner mentioned something about one, but said she was taking care of some other race prep business back at the office. I guess I'll meet her soon enough."

Jersey stuck out her hand. "Pleasure to meet you."

Remington was confused. "Pleasure to *meet* you?" he murmured back. Jersey tugged on the corner of her polo to stretch out the Flux Energy Liquor Racing logo.

"Here she is."

"Are you serious right now?" Remington asked. "*You* are my PR rep?"

"I am dead serious, Rem. I'm excited to work with you. I know this was sort of an awkward introduction and I'm sorry I am just now getting to touch base with you. The boss — you know, Chet — had me cleaning up a few details back at the office to get ready for the season. Guess that comes with the territory as the marketing director for Flux Racing."

"Marketing director? Congratulations, Jersey. That is incredible." Remington was thrilled Jersey would be partnering with him to help build his career. He was also grateful she had apparently forgotten their awkward goodbye, or at least pretended she had. A fresh, professional start was a nice reintroduction.

"So you're finally working in motorsports. I'm so happy for you, Jersey. I know that was what you were shooting for."

"Thank you, Rem," Jersey said. "I ended up getting the social media marketing job I applied for at Sebring International and met Chet at a sportscar race there. Long story short, he asked me to come work for him once he got the Flux team up and running." Jersey slid her sunglasses to the top of her head, revealing her blue eyes. "I always thought it would be cool to work with a new team and driver. You know, a new challenge. Plus, I followed your career since we met at the beach that day. Doesn't surprise me to see you here. I watched you studying sector times on your iPad while the rest of us were partying. I knew good things would happen for you."

"Looks like good things have happened for both of us," Remington said. "All right, tell me where to go, boss."

Jersey laughed as she hopped in her golf cart. "Follow me."

Remington and Lionel trailed Jersey on their scooter, weaving in and out of excited race fans. "Could be worse," Lionel said, leaning over his son's shoulder. "She's cute." Remington gave his dad an elbow and playfully gunned the throttle.

"I think this is your stop here *old man,*" Remington joked as they rolled to a halt next to Jersey outside the media center.

"Congrats on the qualifying by the way, Rem," Jersey said. "I already have it posted to your Twitter and Facebook accounts as well as the team website. I have our writer finishing up a press release as we speak. They'll add quotes from your media appearance and then send it off." Remington was shocked by Jersey's effortless efficiency. "I will make you a household name in no time." Jersey gave Remington and Lionel a confident smirk as she continued to take notes on the clipboard she was carrying. "You make my job easy. You just deliver on the track and let me handle the rest."

Jersey led them up the steps to the infield media center, where a group of reporters were finishing an interview with Helio Castroneves and his team owner, the legendary Captain himself, Roger Penske. Helio had captured the pole position for the next day's race, and his teammates, Will Power and Josef Newgarden, had slotted in right behind him. It was a top three qualifying sweep for Team Penske.

Remington was no stranger to Team Penske's perpetual dominance. With sixteen Indianapolis 500 wins and over a dozen IndyCar championships, The Captain's team was the gold standard of IndyCar operations. Remington had always dreamed of racing for him, but now that he was in the series on a one-car team, he was thrilled with the thought of dethroning the legendary Penske drivers.

The three of them crammed into the corner of the crowded press room as Jersey continued to whisper instructions to Remington. "Rem, you are scheduled to go on in five minutes. You were the highest qualifying rookie so there's already some buzz around this interview. Ganassi and Penske dominated the top six, but then it's you — and people want to hear about that. You beat a lot of great teams. I've watched you interview before and you'll do a great job. Lots of smiles, and don't forget to mention Mr. Buckner and Flux. Wouldn't hurt to mention your team either." Jersey ran through a couple more logistical items and then handed Remington off to the ESPN staff, who took him to the interview stage. He was greeted by Alan Bestwick, who was announcing the weekend's race, as well as a group of ESPN stagehands who prepared them both for the cameras.

"Wonderful job, Remington," Alan said, shaking the young driver's hand as they took their places on the open-air stage overlooking the bay, the palm trees rustling in the evening breeze behind the set.

"Thank you, Alan. I'm thrilled to be sitting up here with you."

"From what I understand, you deserve it." Bestwick shuffled through his notes.

"Gentlemen," the producer said, waving for Alan and Remington's attention from the back of the media room. He held up a finger. "We are on in one minute." Remington took a deep breath as he began to focus on his first live television interview as a professional race driver. He was silently reviewing everything Jersey had mentioned when suddenly, he felt something tickling his left ear. He swatted at the irritant and heard the distinctive laugh of Helio Castroneves just off stage. He turned around to Will Power and Helio swinging a microphone around his head that they had hijacked from the TV crew.

"We are on in five, four, three, two . . . " boomed the producer.

"Don't mess this up rookie," Power whispered in his Australian accent as the two of them disappeared through a side door, laughing. Remington composed himself quickly as Alan struggled to contain his smile.

"Welcome back to our live post-qualifying coverage of the IndyCar Series season opener at the Firestone Grand Prix of St. Petersburg. I'm Alan Bestwick here with the highest-qualifying rookie for tomorrow's race, Remington Mason. Remington, welcome to the Verizon IndyCar Series."

"Thanks, Alan." Recalling Jersey's advice, Remington conveyed confidence as he straightened the collar of his racing suit and leaned in toward his host. "It's an honor to be here."

"I noticed that just before we went live, a couple of your competitors were giving you a hard time. I think I noticed Helio Castroneves and Will Power slip out the back door there." Alan chuckled.

"Yeah, I think they were trying to distract me, but they are going to have to do better than that." Remington smiled as he turned in his chair to make sure the duo had not returned. "I probably just opened myself up to all kinds of pranks with that one." The entire ESPN crew chuckled as Jersey gave Remington a thumbs up from the side of the stage, mouthing the words, "Good job."

"That would not surprise me with those two." Alan tapped his pen on the desk in front of Remington as if to make a point. "Typically, they reserve the pranks for those rookies they think are a threat on the track. So I would take it as a good thing."

"I will choose to see it that way too, Alan."

"Seventh place in qualifying today. That is a phenomenal feat for a rookie at this difficult track, especially with a brand-new team in the IndyCar Series. How did you do it, Remington?"

"To be honest with you, I didn't think I did." Remington looked at ease as the cameras continued to roll. He gripped an imaginary steering wheel and his hands shook. "In the first qualifying session, my nerves were getting the best of me. I hate to admit that as a race driver, but that's the truth. My hands were cramping and I was pretty sure my lungs were out of oxygen. I won't even mention the sweat for the sake of our viewers." Alan chuckled. "So basically, it was my team, led by Craig Doucet, that deserves all the credit for that first session. They gave me a stellar car."

"Nonetheless, a great accomplishment to even make second-round qualifying as a rookie. How did the second session play out?"

"Just making it to round two really helped. I was able to settle in and focus more on driving the car and giving good feedback to Craig on the pit box. Once again, the team put a great car under me and we ended up with some good qualifying times. Not enough to catch the Penske and Ganassi boys, but we're pretty proud of what we accomplished." The interview continued for another minute, with Remington seemingly at ease the whole time.

"I hope you have enjoyed our coverage of today's events and we look forward to joining you tomorrow for the running of the Firestone Grand Prix of St. Petersburg, Florida. On behalf of all of us here at ESPN, I am Alan Bestwick and we wish you a good night from sunny St. Pete." Alan paused, holding his smile as he waited for the director to yell cut. "It was a pleasure to meet you Remington. I have no doubt we'll be seeing a lot more of you in the interview booth. Good luck tomorrow."

"Great job!" Jersey said as Remington jumped off the stage. "You looked like a veteran up there. May I give you an idea of how well you did?"

"Why, please do," Remington said. Jersey dove into a world of social networking lingo and business-speak that made her sound like she was reading from a college textbook. Feeds, analytics, followers, total engagements, Retweets . . . Remington listened patiently to her passionate explanation. She stopped talking somewhere between Facebook and Instagram.

"I lost you, didn't I?" Jersey asked.

"Jersey, I am so glad you manage this stuff and I appreciate your *social* passion. But if this were a race, you took the checkered and I never left the pits," Remington said as he gave Jersey a sympathetic pat on the back. "You want to try again in a language I can understand?"

Jersey laughed. "Basically, you gained a lot of online followers. Online followers are good for popularity, and popularity is good for business." Jersey scrolled through the posts on her phone. "Jax said congratulations and Tweeted a flurry of old pictures of the two of you. But this one from Blonde_Pit_Lizard takes the cake: 'Race Driver Remington Mason, #Hot on and off the track! #Hottest Rookie of the Year?'"

"That's nice of Jax, miss that guy. But what is a blonde pit lizard?" Remington asked. "An iguana with hair?"

"Just you wait," Jersey said. "You will see your share this season. Your typical pit lizard is a beautiful woman anywhere from nineteen to thirty-five, scantily dressed, and draped all over the pit row fences trying to catch the eyes of the best-looking drivers. Our pit area is going to look like a zoo." The three of them laughed. "All of this certainly doesn't hurt our PR efforts."

Remington once again shed the top layer of his driving suit, exposing the fireproof undergarment hugging his body. "I am ready to call it a day. What time is it anyway?"

"Time for you to take a shower," Jersey said. Remington laughed, knowing he had no argument. "No really. You need to get ready for the Flux Energy Liquor Pre Prix Party tonight. There is a clean Calvin Klein outfit hanging in your hotel suite and you are the guest of honor."

"You're joking, right?" Remington looked surprised. "How do they expect me to be rested for the race tomorrow?"

"Welcome to the life of a professional race driver, Rem." Jersey returned Remington's sympathetic pat to the back. "Don't worry, I'll guide you through this."

The Flux Energy Liquor Pre Prix Party was in a high-rise banquet hall on the top floor of Remington's hotel. "She did say she would guide me through this," Remington thought as he debated fastening the top button of his dress shirt. "At least I can get right to bed after the party." A knock on Remington's door forced the decision on the top button. "Come in, it's open," Remington shouted. He grabbed his black dress coat and headed across the room. Jersey had traded her team polo and jeans for a shimmering mid-length black dress and red heals that clicked as she hurriedly glided across the tile floor into the living room of Remington's suite.

"You look amazing, Jersey." Remington paused to observe the transformation.

"Thanks, Rem. You don't look too bad yourself. I did a good job picking out those clothes, I guess." She straightened his collar and stuck a Sharpie in his jacket pocket. "A lot of people up there are really excited to meet you. Business partners of Mr. Buckner, celebrities, fans. They all want a chance to see you. All the drivers and teams will be there, but you are the star of this party. Your sponsor, your night. Be sure to shake a lot of hands, smile for selfies, you get the idea. Just be yourself. Wouldn't hurt to be seen with a glass of Flux in your hands either. I know you don't drink before races, but you can nurse the same glass all night." Jersey took a final glance at her clipboard. "All right, any questions?"

"Just one: could you repeat that one more time?" The two laughed as they headed toward the door.

CHAPTER 10

Race Day

THE KNOCK ON REMINGTON'S HOTEL DOOR broke him from a deep sleep. It was Jersey and Lionel.

"Vrooom!! Vroooooommm!!" Remington chuckled as he rolled over in bed, sweeping the hair from his face. Lionel was hunched over the bed making racing noises as Jersey stood in the background laughing. It was something he had done when Remington was just a child as they traveled the West Coast racing quarter midgets. It was Remington's favorite way to start a day growing up.

"I haven't had a chance to do that for years," Lionel said with a smile. "I hope I didn't embarrass you in front of Jersey. I just could't help it."

Remington finished a quick shower as Lionel and Jersey chatted in the living room, excited for the day's festivities.

"I'm amazed I actually slept last night," Remington said as he joined Jersey and Lionel in the living room. "I see why you had me entertaining at the party. It put me right to bed! I like the way you think, Jersey. What's on the docket for this morning, other than my first professional car race?"

"Mr. Buckner will be here in a while to chat with you, but in the meantime, I know your dad wanted to share a race-day devotional with you, and I have your breakfast on the way up. Other than that, I try to keep race days pretty straightforward for you other than the mandatory interviews and driver's meeting."

It had been some time since Remington had done any sort of devotional on his own. Even the word "devotional" had come to grate him in a strange way. It was one of those "Christainese" words that conjured up an image of a Bible-thumper inviting you over to their home for a potluck and a good old-fashioned witnessing. Remington decided to oblige his father and participate this time. After all, a little prayer couldn't hurt as he embarked on a dangerous career as an IndyCar driver.

"Okay Pop, let's get this devo on the road." Remington cracked a hardboiled egg and took a sip of fresh orange juice as he sat on the couch next to Lionel. "The boss man is on his way up and I need to start getting focused."

Lionel shared what Remington could tell was a well-thought-out story on running the race of life well and ended with a prayer asking God for Remington's protection and success. After Lionel concluded with an "Amen," Remington watched as his father's shaking hand folded the piece of paper he had written his notes on and gently returned it to his breast pocket.

Remington was surprised at the sense of sadness that washed over him as he watched Lionel. He was afraid his dad had noticed his urgency to finish the devotional and dive into his first day as an IndyCar driver. Over the past few years, a relentless surge of annoyance, and then guilt, flared up any time he was exposed to something "Christian." He hated the recurring thorn in his side and wasn't sure why it plagued him, or even why he had drifted away from something he once loved in his childhood. What he did know was that the guilt was a distraction. The only thing that demanded his attention now was his career.

"Thanks, Dad." Remington embraced Lionel in an attempt to cover his restlessness. "I really appreciate the prayers and I'm sure someone will be looking after me during the race today. Who knows, maybe the racing gods will even grant us a win." Lionel smiled, but Rem could see the disappointment in his eyes.

Chet Buckner did not enter Remington's hotel room doing his typical song and dance. His head was down and he didn't say a word as he made his way into the room and sat next to Remington. The awkward pause was followed by a mediocre attempt at a pep talk.

"You're going to do just fine out there today, Rem," Chet said as he tapped his foot and poured the remaining orange juice in a glass. "We have a good thing going here." He took another nervous glance around the room, barely acknowledging Lionel and Jersey sitting across from him.

Jersey had helped Chet prepare a motivational speech the night before and his lackluster intro was not part of the script. She waited for him to start again. He sat silently, swirling the last sip of orange juice in the bottom of his glass. Remington rescued them from the unnerving silence.

"I appreciate that, Chet," Remington said. "And I agree, we do have a good thing going here. Aren't you excited about it? You love this sport. This is your day to celebrate being an IndyCar team owner."

Chet exhaled and finally finished the last sip of orange juice. "You're right, Rem. This is a huge day and I am excited. I just got a case of the damn nerves this morning. We have put a lot in motion over the offseason and I just hope this turns out good for all of us, you know?"

Chet set his glass down and slapped his leg as he stood up. He squeezed Remington's shoulder before walking toward the door. Chet paused, his fingers gently resting on the handle. Remington and Jersey watched silently, trying to figure out this new side of their boss.

"I almost forgot the most important piece of advice," Chet said as he spun around and shook his finger at Remington. "Take 'er easy on the straightaways and give 'er hell in the corners, kid." Chet exited with a wink and a renewed hint of vigor. The room drew a sigh of relief.

"Why is *he* nervous?" Remington asked as he turned to Jersey. "I have never seen him struggle for a single word."

"In all honesty, it doesn't matter," Jersey said, closing her laptop. "You are the only one who has to manage his nerves today. You just focus on *you*. It's race day."

"Trust me," Remington said. "I am more ready than ever. In a race car is where I am the most calm."

"Good. That is what I just posted to your Twitter account. You gentleman ready to head to the track?"

As they waited in the lobby for their transportation, Jersey leaned close to Remington and whispered in his ear. "For what it's worth, I thought it was really sweet that your dad prepared that prayer for you. He loves you a lot."

Remington stared at the ground, embarrassed by his response to Lionel's effort to share something he had worked so hard to prepare. "I know he does. Was it entirely obvious that I really didn't want to be there?"

"You were fine. I think he may have noticed, but I am pretty sure he loves you anyway."

"Thanks, Jersey. After my mom died, I just went away from that churchy stuff, you know? And I have been busy getting to where I am now. I just didn't want anything distracting me from the race today and I let it get the best of me."

"I understand," Jersey said with a look of concern. "I know you are a thousand percent committed to winning. But don't lose focus on the world outside of racing. Racing has destroyed a lot of families. Trust me, I know."

"How much can you have seen in two years?" Remington asked.

"Here's our ride." Jersey grabbed her bag as Lionel returned from the restroom. "That's a story for another time. I'm here to support you on and off the track. My job is to help you stay healthy, win races, and sell Flux Energy Liquor. If that means helping you stay grounded, so be it."

Remington looked out the window as they were escorted past swarms of fans waiting to get into the race, many with a cocktail in their hands at eight a.m. The chauffeur flashed his credentials and pulled into the reserved parking spot next to the VIP tent where Remington's crew was already busy shuttling the day's supplies between their trailer and pit stall. Jersey escorted Lionel to the lounge while Remington entered the side door of the hauler.

Craig greeted him with a fresh coffee in hand. "How did you sleep last night, Rem?" he asked.

"I actually slept great. Jersey had enough planned to thoroughly wear me out last night. The press conferences, the party . . ."

"She's brilliant at what she does. We're lucky to have her." The duo paced through the trailer as they hashed out their plan for the race. "The boys went through the entire car last night and everything looks perfect. I think you'll have a rocket today."

Remington was impressed with the organization of his newly formed team. Coming from a racing circuit where he and his former crew-chief, Mark, did all the work on the car themselves, it felt odd not turning a socket wrench in the shop after midnight with a Red Bull balanced on the right rear. Part of Remington's pre-race routine was walking around his car, tightening the lugs, making sure the driveshaft was free, and putting a little spit shine on the sponsor logos. According to Jersey and Craig, his new pre-race routine would be a little more straightforward. Priority one, focus. After that, stay hydrated and make the fans happy.

In preparation for the dirt and grime that would pelt his helmet throughout the day's race, Remington fastened a set of clear tear-offs to his visor that could be ripped off as his visibility became impaired. He finished just as Jersey entered the hauler lounge to tell him that driver introductions were in thirty minutes.

"You want to sign some autographs on the way to pit lane? May help ease the race-day nerves."

"Absolutely," Remington said. He stuffed his helmet into a bag with his gloves and caught the Sharpie Jersey tossed at him. "I remember how much it meant to me when I was a kid, and a driver went out of his way to talk to me and sign a profile card."

"Well then, let's go make you that driver."

Remington was stunned at the number of fans jockeying for a position to snag his autograph. He'd already had some success in his career, but this was overwhelming: his Sharpie went dry. "Did you hire all these people just to show up and make me feel good before my first race, Jersey?"

"No, sir. This is your new fan base." Remington could see the pride Jersey took in her work, in increasing the length of his autograph line. "I've been telling you all along that you are a PR rep's dream. It doesn't hurt that you get the job done on the track, either." With Remington's Sharpie now leaving nothing but a faint line on the T-shirts, Jersey cut off the swarm of fans and whisked him to driver introductions, the final step before Remington got to strap on his helmet and race.

The Florida heat was already baking the drivers as they pulled on their fire suits. The fans pulled off as many clothes as they could and Alan Bestwick welcomed everyone to "sunny St. Pete" from the broadcast booth. The pit lane bustled with reporters and crews making final tweaks and polishes to the twenty-two cars in the starting field.

Chet Buckner sat quietly on the pit wall in the midst of it all, admiring the beautiful Dallara IndyCar displaying his company's brand. Flux Energy Liquor swept upward off the side pod and trailed back over the engine housing in a flash of blue that stuck out from the car's fluorescent peach body. The nose cone on the car displayed the black number seven that had been Remington's on-track signature since he was a child. Neon green and orange trim tied the rest of the paint scheme together, ensuring the car could not be missed, on or off the track.

Lionel Mason had just been seated in the Flux trackside suite when the booming PA announcer asked all in attendance to rise for a prayer and the singing of the National Anthem. Lionel stood and closed his eyes, echoing everything the pastor said, but tailoring the words to his son who was about to embark on his maiden IndyCar voyage. The National Anthem was belted out seemingly in rhythm with the swaying palm trees. Lionel wiped his eyes with his handkerchief as the rest of the fans cheered and the drivers were called to their cars.

Before the last word was sung, Remington started jumping up and down to loosen his body and nerves. The world around him disappeared and a tunnel of focus was all that was before him. In less than ten minutes, he would take the green flag in his first professional race. He took a final drink from his water bottle and tossed it on the pit box, then pulled up his driving suit and strapped on his helmet. Although his entire crew was making final preparations on the car, the only thing Remington could see was the steering wheel as he stepped over the side pod and lowered himself into the tub of the chassis. That steering wheel was the connection between himself and the 700 horsepower machine he hoped would carry him to victory. He squeezed the wheel as he visualized lap after lap around the circuit. Remington was so focused he could almost feel the rhythmic movement of the car as it sucked into the corner and hopped over the curb as he hugged the apex. It took Craig leaning in to Remington to do a radio test for him to finally acknowledge his surroundings.

"You doing all right, Rem?" Craig asked as he released his radio button.

"Never been better." Remington gave a quick nod.

"You know the routine. You focus on driving the car and giving us feedback on its handling, and we'll do everything we can from the pit box to help you make this thing a rocket. Don't forget, let's try and maintain position for the first half of the race and then make a charge to the front toward the latter half."

Remington did not hear a word Craig said as he re-entered an entirely new world of focus. He subconsciously nodded with approval as Craig patted him on the helmet and returned to the top of the pit box. Remington completed the separation of himself from the outside world as he pulled his visor shut and waited to ignite the ethanol that was as ready to burn as he was to race.

The clanking of tools came to a halt in the barn as an old AM/FM radio crackled in a struggle to find a station. The static gave way to the most famous words in motorsports: "Gentlemen . . . start . . . your . . . engines!" An old barn cat poked her head out of the cockpit as Mark wiped his hands. Since handing the keys over to Craig Doucet, Remington's old friend and crew chief filled his retirement working on the 1952 Kurtis Kraft midget he was restoring in his workshop outside Indianapolis.

"What are you doing in there, you old mouser," Mark said as the cat purred at the touch of his greasy hand. "You want to listen to the race? I'll get you a bowl of milk." The two of them reclined on an old truck bench seat Mark had fashioned into a couch of sorts. He pulled the radio a little closer. His hearing wasn't what it used to be after wrenching on race cars his entire life.

The previous season working as a crew chief for Remington on the USAC midget circuit was his last. He couldn't get the torque out of his weathered hands like he used to. He was now content to follow a career he felt proud to have helped build. Mark had a TV and new recliner in his house, but the crackle of the radio and the surroundings of his old race shop were as comfortable as anything.

"You ready for this, mouser?" The cat happily lapped at the bowl of milk Mark had pulled from the antique Coca-Cola fridge in the corner of the shop. "Let's see how our boy Remington does."

The entire Flux suite leaned forward and peered down the long front straightaway to get a glimpse of the field as they charged toward the waving green flag that signaled the start of the race and the new season. Chet Buckner let out a bellowing yell and pumped his fist as the cars roared by at full speed. Whatever nerves had ailed him earlier in the day had long since departed. Quarterbacks, rappers, oil millionaires, and American Idol winners all seemed to be enjoying the experience, and the Flux Energy Liquor, which was being poured freely. Chet never missed an opportunity to market his product. It paired well with the charcuterie platters circling the suite, evaporating as quickly as the first laps of the race.

Lionel Mason kept a pleasant smile on his face as he talked to Mr. Buckner's high-profile guests. They probably assumed he was some hick from Montana. Maybe it was the flannel shirt in the Florida heat or possibly the leather suspenders with mallards and cattails on them that gave him away. Lionel did not mind. None of them had a clue he was a renowned neurosurgeon and at least as well-off as they were. Mostly, he tried to keep to himself so he could focus on his son and the race at hand. Jersey found a spot next to him in the corner of the suite and pulled out her laptop to track the live timing and scoring of the race and send out social-media updates. She usually avoided the party scene and made her home in the pits with the team, but she felt compelled to keep an eye on Lionel. The two had developed a mutual fondness.

"Jersey," Lionel said, leaning in to be heard over the roar of the cars. "Thank you for all you've done to help Remington."

"Oh, Mr. Mason, this work is a dream come true."

"I can tell," Lionel said. Jersey beamed with pride. "Can I ask you a special favor?"

"Of course."

"You seem like a good soul, Jersey. You have a good head on your shoulders. Would you just watch out for Remington for me? I know it's your job, but outside of that, I just want him to have somebody I trust to keep an eye on things. Over the years I have watched what this business can do to people."

"Mr. Mason, it would be my pleasure." She squeezed his hand. "I know what this business can do better than anyone. My father was an aspiring driver when I was growing up in the eighties. Eventually, he couldn't cut it, and he lost his ride. He had raced his entire life and when he no longer had that, instead of turning to his wife and two daughters, he traded us for a bottle of gin. A year after he lost his ride he decided to leave us, and I haven't heard from him since." Jersey looked at the crowd on the other side of the track as if she were searching for her estranged father. "Sorry. That was probably too much information. I just want you to know I have seen, up close, what this sport can do and I will — "

Before Jersey could finish her sentence, a collective gasp rose from the crowd as they jumped to their feet and pointed toward turn number one at the end of the long front straightaway.

The announcer's voice echoed over the loudspeakers as smoke and car parts erupted. "Folks, there was a hard impact in turn one as a car went airborne. It looks like the number 21 machine of Brody Compton, and there is a second car sliding to a stop upside down. This is going to bring out a full-course caution, the first of the day."

"Can you tell where Remington is, Jersey?" Lionel asked. "That wreck occurred awfully close to where he was running." Jersey scrolled through the timing and scoring to see if Remington's car was still clocking a speed. Chet appeared over her shoulder in search of the same data.

"Remington, you all right, bud?" a calm Craig Doucet said over the radio.

"Yes." Remington's voice crackled through the radio and race scanners lifting the tension on the pit box and in the Flux suite. "The 27 car went right over the top of me. Looks like he was trying to out-brake the 13 going into one."

"Any damage to the car?" Craig asked. The Flux crew, tense and ready for action, awaited Remington's response.

"Not that I can tell, but lots of debris on the track. Let's change tires."

"Good call, Rem. I think everyone will have the same idea." The team already had a fresh set of tires sitting on the pit wall, awaiting the arrival of their driver. "The pits will be open the next time by. Pit then."

The first three-quarters of the race had gone as planned. Remington's nerves settled after a few laps and he seamlessly slipped into the steely focus required to drive on the knife edge, without slipping over. The car seemed to be dialed in, solidly anchoring him in the top ten for all ninety completed laps of the scheduled hundred and ten. It was time for Team Flux to enact phase two of their strategy and move to the front of the field.

Remington veered to the right and hit the brakes. The crew member responsible for changing his left-front tire darted across the pit stall, his feet inches from the front wing, as the car slid to a halt. The air jacks had the car off the ground in a millisecond as the familiar whirring of the impact wrenches started up and the fuel hose engaged the side of his car. Remington only had time to take a couple of deep breaths, and a small sip of water, before his front tire changers threw their hands in the air, signaling they had successfully completed their portion of the pitstop.

As soon as his car hit the ground, Remington popped it in gear and pressed the accelerator. His motor roared, the torque sending his tires spinning in a ghostly white smoke. Remington rocketed from his pit-box, dodging the other cars as they leapt onto pit road and sped back to the racing surface.

"What position are we in after the stop?" Remington asked as he discarded a tear-off.

Craig radioed back. "I was just giving props to the boys. You came in tenth and they got you out in sixth. Now it's all you, Rem."

Remington felt a boost of courage. He'd picked up four spots in the pits and was running on fresh tires. Remington fondly called new tires his 200-mile-per-hour-crampons. They would allow him to break later, accelerate harder, and if the opportunity presented, make a daring pass on the outside of a turn.

Race-control finished radioing the drivers their restart positions as the flagman showed the field the rolled up white flag, signaling they would be back at speed the next time by. Rem ran the potential scenarios of the restart through his mind as his nerves picked up pace in unison with the field of cars. He had good heat in his tires and knew that the initial laps of the final stint would be his fastest before his tires began to wear. The closer he got to the front, the harder each pass would become.

"Green this time by. Green this time by," Craig said. Remington knew his time was now. He tucked the nose of his machine right on the rear attenuator of the fifth-place car as the green flag waved in the searing afternoon heat, and squeezed the throttle to avoid spinning the rear tires as the seven car roared to life. The field bolted down the front straightaway as the packed grandstand melted away at nearly a football field every second. Remington was squarely in the draft of the car in front of him when he snapped his hands to the right, ripping his car from the windless vacuum and pulling even with the fifth-place driver.

Remington cringed as the cars in front of him braked; turn one loomed just ahead. He backed off the throttle and squeezed the brake pedal, hoping his car would slow in time for the turn, but maintain the right amount of speed to edge out the car inches to his left. He gingerly guided his race car into the sharp right-hander.

Suddenly, his car snapped to the outside of the turn, placing his left rear wheel squarely on the side pod of his competitor. The contact bounced Remington's car back into the racing line and he immediately grabbed the throttle, blowing past the car and into fifth place. His pass did not cost him as much time as he thought it would and he once again found himself trailing his next victim by a split second, the small rubber marbles, shed from his competitors' tires, ricocheting off his visor. He composed himself and began to plan his next maneuver.

Remington knew he needed to make another move quickly, as each corner ripped the life from the surface of his Firestone racing tires. He would not have to wait long. In an instant, Remington realized the fourth-place driver had under-braked going into the next turn and was drifting toward the outside of the corner. Remington slung his car to the right, centering it squarely on the inner curb. He hoped to take advantage of the narrow gap that had materialized to slide under his competitor and into fourth. As the bottom of his car came into contact with the curb, it was instantly propelled a foot into the air. The sudden loss of traction left Remington sawing the steering wheel of his car like he was trying to swat a bee. As he wrestled his own car from the grip of peril, the sixth-place car was able to skate by both of the drivers and Remington suddenly found himself in sixth place once again.

Remington took a deep breath to dampen the adrenaline that surged through his veins. He reassured himself that he still had plenty of time to pick up spots, if his tires would allow. The lead drivers had raced their way out of his sight in a battle of their own, but the other two cars he was competing with were still right in front of him. Once again, the chase was on.

Remington caught another good draft going down the front stretch and was able to pass the fifth-place car for a second time. With just five laps remaining, it was going to be a stretch to reel in fourth-place. Remington pressed on. One sector at a time, he was able to chip away at the tenths-of-seconds between him and a top-four finish until at last, he could feel the turbulent draft rumbling off the car in front of him.

"You'll be getting the white flag this time by," Craig said over the radio. "You can get this guy, Rem. Let's go!" The white flag signaled the final lap. It was now or never.

Remington positioned himself two car lengths behind the fourth-place car going through the quick dogleg that made up turns 11 and 12. If he could get a good enough run, it would be a drag race going down the front straightaway to the finish line. Remington accelerated hard coming out of the final turn, his throttle drawing upon every fiber of grip left in his depleted rear tires. With a squeal and chatter, they catapulted him even with his contender. The two cars ran inches apart as they approached the waving checkered flags and ripped across the finish line. A burst of excitement erupted from the crowd, standing for the spectacular finish.

"Did I get him?" gasped Remington on the radio.

"Did he get him?" Chet Buckner asked Jersey with a fist still in the air.

"He beat you by one-tenth of a second, Rem," Craig said. "Outstanding race. We're going to do good things this season."

The cat purred on Mark's lap as he turned off the old radio and cupped his hands in front of the space heater. He sat in silence, gazing at the racing memorabilia that hung throughout his shop. He could almost hear the antiquities applauding the performance of Remington Mason's rookie debut. Or, it could have been the cold wind howling through the cracks in the barn. Mark smiled as his eyes landed on the picture of himself and Remington in victory lane.

"Mark! Dinner," his wife yelled from the front porch. He turned off the space heater, grabbed his jacket, and took another look around the shop.

"Let's hope Remington has more races like that, hey mouser?" The cat purred and bolted ahead as Mark shut the door and followed her up the snowy driveway.

CHAPTER 11

Foster the Season

THE GYM IN THE HOTEL was still vacant at six in the morning as Remington set the incline to four and the speed to seven. He always felt he was gaining on the rest of the world at this hour. While they were sleeping, he was perfecting his body and his mind. The digital miles melted away as he visualized lap after lap and pass after pass on the racetrack. Flux Energy Liquor Racing was about to enter its third contest as a professional race team, and Remington had already mastered a routine. His alarm signaled the kickoff at 5:00, followed by a protein-packed breakfast while studying film from past races. His focus was relentless, and he felt a responsibility to everyone on his team, and to his dad, to foster the opportunity he had been given and had worked so hard to create.

It wasn't until mile marker six that Remington realized he was no longer alone in the gym. Mile ten came in no time, and he pulled the stop cord on the treadmill, signaling his transition to the weightlifting portion of his workout. After a squirt of sports drink and a quick adjustment to his headband, Remington was standing over the rack of free weights when he finally noticed the woman glistening with sweat on the elliptical behind him. He quickly grabbed a set of dumbbells when their eyes unexpectedly met in the mirror. Thankfully, the dumbbells were about the right weight. Remington pretended to check his foot position to avoid another such occurrence. But after two sets of bicep curls, an invisible, relentless tug pulled his eyes toward his early-morning counterpart in the gym. A chink in the armor of his focus had come in the form of bleach blonde hair, a pink tank top, and yoga pants.

Remington's fitness was his livelihood, and it gave him an edge on the track. While his physique matched those of bodies strutting the sands of SoCal's beaches, he was there for one reason: to win the IndyCar Grand Prix of Long Beach.

After Remington fumbled a few awkward attempts at avoiding the woman on the elliptical, she finally flashed a smile and stepped off the machine. There was nothing he could do but smile back.

"Hi. I'm Mabel Foster," she said as she approached Remington with her hand out.

"Remington Mason," he replied, surprised at her firm handshake. "I guess all the awkward looks were either going to lead to this, or one of us was going to have to end our workout early."

Mabel laughed as she removed a hair tie, and with a slight shake of her head, unfurled a stampede of wavy blonde hair that made its way to the middle of her back. "There was nothing awkward about it. I mean, you looked a little eighth-grade-dance-ish trying to dodge all my looks, but shouldn't you be used to that by now?" Mabel smiled, her piercing blue eyes surveying Remington's arms. "After all, you are the hottest new rookie to come through the IndyCar Series in a while. You must get women looking at you everywhere you go."

Remington was a little taken aback, but was amused by Mabel's boldness, and without question, he liked her looks. "So you're a race fan then?" Remington asked, wiping his face with his gym towel.

"A *race* fan?" Mabel said, with a manufactured look of annoyance. "I am insulted. I have not missed an Indy 500, in person mind you, since my parents took me to my first one twelve years ago. And I hit all of the West Coast circuit stops as well. So, a *fan*?"

"I am sorry, and as equally impressed."

"No hard feelings, rookie." Mabel smiled mischievously and gave Remington a wink. "Mind if we get a selfie? My girlfriends will die when they see who I met in the hotel weight room. Every year, we do a girls weekend at the hotel for the race and have a friendly competition to see who can get the best selfie. This will be the winner. I came to watch the race, but they all came to see you."

She pushed her body close to his, striking a sexy, well-rehearsed pose. "Click!" He quickly removed his arm from her waist, realizing his gesture may have been a little too familiar. Especially for someone supposedly not interested in promoting any type of romantic relationship.

"One more," Mabel said as she quickly grabbed his hand and placed it back on her hip, this time, a little lower. "This one is for me." Their embrace released after the digital image was captured. Remington's hand slowly dragged across Mabel's back as she turned to him, flashed a sexy smile, and placed her index finger squarely on his chest as she backed away. "Good luck this weekend, rookie. We will see you on race day."

Mabel disappeared into the hall as Remington returned to the weight rack. He hadn't been lifting for the past few minutes, but his heart was racing. He picked up two dumbbells, trying to refocus, but all he could think about was Mabel's last touch on his chest. She was probably about to get on the elevator, and here he was talking to himself with sweaty palms and weights hanging at his side.

The elevator door was just opening when Remington slid around the corner at a pretty good clip. Thankfully, a large family of tourists stuffed themselves and their bags into the elevator just ahead of Mabel, forcing her to wait for the next ride.

"Hey, rookie," Mabel said as Remington slid to a stop. "Done with your workout already?"

"The most strenuous part of my workout was sprinting down this hall after you. It *would* have been a serious rookie mistake not asking you to grab a cup of coffee. So, how about a cup of coffee?" The second elevator door opened, cuing Mabel's departure. She stepped into the elevator and slowly turned, tousling a lock of hair that now covered half of her face as the door began to shut.

"I'll think about it." The door slipped to a close. Remington turned around in frustration. It took him a second to realize, via the lobby mirror, that the elevator door had opened back up. He could see the mischievous smirk on Mabel's face.

"What time and where, rookie?" Mabel asked with her hand on her hip as the door started to close again. "Think fast!"

Remington spun around. "Beachside Bistro, eight a.m." He got his words out in the nick of time. Mabel gave him a subtle wink of acknowledgement as she disappeared from sight.

If the first three races of the season were any indication, Remington and Flux Racing were a magical combination. Remington's on-track performance was impeccable: no "Did Not Finish," or DNFs; all top-tens; and a solid fourth place at the Grand Prix of Long Beach. Flux Energy Liquor had seen a substantial boost in sales through the first quarter of the year and the Flux crew was coming together as a high-performing team. As for Remington, he was living a dream. He was quickly becoming the new face of the IndyCar Series, his raw talent and aggressive driving style being pitted against the wily veterans of the series, determined not to relinquish their throne as IndyCar royalty. The David vs. Goliath story, with the one-car Flux team consistently beating the multi-car mega-teams, was a boon for TV ratings and the key storyline approaching the month of May, the most important, and trying, 31 days in the life of an IndyCar driver. It was the month Remington had been waiting for his whole life.

CHAPTER 12

Memorial Day

THE LIGHTS OF THE PAGODA were a beacon piercing the dark sky over the racetrack. They would soon serve as a guide for multitudes of race fans descending upon the Indianapolis Motor Speedway, just as they had every Memorial Day weekend for more than a hundred years. Remington squeezed the cup of warm coffee in his hands and propped himself up on the front-stretch wall straddling the legendary yard of bricks. The grandstands were quiet except for the occasional employee preparing each seat for 350,000 roaring fans. Remington could already hear their cheers echoing through the cathedrals of the modern-day Coliseum where, in eight hours, he would prepare to do battle.

Remington's hotel room had served as a prison cell throughout the night as he tossed and turned, unable to sleep. Excitement, mixed with understanding the dangers of racing at more than 230 mph, kept the most seasoned drivers from a good night's sleep. As a rookie driver preparing for his first Indianapolis 500, Remington was awake at four a.m.

The American and checkered flags atop the Pagoda swayed in the early morning breeze. Remington vividly recalled the morning Lionel turned their rental car southeast on Crawfordsville Road. It wasn't long before he saw the massive turn-one grandstand jutting from the flat Indiana ground.

"This is it," Lionel said as he pointed toward the main gate of the speedway, returning to a place he had been many times before. At six years of age, Remington was overcome with a feeling of awe, mixed with a surprising sense of sadness as they drove past the speedway's corporate offices and headed north down Georgetown Road. The expansive length of the grandstands were still shrouded in early-morning mist as banners of winners past slowly appeared, looming down as they drove the length of the front straightaway. Remington had watched enough races and listened to his dad long enough to understand the significance of these legendary grounds. He knew the stories of heartbreak and success, of names made and families broken. For every victor looking down from the back of the grandstands, there was a blank wall and indescribable loss experienced by so many more.

The grief, the awe, and the glory combined in a rare elixir of emotion that left Remington's heart aching, yet simultaneously filled with a sense of wonder and passion. The sleepy town of Speedway, Indiana, was hallowed ground that served as a bridge between life and death and in a way, made both seem more worthy. The drivers who dared to turn a lap at this place embodied the individual Teddy Roosevelt spoke of when he referred to those "who spend themselves in a worthy cause; who at the best know in the end the triumph of high achievement, and who at the worst, if they fail, at least fail while daring greatly, so that their place shall never be with those cold and timid souls who neither know victory nor defeat." The Indianapolis Motor Speedway was a monument to those who have dared greatly.

And Remington was now one of those men; he had sensed it when he first approached the gates of the Speedway and looked down the tunnel-like front stretch that he was now barreling through as an IndyCar driver himself. As he finished his last sip of coffee, he realized how lucky he was to have found his way from the other side of the catch fence to where he stood now, on the brink of his first Indianapolis 500.

The blast of the cannon that signaled the opening of the track rattled Remington from his reflection as throngs of fans began to pour through the gates, waking up the sleepy grounds. Remington glanced at his watch out of habit as he took a deep breath, attempting to keep his nerves at bay. The gnawing suspense in his stomach would continue to eat its way through his body until about lap three, when he could finally settle into just driving the car.

The pre-race routine for every driver was unique. Some found comfort in a quick bike ride to get their blood flowing, while others liked to mix it up with their fans or hunt down reporters to snag some airtime. Some find their focus in being alone, others in the hub of the race-day activity. Remington found his peace by spending time with Mabel Foster.

Remington popped out the kickstand on his moped and strolled into the Brickyard Cafe. Mabel smiled at him from the corner booth. Fans stared and pointed as he wove through the maze of tables scattered through the room. The corner booth served as a finish line as Mable threw her arms around Remington and planted her pink lipstick on his cheek.

"You look stunning," Remington said.

"I *am* the girlfriend of a professional race driver and this *is* the Indianapolis 500," Mabel replied as she sheepishly smiled at Remington across the table. "If there was ever a time to look my best, today would be the day." Remington smiled, his race-day nerves temporarily soothed by Mabel's presence. Their first cup of coffee in Long Beach, just a couple of months earlier, had led to drinks, dinner, a kiss, and eventually a relationship. Mabel's modeling career afforded her the flexibility to meet up with Remington wherever he was on the racing circuit.

"How did you sleep last night, babe?" Mabel asked.

"Horrible," Remington said. The waitress delivered two vanilla lattes, a foam heart floating on top of each.

"I'm sorry," the blushing waitress said. "I just have to say that I am a huge fan, Remington, and you two are a great-looking couple. Good luck today."

The minutes quickly built to an hour — one hour closer to the start of the race. The solace of distraction Remington had found in chatting with Mabel disappeared as quickly as it had set in as they mounted Remington's moped and headed to the Pagoda for the mandatory race-day drivers' meeting. He reminded himself that the nerves were not all bad, a necessary concoction of fear, confidence, faith, and excitement. The feelings in his head and heart were what scared him, drove him, and made him who he was. It was the closest thing he had ever experienced to a drug. He lived for it; he loved it and would pursue it regardless of the price. This feeling *was* Remington Mason. He was making a living by being himself.

The cameras clicked as Mabel dismounted the moped. Remington clasped her hand and walked toward the Pagoda green room. The press did everything they could to get a word from the couple, to no avail. But his smile and confident wave gave them something for that evening's news. He was marketing gold and his new girlfriend added to the mystique of auto racing's latest heartthrob. Their story was followed by every small-town mom and pop publication covering the local races. After all, Remington was one of them, the pride and joy of every

Saturday night short-track dirt slinger with Indianapolis piercing their dreams. In an age of imports, Remington Mason was a beacon of small-town American hope in the bright lights of Indy.

"Do you not know that in a race all the runners run, but only one gets the prize? Run in such a way as to get the prize. First Corinthians, chapter nine verse twenty-four," Brody Compton said as he closed his Bible on the makeshift pulpit in the Pagoda green room. "I will not lie — I hope I'm the *one* that gets the prize today." Brody shrugged as his fellow drivers ribbed him back. "You know, growing up watching my dad race, that was a Scripture that always stood out. As a boy, I loved it because it fit motorsports. But as I grew older it came to mean more. It was something tangible that helped me understand an intangible God. It also became a mantra for how I live my life. I wasn't only put on this earth to drive cars faster than all of you." The hooting continued. "I was put here for a greater purpose, to glorify God with my life, and professional motorsports just happens to be the way I do it. I want to leave you with one thing as we all get ready to walk through those doors and run for the greatest prize that motorsports has to offer. Regardless of whose face is on the Borg Warner at the end of the day, just remember that the ultimate prize is a life lived for Jesus. A life that gives hope to others through love." Compton folded his hands in prayer.

"Father God, I ask that you protect each of us today. Protect the fans, our crews, and everyone that is a part of this great event. Above all, help us to run races that glorify you. It is in your name we pray, Amen."

"Wow. The *preacher* was really going hard today," Mabel said as they left the green room and headed back to Gasoline Alley. "Does he always get that fired up before the drivers' meetings?"

Remington laughed. "Brody is such a good guy, and a hell of a race driver. He *could* be the one that gets that prize today — he's starting on the second row. He drives as hard as he preaches and I hand it to him, he lives out what he says in there. Not many people do. He doesn't speak before every meeting, but I like it when he does. Somehow I feel it sort of protects me. Protects us. I'm probably being superstitious. It's these quick hands of mine that protect me."

Remington and Mabel were about to enter the Flux motorsports stall in the garage area when Remington received a firm slap on the back. "Run for the prize, rookie," Brody Compton yelled as he rolled by the couple on his moped, his wife on the back. "Praying for you bro. Run hard out there today!" Brody pinned the throttle on his moped, swinging one hand in the air like a bull rider, smoke pouring out the back of the scooter.

Brody Compton had been a staple in the IndyCar series the past five years: rookie of the year, seven race wins, handsome, with a beautiful wife and two kids. He was an IndyCar hero with a heart as big as his personality. It was impossible not to like the man. Brody was respected by his peers and was an anchor of hope and solace during the trials and triumphs that come during an IndyCar season.

Remington slipped his race suit on while Mabel sat on the couch in his hauler, Tweeting about her man's first Indianapolis 500 start.

"Can I be honest with you about something?" Remington asked. He threw his gloves in his helmet bag and pulled his fireproof undershirt down.

"Of course, Rem." Mabel set her phone aside and patted the couch. Remington sat beside her. "What's up?"

"I had a bad dream last night. I couldn't really sleep, but somehow, I apparently slept long enough to dream." Remington rubbed his neck as he stumbled with the cloudy images from the night before. "I don't think I can recall the exact details, but I had a dream something bad would happen today."

"I'm so sorry sweetie. Please, tell me more." Mabel squeezed his hand and took over the duty of rubbing his neck.

"I mean, I'm sure it's nothing and I don't want to worry you, but I just couldn't shake it this morning and figured it would do me good to get it off my chest."

Mabel leaned even closer and, with her lips touching his ear, whispered, "Not only are you sexy, you are the best damn driver in the field today, and no one is more prepared to win the Indy 500 than Remington Mason. You just put this little vision of yours right out of your mind, replace it with checkered flags, and go kick some ass."

Remington laughed as she giggled and kissed his ear. He knew he had fallen for her for a reason and in this particular moment, her humor cleared his mind. Mabel's presence at the track had kept him motivated and focused throughout the month, and her fun-loving personality was a welcome balance to his demanding schedule. She sprayed champagne with him after his first podium finish in the IndyCar Grand Prix and had checkered cupcakes waiting in their motor coach after he completed rookie orientation. Her smile greeted him from the top of his pit box after every hour of on-track testing and he would never forget her running down pit lane and jumping into his arms after he qualified for his first Indy 500.

After a quick media tour through the Flux VIP area, Jersey led Remington past the growing mass of fans pressed against the fence leading to the garages. Sharpies and programs resembled little swords and shields as they were waved furiously in Remington's direction with hopes of snagging an autograph. Jersey kept a close eye on her watch, letting Remington know when it was time to make the next stop.

The helicopters buzzed low overhead and small planes defied physics as they pulled banners four times their size promoting everything from beer to insurance. The infamous Snake Pit party was well underway as DJs sprayed Champagne on a buzzing crowd. The Purdue University band circled the raceway in rhythmic pomp kept in time by the "World's Largest Drum," and movie stars graced the red carpet on the front straightaway as they had for years. The "Yellow Shirts" and their whistles herded the masses, while accident response crews circled the track like hawks, looking for anything that might affect the safety of the racing surface. Small wonder the Indianapolis 500 was deemed the Greatest Spectacle in Racing. Remington had experienced this show many times before from the outside, but today he could not hear the driving beats of the Snake Pit or see the red carpet. But as he reviewed the day's race strategy with Craig Doucet, he could feel the monumental pulse of the event.

Driver introductions were over, the traditional photograph of the starting field captured, and the cars aligned in their starting positions on the front straightaway. TV cameras and reporters wove their way through the colorful mass of machine and humanity, hoping to get a final word with one of the drivers as fans rushed to find their seats before the final pre-race festivities. Around the Speedway, 350,000 spectators removed their hats in unison for a prayer of thanks for our country and veterans and a word of protection for the drivers, itching to don their helmets and start the race. Only the dull buzz of the helicopters could be heard in the distance as "Taps" echoed hauntingly through the grandstands before the National Anthem was sung.

Lionel Mason wiped the sweat from his forehead, the Indiana humidity, and the anticipation of his son racing in the Indianapolis 500, taking their toll. The Flux VIP trackside suite was starting to fill with celebrities fresh off the red carpet, greeted by Flux girls strolling through the room serving ice-cold neon shots of Flux Energy Liquor and decadent hors d'oeuvres. Chet Buckner loudly entertained a group of well-heeled businessmen in one corner of the room, and Jersey clicked away on her laptop, posting photos of the morning's events to Remington's social media accounts. The room was ablaze with excitement. Lionel sat quietly outside of the suite, his prayers for his son's safety drifting heavenward with the traditional release of balloons as "Back Home Again in Indiana" echoed through the infield. The moment had finally come.

Mabel wrapped her arms around Remington's neck and gave him a kiss. "Please be safe out there, Rem. I love you."

"I love you too," Remington said as one of his crew members handed him his helmet. "See you in victory lane in about four hours?"

"I'll be there."

With a final wave to the fans, Remington pulled on his helmet and slid into the driver's seat. The crew cinched his harness and attached his HANS device as Craig leaned in to give Remington final instructions.

"Be patient out there. This is the longest race you have ever been in — by far. I need you in one piece for the last fifty laps so we can make a run to the front. Keep doing what you have done all season. Race your race." Remington gave Craig a confident wink from under his mirrored visor and squeezed his hand. An entire month of preparation had come down to this: the start of the Indianapolis 500, four hours that could change the life of any race driver.

"And now, for the most famous words in motorsports," boomed over the loud speaker as Mari Hulman George was escorted to a microphone on the victory podium.

"Lady and gentlemen, start your engines!" Mrs. George said with a quiver. Crank starters whirred and thirty-three roaring engines were commanded to life by her feeble voice. After a handful of pace laps, the drivers would be off.

The pace car roared as the driver sped up, distancing himself from the pack of cars that growled hungrily behind him, and dove into pit lane. Fans craned their necks to catch the first glimpse of the cars coming off turn four with their pent-up power urging to be turned loose with the wave of a green flag. More than 350,000 hearts quickened as the muted roar built to a howl. The crowd silenced in anticipation and a rumble crescendoed through the metal mass of grandstands.

Remington's blood pulsed through his veins, causing his harness to further constrict his body. His hearing faded and his vision narrowed as ancient hyperarousal, physiological responses sharpened all of his senses for a perceived threat — in this case, the start of his first Indianapolis 500. Remington did his best to take a deep, even breath, staring down the tunnel of fans composing the front straightaway. The track looked dauntingly narrow with the grandstands full and four rows of cars tightly aligned three abreast in front of him and the rest of the field behind, longing to steal his spot. The pace of the field began to pick up as if he were being sucked into a swift current. There was no turning back.

"Green!" Remington's spotter shouted over the radio. Remington squeezed the throttle; his car rocketed forward down the front straightaway. His two row-mates pinned him to the outside of the track and dove wheel to wheel into turn one. His first impulse was to remain three wide going in with hopes the other two drivers would lift, but Craig's advice echoed its way into Remington's crowded mind: "We need you in one piece for the last fifty laps." Remington had seen it too many times: first lap jitters numbing a driver's senses, and they'd think they could win the race on the first lap. Remington breathed the throttle and tucked in behind the other drivers. A split-second later, he was back on the gas through the short chute and into turn 2, inches off the gear box of the fourteenth-place car. The draft gave Remington's car a boost heading down the backstretch. He veered to the left and blew by his competitor. One down, thirteen to go.

"Easy, easy," Remington's turn three spotter said over the radio. Remington had the race plan ingrained in his mind, but was caught off guard at how quickly his car had come up to speed. Turn three was bearing down on him almost as fast as he was approaching the thirteenth-place car. It was too late to move back to the outside of the track and follow the best racing line. Remington kept his foot on the gas and dove aggressively toward the apex of turn three, hoping he would clear the car beside him and that his car would stick to the racing surface. He did, and it did. The short chute and final turn melted away and Remington felt the subtle vibration as he crossed the yard of bricks to complete lap one of the Indianapolis 500.

It wasn't until halfway down the back straightaway on lap two that Remington remembered taking his first breath of the race. "I have to calm down," he thought. "My adrenaline is racing and I still have 497 miles to go."

Lionel's nerves were getting the best of him, too. Remington's fast and steady start was helping to take the edge off, but Lionel's prayers continued for his son as the first set of green flag pit stops approached. Lionel evolved from silent prayers to prayers intermixed with a dose of loud cheering each time his son passed the Flux suite. Chet Buckner's VIP guests shared in Lionel's excitement as they applauded Remington's early race performance.

"He's looking great so far, Lionel," Jersey yelled over the noise as she sat down next to him. The more Jersey spent time with Lionel Mason, the more she liked him. She admired his wisdom and professional accomplishments. Above all, she adored the love and concern he had for his son, something she lacked growing up with a father whose racing left her as a lonely spectator, observing his career from afar.

She gave her dad credit for her love of motorsports, and her mother credit for everything else she had become. Jersey's mother always said, "It wasn't racing that took your father from us. It was his choices." Jersey knew her mother's love, wisdom, and support were why she was pursuing her passion now.

"You let me know if you need anything, Mr. Mason." Jersey squeezed his shoulder as she popped up to continue working. "Your boy is doing amazing."

Mabel Foster cheered from her seat atop the pit box as Remington slid to a halt and a flurry of crew members dove over the wall to service his car. She was ecstatic to be sitting trackside for the Indy 500 and to be dating one of the sport's hottest drivers. Mabel's enthusiastic support of Remington quickly caught the attention of the camera crews covering pit lane, her excitement and stunning looks making a great side story to the day's events.

Remington felt the air jack drop and punched the throttle. "Good stop boys!" he yelled over the radio, careful to avoid the potential for carnage as cars weaved in and out of their pit boxes like prairie dogs diving for cover in their burrows.

"Good job yourself," echoed Craig. "Stay smooth and calm out there, Remington. You're doing just what you need to do. Keep letting the car come to you. We'll get it to where we have a good shot at winning this thing by the end of the day."

The first three-quarters of a relatively clean race evaporated, with only one caution flag for debris on the track. Remington had run consistently around the middle of the pack for most of the day, an outstanding feat for a rookie. But as the last fifty laps of the race approached, a competitive burning in Remington's heart wanted more, and he felt his car had the juice to deliver a top-five spot. It was time to stop saving the car for the final fifty and start using the car to climb the standings. Craig Doucet agreed.

"Okay, Rem," Craig crackled over the radio. "Fifty-three laps to go. Any changes for the final stop?"

"None," a calm Remington replied as he blew past the Flux pit box at 230 miles an hour. The car was perfect. Remington felt he could drive just about anywhere on the track and was ready to make his mark on Indianapolis 500 history.

Each lap, the vibration of the last remaining strip of original brick racing surface marking the finish line, was a reminder of why every driver was there: an hour glass marked in laps, counting down one driver's destiny with racing immortality. Win this race, and you become legend: the remaining results of your career, good and bad, covered by the shadow of the Borg Warner trophy.

Fatigue was starting to set in. Remington's hands ached and sweat stung his eyes. The G-forces continued to pound each driver further into the recesses of their seat until they were one with their machine. The battle had long since stopped being merely physical. Whichever driver was able to wring every last ounce of courage and focus from within would stand victorious, sipping milk in victory lane. Fifty. More. Laps.

Remington took a deep breath during his final pit stop, hit his water button to hydrate, and removed a final tear-off. His engine gave sharp staccato warnings as his car hit the rev limiter leaving his pit box. His team's quick work and his aggressive exit to the second lane of pit row gained him two positions. By the time the remaining cars would pit, he'd cycle out in the tenth position, an ideal spot for a shootout to the checkered flag. Ryan Hunter Reay, Helio Castroneves, and Brody Compton had dominated every stage of the race to this point, but there were a slew of fast cars waiting to make a charge to the front of the field — including Remington Mason's number seven.

"Welcome back to ABC's coverage of the 105th running of the Indianapolis 500. I'm Alan Bestwick, joined by Eddie Cheever and Scott Goodyear. Folks, you are in for a treat. This is shaping up to be a phenomenal finish. Ryan Hunter Reay has been absolutely dominant for Andretti Autosport today. Helio Castroneves and Brody Compton round out the top three and you could toss a blanket over all three of them, but there are some hungry drivers charging toward the front. How about rookie, Remington Mason, in his Indianapolis 500 debut? His consistency throughout the day has been impressive and I think that car has even more to offer as we approach the final laps of this race. If his record is any indication, he will be near the front of this field when the checkered flag falls."

"I agree with you, Alan," Eddie said. "I have been so impressed with this kid's composure, not just here at Indianapolis, but through the entire season so far. His maturity, both on and off the track, has been incredible. Remington Mason finds himself running P10 as we approach the end of this race — that speaks volumes about his talent."

"I agree," Alan said, "but we still have a thirty-lap dash to the finish. Let's see how things play out."

"Get off that table you darn cat!" Mark scrambled to the workbench to re-adjust the aluminum foil precariously snaking toward the shop window from the antenna of his AM/FM radio. The radio crackled back to life. "You want to miss this, mouser? Our boy Remington is making his way to the front. You're lucky I'm even letting you listen. I'm nervous too, but you don't see me batting at the antenna." Mark slid a placatory slice of salami to the cat who happily chomped on it as he turned his attention back to the race. "C'mon, Rem. Twenty more laps. Make your move."

"And here comes the field out of turn number four. Nineteen laps to go. Remington Mason in the number seven Flux Energy Liquor car has a good run going down the front straightaway. Will he have time to make a move? Yes, yes! Mason makes a daring pass, darting under Chris Farrington into turn number one. That car is on rails. Will the Flux machine be able to continue this climb? It's only going to get more difficult the higher the 7 car moves up the scoring pylon." The excitement in the announcer's voices tumbled through radio waves and poured into Mark's shop. Their words rejuvenated the antiquated racing memorabilia hanging in the barn, and the roar of the cars rattled the socket sets on Mark's work bench.

"Fifteen laps to go in the 105th running of the Indianapolis 500 and your leader is still Ryan Hunter Reay, with Brody Compton now in command of the second position. But the real race is a little further back in the pack as Remington Mason is trying to work on the number 27 car of Marco Andretti. Oh no! James Hinchcliffe touched wheels with the eight car as they headed into turn number three. Andretti and Mason are rapidly approaching the slower cars."

Mark sat silently shaking his head, imagining the potential for disaster unfolding in front of Remington. He had seen it before.

"Mason darts to the outside of Andretti into turn three just inches from the wall. He is going to have to adjust quickly to avoid disaster . . . and he does! He clears the back of James Hinchcliffe's car by inches. Remington Mason averts carnage and jumps three positions to find himself in the sixth spot. What a race this is!"

Mark paced through the maze of old sprint cars and midgets, fidgeting with the corn cob pipe dangling from the side of his mouth. "C'mon, Rem, c'mon," he mumbled to himself as the pace of his steps and heart quickened.

"I don't think Remington Mason backed off through that entire ordeal as he is already flirting with the draft of the fifth-place car. Where will this phenomenal rookie end up?"

Remington was clueless to the buzz he was creating on the radio broadcast. Had he heard their assessment of how calm and collected he was in the car, he would have laughed. His nerves were raging from the narrow miss the lap before and at the thrill of catching two more cars before the checkers waved. He could now feel himself firmly inside the draft of the fifth-place car, a sure sign he had a good run going. The time was now. Remington pulled within inches of the gear box of the fifth-place car, then turned left into the wall of wind outside the draft just as he crossed the start/finish line. His momentum catapulted him ahead of his opponent in time to drift back to the outside wall coming into turn one. A textbook pass. Remington pushed hard, careful to not outdrive his car on a set of Firestone tires nearing the end of its life.

With just two laps to go, Remington was looking to make a move on the fourth-place car. He went through all his mental calculations to determine the exact spot on the race track he would attempt a pass. Judging by how quickly he was gaining, Remington decided turn one of the final lap would be the moment.

"One to go, Rem," Craig informed his driver from the pit box. "If the car has anything left, you need to make your move." Before Craig could even finish his message, Remington shot to the outside of Helio Castroneves going into one. The audience roared as Remington's car drew even with its target. Before he could react, he realized both cars were far too high entering the turn. Marbles began to pelt his helmet and suddenly he felt as if he were in a Montana winter driving on a sheet of black ice. The car snapped violently toward the outside retaining wall, skidding on the deposit of little rubber balls shed throughout the course of 500 miles. Remington had no time to think, only react. He completed the unnatural maneuver of snapping the wheel toward the wall in the direction of his slide and kept his foot on the throttle. Miraculously, his left front tire found a clear patch of asphalt and pulled his car back to the racing line, like a father might pull his child back from a busy street. As Remington held his breath, the Flux crew breathed a sigh of relief, and Mabel removed her cupped hand from her mouth. Remington checked his mirrors as he accelerated through the short chute, knowing the sixth-place car would be bearing down on him at full speed. He kept his right foot at three-quarters throttle through turn number two to ensure the marbles had detached themselves from his racing tires before accelerating down the backstretch and once again hitting turn three at full speed.

"Please stick; please stick," Remington gasped to himself. With no room for doubt, and the sixth place car now in tow, he turned left into turn three at full throttle. The car stuck. Remington checked his mirrors one final time in the short chute before maneuvering the last turn of the race.

Remington climbed from the car drenched in sweat, rubber, and oil. Mabel leapt over the pit wall and jumped into his arms, delivering a much-deserved, juicy kiss.

"I am so proud of you, Remington!" Mabel said with a spot of grease on her cheek. "A fifth-place finish in the Indianapolis 500 and rookie of the race to boot. Hot damn!" Remington lifted her up and twirled her as the rest of his team gathered around, congratulating him. The Flux Energy Liquor VIP suite was electric with excitement too. Chet Buckner had built a team around a promising young talent, and their place as a legitimate force to be reckoned with in the IndyCar Series was already being solidified. To everyone in the suite and on the Flux team, Remington's performance was a solid win. The Indianapolis Motor Speedway had smiled upon Remington Mason. Any feelings of grief or sadness he ever had here were a distant memory — he was a part of Indianapolis 500 history.

CHAPTER *13*

Mackinac

THE TROLLING MOTOR GARGLED AND HUMMED as it stirred the water off the stern of the boat. For Remington, it was a welcome contrast to the screaming roar that permeated the grounds of the Indianapolis Motor Speedway throughout the month of May.

"Let out just a little more line, Rem," Lionel said as he gently increased the speed of their small fishing boat. "Perfect! Hold it right there." Remington kicked back in his chair to stand guard over his fishing pole as his father flipped the bail and let his own line out.

"If we don't hook into a good lake trout here, fire me as your guide." Lionel wedged his rod under his leg. "I fished this spot hundreds of times as a kid and it never let me down. But I'm sure it gets fished more than it used to."

"I am happy either way, Pop. It's nice to have this time away from the track." Lionel had looked forward to the trip as well. They already spent too much time apart.

"Rem, look," Lionel whispered. "Your line is moving." Remington sat up in his seat and slowly reached for his fishing pole.

"Give him time. He is toying with the lure. You will know when he hits it." Remington readied himself. "Wait . . . wait . . . wait . . . now!" Remington set the hook as the line began to rip off of his reel. "That's what I'm talking about!" Lionel shouted as he retrieved his own line to avoid a tangle. "Work him in nice and slow."

Remington was having fun with the hard tug on the end of his line as he battled what felt to be a nice fish. But even more, he enjoyed the look on his father's face, one he had seen many times before. He had seen it when he caught his first cutthroat trout on a fly rod floating a big grasshopper down a Montana stream in late August. He had seen it when he bagged his first deer shortly after completing his hunter's safety course, and when he won his first race as a novice quarter midget driver, blowing past the finish line at an impressive 34 miles per hour. He had seen it again just a couple of days before, when he received his rookie of the race honors at the Indianapolis 500 Awards Banquet. A look that built inside a young man, that gave him courage, confidence, and the knowledge that his father believed in him — that his father loved him.

Remington became so caught up in the moment he almost jerked the fish right out of the water as it approached the boat.

"Whoa, whoa! Don't horse it," Lionel said as he scrambled for the net. The beautiful fish flashed its white underbelly just a few feet from the boat, churning the surface of the water. Remington eased the fish closer as Lionel scooped it into the net.

"All right, buddy!" Lionel slapped his boy on the back. "That's exactly how I remembered this spot. What a beautiful lake trout."

A couple of pictures captured the moment as the sun began to set over Lake Huron. Remington pulled up the trolling motor as Lionel fired up the seventy-five-horse Johnson motor and pointed the boat toward the dock. They were in no rush to get back as they glided along the glassy surface reflecting the sun as it melted into the western banks of the lake. Neither of them had to say anything to appreciate the other's company and the raw beauty that surrounded them. Some moments are simply better left silent, a pact well understood among outdoorsmen.

Remington tied a final cleat hitch before they began the walk up to their rooms at the Mackinac Island Grand Hotel, where they would be staying for the following three nights. They planned to fish as much as humanly possible before heading south to the Milwaukee Mile for the next stop on the IndyCar schedule. Before turning in for the night, they stopped in the main dining room for a plate of fresh strawberries, angel food cake, and whipped cream.

They checked out of the Grand Hotel feeling rested, having added quite a few lake trout to their fishing tally. The Masons rarely came home empty-handed.

They talked all the way down on the drive to the track in Milwaukee. Lionel would be heading back to Montana after the race and Remington had a full schedule of races and promotions lined up for the rest of the season.

At the track, Remington set a blazing-fast time in the first practice session of the weekend, fast enough to put him on the first row. The remainder of his weekend followed suit, with a third-place qualifying run and second place finish in the race.

Lionel, Jersey, and Remington dropped the rental car off at the airport and checked in for their flights: Remington and Jersey to Florida, Lionel to Montana.

"This has been a couple of the most amazing weeks of my life," Lionel said. "To see you succeeding in a sport you love so much . . . it brings me great joy. Jersey, it was an absolute pleasure to get to spend more time with you. I am glad Remington has you to look after him. Take good care of my boy, all right?"

"Don't you worry Mr. Mason," Jersey said as she embraced Lionel in a hug. "I'll do what I can. Maybe make him famous in the process, too." They thanked the barista for their coffees and walked Lionel to his gate.

"I love you, Dad. You take care in Montana, and I'll try and get up there after the season so we can chase some ducks."

"I'd like that very much. I wish I could get to a few more of your races, but I better save up some energy for next season. But you better believe I will be glued to my TV."

"I know you will. I couldn't ask for a better fan. Thanks for helping make this real for me." Remington and Jersey gathered their bags and began the walk to their own departure gate.

"Your dad is precious, Rem," Jersey said as she sipped her latte. "You are blessed to have him around." Remington paused for a moment as Jersey spoke and glanced back to take a look at his father, sitting alone at his gate. He couldn't help but wish his mother was sitting beside him. It hurt Remington to know his dad was lonely, but he also knew he would be all right. He was a man of tremendous character and had plenty of passions to keep him busy back in

Montana. He looked so much smaller than he used to, almost swimming in his Flux Energy Racing Team shirt as he sipped his latte and smiled at travelers in the terminal. Remington would miss him.

When they arrived at their gate, Rem and Jersey found a window seat to avoid the attention Remington was drawing in the waiting area. The terminal was crawling with race fans returning home, and Remington had captured their attention. His social media accounts were buzzing, and he was on the front page of the complementary *Milwaukee Journal Sentinel* that was in the hands of almost everyone in the terminal. He was gracious to a couple of young race fans and their parents who picked him out of the crowd and asked for an autograph and picture. A couple of older women did the same.

"We are going to need to start ordering Sharpies in bulk," Jersey said as he signed a final autograph while they boarded the plane and settled into their first-class seats. "I have a marketing gig that is probably going to add to your demand."

"Oh, really?" Remington said.

Jersey pulled out her laptop and showed him an assortment of emails. "I still have a couple of details to work out, but I think I may have landed you on the cover of the August edition of *Men's Health* magazine."

"Are you kidding me, Jersey?"

"No joke. They reached out to me after your finish at Indy to see if you might be interested. We have been corresponding ever since, trying to work through some of the logistics, but I think it's a go. The editor wants to do a feature article on the dangers of motorsports at the professional level. This is a big deal, Rem. Talk about building equity in your brand, this is how you do it."

By the time their plane touched down in Miami, Jersey and Remington were fast asleep, exhausted from their respective work. "I am so sorry, Rem," Jersey slurred as she rose from his shoulder. "This is so embarrassing. Not to mention unprofessional."

Remington laughed. "Don't worry about it. You work so hard for me, the least I could do is serve as a pillow. I need you rested so you can keep landing me these sweet gigs." Remington helped Jersey with her bags and walked her to section B4 in long-term parking.

"I should know by tomorrow if we got the cover spot," she said. "I will let you know right away because they want to do the shoot before your next race at Belle Isle."

Remington thanked Jersey for all of her efforts as he shut the door of her BMW. "Drive safely, Jersey. I will see you soon." She gave him a wistful smile as she rolled up her window and drove off.

Remington's phone woke him from a dead sleep. It felt like minutes after he'd fallen into bed. "We got it, Rem!" Jersey was already at her desk at the Flux Racing headquarters. "You are the August *Men's Health* cover model."

"Model? Are you kidding me? You never said anything about being a model. That's what my girlfriend does. I'm a driver."

"Sorry, Rem. Part of the gig. That's what you get for being handsome. Oh yeah, I'm sorry, *and* a race driver. I need you to be at First Cut studios on Wednesday at 10 a.m. for fitting and makeup. I will meet you there and run over the day's schedule."

"You're the boss. See you there."

Men's Health was going to have an unusually heavy female reader base for the August issue. Remington Mason was made for the cover of the magazine. His abs flexed from his unzipped Flux Energy Liquor driving suit, and his race helmet hung to his side in one hand. The South Beach wind disheveled his hair, cameras capturing the scene as onlookers did the same. The occasional wolf whistle echoed out from a passing group of bikini-clad observers.

"Okay, Remington," said the director of the shoot. "For this one, we want you sitting on the side pod of the car with the glass of Flux in your hand. Give us that look again where you are present, but your eyes tell us you are somewhere else . . . focused on winning your next race." Jersey brought the bottle of Flux to Remington, wiping it with a cloth.

"You are doing great, Rem. I know this isn't necessarily your thing, but it's going very well." Jersey nodded toward the swooning group of onlookers. "Appears *you* are going to sell some magazines."

"That's a wrap on photos," the director said. "Good job everyone. Let's get Remington some clothes and shoot the interview for the YouTube channel." The camera crew started their cleanup as Remington was whisked back to the studio by Jersey after signing a couple of autographs. She handed him a list of the questions they would be asking in the interview. Much to Remington's delight, they were legitimate questions about racing.

"Are we ready?" asked the interviewer from *Men's Health*. "We are rolling." Jersey snapped a few pictures for Remington's Instagram as the interview began.

"Remington, thank you for taking the time to chat with us here at *Men's Health*. We are thrilled to have you on the cover. You are clearly a rising star in IndyCar. What's it like to have found success so quickly in a sport that sometimes takes years to even make a ripple in?"

"Great question. In all honesty, I don't feel like it happened quickly at all. This is my first season with the IndyCar Series, but this is something I've worked toward and prepared for my entire life. This is just the result of years of hard work on and off the track. And I was lucky enough to join with such a great partner in Chet Buckner, who is really the mastermind behind this team."

"Chet Buckner is quite the character. Is what we see on TV the same Chet Buckner you know behind the scenes?"

"It is. Chet is a genuine guy. He is also one of the best business minds I have ever been around. Don't let his public persona fool you — Chet absolutely gets things done, but he keeps the mood light."

"So, we have to know. Do you drink Flux Energy Liquor yourself?"

"What kind of an ambassador would I be if I didn't?" The camera crew chuckled as Remington repositioned himself in his chair. "No, in all seriousness, I stay away from it during race weekends to keep my reflexes as sharp as possible, but I absolutely enjoy Flux on my off days. It makes for a good party."

"As a magazine that focuses on health and fitness, I have to ask you about your training regimen. You look more like a football DB or safety to me. What is your workout routine and how does it apply to what you do on the track?"

Remington laughed as he dove into his next answer. "Fitness, combined with a strict diet, is everything for me. There is a direct link between how I eat and train and how I perform on the track. For me, it is more of a lifestyle than a regimen. I used to follow workout and diet plans, but they have become second nature at this point."

The director cut to a different shot of Remington. "When it comes to my workouts, it is a pretty heavy dose of upper body exercises combined with even more cardio. The upper body strength helps battle the G-forces we experience during the course of a race, and the cardiovascular fitness allows us to sustain that for three to four hours."

"That sounds like a solid routine, and it obviously has proven successful on the track for you this season. What about the dangers inherent in motorsports? How does that impact the way you approach the sport and your life? It has to have some effect."

"It really doesn't — or at least, not the way you'd expect. If the potential danger of the sport affects how you approach your career as a driver, you will probably never be successful in this sport. It goes back to the mental preparation I mentioned before. If there is one sliver of doubt or distraction in your mind as you buckle into your car for a race, it could be that sliver of doubt, fear, whatever it may be, that ultimately ends up biting you."

Remington shifted uneasily in his chair. "I don't think race drivers are fearless. Most of us have a healthy respect for what could happen to us on the track. But we find ways to deal with it. For me, the possibility of getting hurt — or even killed — is something I am willing to live with to do what I love. I also have an extreme amount of faith in IndyCar and our Dallara race chassis. The focus on safety in the cars and at the tracks has come a long way. From SAFER barriers to cars that dissipate energy in an impact, safety technology is getting better and better. As long as the car is on the ground, an IndyCar is the safest car in the world. "

"That's a wrap everyone. Remington, we greatly appreciate your time, and congratulations on being a *Men's Health* cover model. We are looking forward to following your career."

Remington opened the door for Jersey as they left the studio.

"You were a natural today, Rem," Jersey said.

"Sure didn't feel natural," Remington replied. "Letting my chest hang out of my race suit in front of a bunch of strangers was a little awkward. And to think it was all photographed . . . I'll stick to driving." Jersey laughed and slipped on a pair of shades. "Can I buy you lunch as a thanks for landing me this gig?" Remington asked.

Jersey was surprised by Remington's offer. "Of course. I would really like that, Rem."

Remington knew a good beachside grill just around the block. "Best fish tacos I've ever had," Remington said. "This place okay with you?" Jersey agreed. The hostess sat them on the patio overlooking neatly aligned rows of sport-fishing boats and it was not long before Remington and Jersey were deep in conversation.

"I'm really enjoying our time, Rem. It's nice to catch up away from the track," Jersey said. She rested her chin in her hand and smiled at Remington across the table.

"I agree," Remington replied. "I think this is the first time you and I have talked about anything other than racing since we met." Jersey beamed at Remington's mention of the day. "What do you say, a quick walk on the beach for old times sake? We can take the long way back to the parking garage." Jersey was giddy as Remington signed the check and the two of them started toward the water's edge. Jersey had just kicked off her shoes and curled her toes into the sand when Remington's phone rang. It was Mabel.

"Jersey, I'm sorry, but I have to take this," Remington said, covering his phone with his hand. "It's Mabel and I promised her I would tell her about my shoot. Can I take a raincheck on the walk?"

"Of course, Rem. Tell her hi for me." Jersey masked her disappointment as Rem gave her a quick hug and headed back toward the restaurant. With her shoes in hand, Jersey continued onto the beach, surprised by the feeling of rejection that had draped itself over her heart. She hoped the rhythmic hiss of the surf would ease her mind as she took the long way back to her car.

CHAPTER 14

Rookie of The Year

REMINGTON WAS LIVID ON THE RADIO. "What did you do to the car? I've got no rear grip. I'm going to crash!" The lead Remington had accumulated under the lights of the Las Vegas Strip in the inaugural Streets of Vegas Grand Prix had been slashed to inches. Helio Castroneves veered through Remington's slip stream, taking even more downforce off the rear of the car. "I can't hold on out here. Tell me what to do."

"Track temp is coming down now that the sun has set, Rem," Craig said from the pit box. "We adjusted the car so you won't be too tight toward the end of this race."

"I'm not going to be around for the end of this race the way this car is handling," Remington said, shaking his fist as he flew by pit row. "I'm coming back to the pits next lap."

"Negative. Stay on track. Let the car come to you. Just make your car as wide as possible, and keep the 3 car behind you."

Remington took a deep breath and checked his mirrors as he raced by the Fountains of Bellagio. Craig was right, he needed to let the car come to him. He had driven flawlessly; a few bad laps could not define his race — it was his to win.

Remington continued to wrestle with his car, but the steering wheel that just a lap earlier was attempting to pry itself from his grip through every corner, was beginning to settle. He could feel the balance of the car returning. He braked later, accelerated earlier, the car responding with increased grip and precision. Craig was right . . . the Flux car was back. "You called it! You called it. This thing is back boys. What did you do?"

"Doesn't matter," Craig responded. "Just drive your race." Craig fist bumped his engineer sitting on the pit box next to him, knowing their race strategy was paying off. "Looks like Castroneves and the Penske crew are on the same plan, so be ready for another charge from Helio." Remington was ready, he was more than ready. He was hungry for his first IndyCar win and no one, or team, even Team Penske, was going to steal this race from him.

"Two turns to go, Rem," Craig said. "You're going to have to push hard; the 3 is locked onto you." Remington hit a perfect apex in the final turn and felt he had a good run heading down the front straight. He checked his mirrors again. Castroneves had not given an inch. Remington veered toward the pit wall to try and shake the Penske car from his draft as he accelerated toward the finish line. Helio mirrored his every move. Remington could see the checkered flags waving ahead. He glanced behind him one more time . . . Helio was attempting a pass! Remington ripped his car to the other side of the track to block, but Castroneves executed a crossover move and began drawing even with Remington as they barreled toward the finish line. Remington felt he would break his throttle pedal if he pushed any harder, but at this point, it was all he could do. He watched helplessly as the nose of the three car drew even with his, and as quickly as Helio had made his final move, it was over.

"Did we win?" Remington shouted over the radio.

"If you could see your crew leaping off the pit wall right now, you would know," Craig said. "You are an IndyCar race winner, Remington. You beat Helio by one-tenth of a second. Congratulations!" Remington yelled underneath his helmet, pumping his fists as he drove past the cheering fans and rolled to a stop in turn 1. "You know what to do next buddy; light 'em up!" Remington buried his foot in the throttle and did a Vegas-worthy burnout, smoke swirling into the night sky as he came to a stop and unbuckled. He climbed on top of his car, still veiled by smoke, and when it cleared, was greeted with a roar of applause. The burnt rubber stinging his eyes was the only thing reassuring Remington he was not dreaming, that he *was* an IndyCar race winner.

Remington's victory did not come as a surprise to anyone. It was a pinnacle on a foundation of success built by the Flux team throughout the season. The bright lights of Sin City magnified the talented young driver and his liquor sponsor as they toasted the top of the podium for the first time. The ensuing Flux party fit Vegas like a quarter fits a slot machine.

Remington stepped off the elevator and started down the hallway toward his hotel room before he noticed Jersey filling a bucket of ice near the vending machines. "I didn't see you at the party tonight," Remington said, pre-nursing his imminent victor's hangover with a soda water and Advil.

"You know me, Rem," Jersey said. "The party thing isn't really my deal."

"But we wanted to celebrate *you* too. Our win tonight was your win."

"I appreciate that, but I like being the force behind the scenes who keeps things moving forward. Plus, I volunteered —" Jersey was interrupted by an intoxicated Mabel Foster.

"There's my man." Mabel slurred and gave a flirtatious tug on Rem's T-shirt. "Come back to me. I'm not done with you." She finally noticed Jersey as Remington steadied her swaying torso. "Oh, hey Jersey."

Jersey gave Mabel an awkward wave. "I'll leave you two alone."

Remington mouthed the word "sorry" as he was playfully pulled down the hotel hallway, with Mabel trying to kiss his ear.

The swing through California to end the IndyCar season could not have gone better for Remington and the Flux team. With a fourth-place finish at Sonoma and another second on the two-mile oval at the California Speedway, Remington had easily locked up rookie-of-the-year honors and a solid third-place finish in the point standings. It was an incredible feat for a rookie. Remington's stock as a premier driver and marketing symbol were soaring. Flux Energy Liquor sales had hit record levels. On and off the track, success was squarely in the draft of Flux Racing, following the team wherever they went. Remington Mason was in a seat envied by every aspiring driver. Life was good. The only thing Remington needed was rest, and the season-ending team awards banquet was the final lap before the checkered would wave-in the offseason.

Remington looked fabulous in his tuxedo, but he was severely overshadowed by Mabel Foster adorning his arm in a red Versace dress. Her blonde hair glowed against her skin, her cherry-red lips perfectly matching the dress. The couple made their way through the banquet as bubbles of Champagne mirrored the excitement of the season and anticipation for the next. It seemed Remington was congratulated by everyone in attendance, and he looked forward to his turn at the podium to thank his team. His speech was an eloquent blend of gratitude and inspiration, of words that lit a fire within his team to take their success to the next level.

"A toast to each of you," Remington said, raising his glass to the room. "To the successes of this season, and many more to follow. Finally, a toast to the vacation I am about to take. Thank you all."

For a moment, the tranquil blue world that surrounded Remington 90 feet below made him feel as if the God he once believed in was speaking to him, calling him back to a younger day, and a way of living he had discarded as naive and immature the moment his mother died. Scuba diving was the closest thing to spirituality Remington had ever experienced. The wonder of being suspended on a shear coral cliff plummeting to uninhabitable depths with some of the world's most fascinating creatures was other-worldly and mysterious. What alien life form would appear next from a coral crevice as the small group of explorers weightlessly dangled off the edge of the reef? Remington crossed them off on his aquatic identification card; lion, angel, and drum fish, eels, nurse shark; all leading characters on the stage of the Mesoamerican Reef.

An hour later, Mabel's blonde hair floated in the breeze as Remington popped a lime in a beer and joined her on the bow of the boat to dry out after their final dive of the day. Of all the magnificent specimens he had seen that day, Mabel's toned body was Remington's favorite.

"Can you believe how close we got to the nurse shark?" Mabel asked as she cuddled closer, placing her hand on his chest. "I swear I could have touched it. What do you think? Five feet from us?"

"At a maximum. That was incredible. What about that eel in the tunnel we dove through?"

"I know! So amazing. Thank you for bringing me to Belize, Rem. This place is incredible — and we finally get some alone time." Remington raised his Belikin bottle in a toast of agreement as they soaked in the sun and each other's company.

Later that evening, Remington and Mabel talked and flirted their way through an expensive dinner.

"Do you ever think about marriage, babe?" Remington's question seemed to catch Mabel off-guard.

"Never. Why, do you?" she asked. Remington was now the one off-guard. Mabel came to his rescue. "You should have seen the look on your face. Of course I do."

"And what did you think, exactly?" Remington asked.

"I mean, you're unbelievably sexy, and a superstar race driver. Who wouldn't want to marry you?" Mabel said. "On the flip-side, we both have careers that would make marriage impossible right now." She gave Remington's leg a tight squeeze. "Have you thought about it? Doesn't really seem like your type of thing."

"I mean, yeah, the thought has definitely crossed my mind. I could see spending the rest of my life with you, but I agree. We both love what we do, and we should probably just leave it at that for now. We can always re-evaluate things down the road."

"Phew! Glad we got that out of the way," Mabel said. "I love you, Rem. Now, how about a shot of tequila?"

As they were finishing their coconut ice cream, a Jimmy Buffett tribute band started up in the corner of the bistro. Mabel grabbed Remington's arm and pulled him to the dance floor. He wasn't much for dancing, but the combination of a little alcohol and a lot of Mabel quickly erased any doubts he had. Her hips swayed perfectly to the rhythm as her hands clasped behind his neck, her short yellow skirt keeping time with her body. She sank into him as they began to move as one.

Remington had always been a horrible dancer. He always seemed to get in his own way, and wound up stepping on his date's toes. Tonight was different. There was something magical about being so close to this new woman in his life. Her skin glistened as she danced in the tiki light. Remington was in love. He knew he would eventually marry Mabel Foster. It was just a matter of time.

From the deck of their oceanside bungalow, Remington could see Mabel's blonde locks covering her bare back when the ocean breeze parted their bedroom curtains. He had come a long way from vowing to avoid a relationship until his career was more established. Mabel Foster changed all of that. His career was rocketing forward, and he certainly did not find Mabel a distraction. Quite the contrary. She helped supply motivation, energy, and balance to the demands of being a professional athlete.

Remington crawled back into bed and caressed Mabel's hair as she began to wake. The moment felt perfect; a surge of adrenaline and emotion charged through his body. But, it came again: the small snake of guilt that plagued his adult life slithered its way into his heart as he lay beside her. How could he shake these tiny, yet relentless, impulses that seemed to ruin the moments he enjoyed most? He had long since left religion behind, but something his parents had taught him still bounced around somewhere deep in the recesses of his subconscious. He hated it when his own principles were taken hostage by those of his parents, or anyone else's for that matter. He wished he could cauterize the "Holier than though" synapses delivering the little messages of shame, never to hear from them again.

"You all right, handsome?" Mabel's smile staring back at him from the pillow evaporated every other thought.

"How could I not be, next to you?" Mabel pulled his head to hers and kissed him passionately — just long enough to gather a pillow in her hand and smack him over the head. Luckily, room service knocked on the door with breakfast. Mabel quickly covered up as Remington slid a tip to the attendant and pulled the cart in. They devoured the breakfast on the foot of the bed before lacing up their sneakers for a run on the beach, kicking off their last full day of vacation.

"No!" Mabel pouted from under her Flux Energy Racing ball cap, standing near her connecting gate, her arms still wrapped around his neck long after they had called her seat.

"I'll see you soon, babe. I promise. You have modeling gigs lined up for the next month and I have to get ready with the race team. But after that, I'll come see you in California."

"Do you promise?" Mabel's pout concealed a hidden smile.

"I promise."

Remington walked her to the gate and gave her an ardent kiss goodbye as the airline crew looked on, waiting for their final passenger to board.

"Sorry," Remington said to the crew as Mabel handed them her ticket. "She's hard to say goodbye to."

"I do not blame you, sir," said the attendant. "The good ones always are." Mabel blew him a final kiss as she disappeared around the corner of the jetway. Remington was just leaving the gate when the same airline attendant asked, "Excuse me, sir. Isn't that you on that billboard?" Remington had not even noticed the Flux Racing IndyCar banner covering an entire wall of the terminal, prominently displaying him in his driver's suit. "Yes ma'am — why, it most certainly is."

"Good luck this year. Miami is pulling for you, Remington."

Remington thanked the attendant and left the terminal as determined as he had ever been in his career. He was refreshed, refocused, and bent on bringing home an IndyCar championship for Flux Racing, and Miami.

CHAPTER 15

Rock On

REMINGTON HAD BEEN IN THE SEAT for fifteen minutes when his iPhone rang. "Craig!" he shouted across the race shop. "Can you answer my phone for me? It's on the side pod, and I can't move." Craig hustled across the shop to where his driver was sitting in the clay mold for his new race seat. Remington had forty-five minutes left before the fitted seat would be perfectly contoured to his body and was itching for something to entertain him. He answered the call.

"Remington, it's Jax. How are you?"

"Jax! I am doing well, man. It's been a long time. How are you?"

"I'm doing all right. Is this a good time?"

"Couldn't be better. I'm stuck in a tub of some weird goo waiting for it to mold to my ass. So yes, your timing is impeccable."

"Oh, the tough life of an IndyCar driver. I feel *horrible* for you having to sit in that amazing seat. I would have gladly taken your spot a year ago."

"Why wouldn't you take it now? You never know, things continue at this rate, and we may be looking for a second driver. I could put in a good word for you."

"I'm done racing, Rem."

"*What?* Are you kidding me? Why?" Remington had to will himself to stay in the seat.

"It's not worth it anymore, man. Did you know Davey Nguyen, the Australian driver?"

"Yeah, I know him. Hell of a driver. Is he all right? You're scaring me."

"He has been in a coma for two weeks now. Even if he wakes up, he is going to be a vegetable. Dude, I was the one who caused the wreck." The line went silent.

"Jax, I'm so sorry. That has to be hard."

"You have no idea, Rem. I could be — I mean, I'm responsible for ending his life."

Remington could hear the pain in Jax's voice, but he was not about to let his friend blame himself for another driver's injury. "Look, Jax, you are *not* responsible for his life. I know you feel bad, but both of you jumped into those cars knowing full well that it could have been either one of you in that hospital bed. We are race drivers. We take that risk and accept it because we are doing what we love. It is going to take some time to work through this in your mind, but this is *not your fault*, okay? It could have been anyone. These things happen. You have to forgive yourself."

Silence echoed eerily through the phone line. "You still there, Jax?

"Yeah."

"Do you understand that or not? I am not trying to be hard on you, but you can't let this ruin your career. You have too much potential, whether it is in a race car or somewhere else."

Jax choked up, and there was a pause before he said, "Thanks. I understand. Listen, please be extra careful out there this season. It's crazy that it took this wreck to snap me out of my ridiculous belief that we are invincible. Life is fragile. It just sucks this had to happen to Davey for me to learn that. Just be careful, Rem. I couldn't stand to have to deal with something like this again."

"Jax, don't worry about me. I'll be fine. There hasn't been a serious injury in IndyCar for some time. These cars are bulletproof. And I just told you, I accept the risks of what we do. I appreciate your concern, and I am really sorry for what you are going through, but don't let worrying about me make it any worse, okay?"

"I appreciate it. Good luck this year. Make it a repeat of last season, huh? Do it for me."

"Will do, Jax. You take care. Call me anytime."

"Thanks man and hey, one more thing. Your old man is right, Rem. There is more to life than what we see. Just take care."

Remington hung up his cell.

"What was that all about?" Craig asked.

"Some guy we used to race against got hurt in a sprint-car wreck. Jax thinks it's his fault the guy is a mess. We all know this stuff happens."

"That's tough," Craig said. "Amateur racing is one of the most dangerous jobs in the world. Thank God you finally made it to IndyCar, huh?"

"Yeah, thank God. Or whoever."

Offseason testing was over, and the blank Dallara canvases were dressed in sponsor-laden liveries in preparation for the first race of the season. St. Petersburg was one week away, marking Remington's second season as a professional race driver. Coming off of a glowing rookie campaign, expectations for Remington Mason's second season in the IndyCar series were through the roof. Craig Doucet had three wins on his list of goals and Chet Buckner had doubled Remington's public appearances. Success equals sales; sales equal cash; cash equals a better race team.

Chet Buckner was telling his executive team the specifics of the rise in their brand. The board room at Flux headquarters was adorned with flip charts and flashy PowerPoint presentations as its CEO thundered through the room, pointing out the success of last season and showing its direct correlation to momentum going into the next.

"Look here," Chet said. "Do you see these trends? The success of this racing team caused sales to skyrocket. And look at the correlation with Remington's social media presence. Brilliant work by Jersey. You have all paved the way for this team and this company to go to the next level. I hope I am conveying just how excited I am about this opportunity." Subtle laughs echoed through the room; there was never a moment that anyone didn't know exactly what Chet Buckner was thinking or how he was feeling.

As the room dispersed, the business team wished Remington good luck on the upcoming season as he stayed behind, studying the detailed schedule of events for the upcoming year.

"That's a lot of appearances, isn't it?" Jersey asked.

"No kidding. Will I still have time to race?"

"Don't worry, Rem. I have you covered. We are in this together," Jersey said.

"Hey, I never got back around to asking you about the volunteer thing you were doing in Vegas. I had no idea you had any spare time."

Jersey laughed. "I won't this year. No, in all seriousness, I really love speaking to kids. I have talked to civic organizations and school functions, even churches."

"What do you talk about?" Remington asked.

"A lot about racing. My message always centers on hard work, making a difference in people's lives, you know, that kind of thing. But it's always rooted in the world of racing. And I usually get a great response from the kids."

"That is so cool you do that. I had no idea."

"You should come along sometime. The kids would love to meet a real driver."

"I'd be up for that," Remington said. "I've been so wrapped up in building a career — I should start branching out a little."

"I'll let you know next time I go. Maybe you can tag along?"

"I'd appreciate that. Keep me posted."

"By the way, it's pretty cool you and Mabel are in the Flux ad together. You look like the cover of *GQ* and *Cosmo* all wrapped into one." Jersey slid the magazine over to him.

"Thanks. Yeah, that was a fun shoot. Never thought I would get to do a commercial with a supermodel, and I definitely never imagined she would be my girlfriend." Remington tossed the magazine back at Jersey. "I'm just ready to go racing. Enough of this modeling stuff."

"Amen. Let's go racing." Jersey gave Remington a high-five as she spun in her chair, grabbed her belongings, and headed for the door of the boardroom. "See you in St. Pete, Rem."

Lionel was carefully examining the newest addition to his collection when the phone rang in his shop. It was Remington.

"Hi Pop. How are you?"

"I'm puzzled. I'm sitting here looking at an old Ward Brothers decoy I just bought at auction — ducks must not have been as smart back in the day. The darn thing is worth a fortune, but what duck with any self respect would be attracted to this shot-up chunk of wood?"

Remington laughed, happy his dad was keeping busy. "You planning to come to any races this year? I can fly you out and put you up in the team hotel."

"I have already gone through the schedule and picked my races."

"Great! Which tracks are you thinking you want to see?"

"You know I wouldn't miss Indy for the world. After that, I am excited to see you boys tackle the new two-mile oval up in Seattle. They have been trying to bring racing to the Seattle area for some time now, and I want to be a part of the inaugural show."

Remington was excited for the new track as well. It had been specifically designed for IndyCar racing and was going to be one of the fastest tracks on the circuit. His time in the simulator was the only thing that prepared him for the new track, but he could already imagine the G-forces the sweeping corners would produce and the turbulence of the draft as they shot down the long straightaways. He even felt he had identified some good spots to pass if he could under-brake his competitors into turns 1 and 3. It was sure to be a great race, one Remington wanted to commemorate with a first-place trophy in his man cave.

"All right, you let me know if you need anything, and I will have all your pit and suite passes waiting when you get there."

"Thanks. I have been praying for your success this year and of course, that God will keep you safe. I love you, Rem."

"Love you too, Pop."

Flames roared as Jim Foster flipped hamburger patties on the grill. Rem felt great to be back in Long Beach.

"That was an impressive drive today, Remington," Mabel's dad said. "What a way to follow up your win at St. Petersburg. Mabel told me you were good, but man, you're the IndyCar Series points leader." Mabel clung to Remington's arm as the two men talked.

"Thanks. The team is off to a great start so far. Hopefully we can keep it going at the new track up in Seattle this weekend."

"I heard that was supposed to be a wicked-fast track. Another glass of Chardonnay?" Jim poured Remington and Mabel another glass of wine.

"The fastest outside of Indianapolis," Remington said. "We were turning simulated laps around 220 miles an hour in our offseason testing. All the teams had hoped for actual track time, but par for the course in the Northwest, rain shut us down. It should be a good race if we can get it in between the rains. I thought they should have scheduled the race for the second half of the season, once things dry out a little up there."

"It's great to have you here, Remington, and thanks again for the VIP passes today. That was incredible. You guys ready to eat?"

Mabel led Remington through a gate at the edge of her family's yard overlooking the Pacific Ocean. A daunting staircase zig-zagged its way to the beach below.

"What a beautiful way to end a race weekend," Remington said. "And there's no one else I would rather spend it with." A cool evening breeze stalked them along the beach. Remington held Mabel close as she wrapped herself even tighter in the blanket she had brought along.

They walked to a small rock outcropping that looked over the open ocean, a perfect place to watch the sun set over the Pacific. "I'm so glad we get the next week together, Rem. I can't wait to travel with you to Seattle. That sounds like a really exciting race."

"We needed some time together. Work has been pulling us in different directions lately. I'm glad we could finally get our schedules lined up." Mabel pressed into Remington and put her soft lips on his. Her perfume and the taste of the sweet white wine still lingering on her breath made Remington's head spin.

It was the final push he needed. Remington dug through the pocket of his jeans until he felt the tiny box and concealed it in his hand. He pulled his lips from hers and looked intently into her eyes. They reflected adventure, a zest for life: everything Remington loved about her. In his deepest hopes, they represented commitment as well. He was about to find out.

He tucked a lock of her golden hair behind her ear as he scooted away from her on the blanket and found his way to one knee. He unveiled the tiny box with shaking hands and popped it open. "Mabel, you mean the world to me. You inspire me to be better, to drive harder, live louder, and climb higher." Mabel tried to interrupt as tears welled in her eyes, but Remington was determined to finish. "I love you. A few months ago, we talked about how content we were with our relationship, but I couldn't shake the thought of how I almost let you escape my life on the elevator the day we met, and I cannot live with the thought of repeating that mistake. I want to live the rest of my life with you. So, Mabel Foster, will you marry me?"

Mabel's mother jumped, spilling red wine on her plaid shirt when the door burst open to the rec room, where the family was watching a movie. Mabel flipped on the light, exposing the stunned looks on her family's faces.

"I'm getting married!" Mabel leapt onto the couch next to her mother and father as her younger sister raced across the room and grabbed her hand.

"OMG Mabes, that is so beautiful! I am jealous. You are so lucky," Mabel's sister Emma said, as she examined the stunning rock adorning her sister's ring. "Jealous, but so happy for you two." She jumped off the couch and gave Remington a hug. Her parents followed, wrapping both Mabel and Remington in their arms.

Jim left the room and returned moments later with Champagne glasses clinking in one hand and a bottle of bubbly in the other. "This calls for a toast," Jim said as he popped the cork from a bottle of Dom Pérignon. "I have been waiting for the perfect occasion to open this bottle. The time is now." The expensive drink flowed over the top of the tulip glasses as he poured, and Emma passed them around. Jim gave a passionate toast, and the story of the proposal was explained, no detail spared, at Mrs. Foster's request.

"You two better get packed," Jim said as he poured the last drop of Champagne in Remington's glass. "I'm taking you to the airport to catch your flight to Seattle at five a.m." Mabel kissed her father on the cheek, then ran across the room and leapt into Remington's arms, wrapping her legs around him.

"I think I'm too excited to pack!"

"I could just leave you here," Remington said as he swung her around.

"Are you *kidding* me? I am your fiancee. You are stuck with me now!" Emma giggled as she pretended to push the couple out the front door. Remington playfully fought back, grateful for his new family.

CHAPTER 16

Pacific Northwest

THE RAIN PELTING THE WINDOW drew Remington from a sound sleep. His hand crawled through the sheets to find Mabel still resting. Morning rain was a menacing sound for a race driver. It was hard enough to manage nerves, and any delay was fertile ground for worries to grow. Remington stepped onto the balcony of his suite overlooking the Seattle skyline. Gray clouds cloaked the tallest buildings as the weather swept off of Puget Sound and dammed itself up against the Cascade Mountains.

Mabel quietly slipped up behind Remington, wrapping her arms around his waist as she lay her head on his back. "Hopefully this blows over," she said.

"I hope so too. We aren't going to race in this weather. Even if they do get the track dried, it will be slick with all the tire rubber washed away from practice and qualifying. How did you sleep?"

"Like a baby. I was freezing until I cuddled up to you."

"*That's* why I was so hot last night."

"That's your duty! I am a Cali girl. Not to mention your fiancee." She waved her new diamond ring in front of his face. "This city is beautiful, but the weather . . . " She shivered and pulled Remington closer.

By the time they arrived at the track, the sun was beginning to unwrap itself on the horizon as clouds still shrouded the Cascades off to the east. The moisture evaporating from the racing surface created an eerie inversion of steam, the brand-new front stretch grandstands majestically rising from the mist. The speedway staff seemed to float in and out of the fog as they walked up and down the bleachers preparing for the day's festivities. The new two-mile oval was an instant favorite among the drivers. Its moderate banking allowed intense speeds and made for perfect two and three-wide racing conditions with plenty of room to pass. It was a driver's track, requiring minute attention to breaking and throttle control, placing success squarely in the driver's hands.

The off-track amenities were as impressive as the racing surface. A roaring waterfall cascaded over natural river rock from the front-stretch suites, a Northwest welcome as fans came through the main gate. Escalators quickly chauffeured spectators to perches overlooking the entire track, a rarity among super-speedways. Nestled throughout the grounds, food shacks served local cuisines, from smoked salmon to bison burgers, and microbreweries offered samples of their huckleberry ciders and hand-crafted IPAs. Giant bronze umbrellas provided cover from the elements.

On the infield, condos for drivers and teams spanned the length of the backstretch and included two dining areas staffed by gourmet chefs. Each pit stall included data ports for the team's communications equipment and came with a sink and first aid station. Because it was brand new, the track was designed with cutting-edge safety features, including SAFER barriers that provided instant feedback to onsite doctors in the case of an impact. The venue was world class on and off the track, and the anticipation for the inaugural race had drawn a sold-out crowd. The drivers were ready to put on a show.

Remington and Mabel sipped on coffee as they walked toward Flux's area in the paddock. "This place is remarkable," Remington said. "I always dreamed of being able to race somewhere like this, at least somewhat close to home." He stopped to sign a couple of autographs.

"Yeah, it's all right," Mabel said.

"Just all right? You don't agree this place is amazing? Look at the view behind the backstretch. This is the best track on the circuit. Are you okay?" Remington jokingly shook Mabel's shoulders.

"I agree. It is a spectacular facility." She paused for a moment. "You're running so fast out there. I just wish it wasn't pack racing."

"Oh, come on babe. This is *such* a safe track. If we are going to race wheel to wheel, I want to do it here. And the fans love it. This is good for the sport. You seemed fine yesterday during qualifying. What changed?"

"Oh, I don't know. I'm probably just worrying too much."

"I know you better than this. What happened?"

Mabel sighed and stopped walking so she could face Remington. She spoke softly. "I was hanging out in the paddock yesterday before the driver's meeting and I overheard Brody Compton's wife pleading with him not to race this track. I guess she just had a bad feeling about it. Brody said it was all in God's hands and he just wanted Jesus to be glorified or something. He didn't waver for a second, but his poor wife nearly lost it."

Remington put his arms around his fiancee and pulled her close. "Listen, I am sorry that got to you. We're going to be fine out there. I'm sure Brody is right. If there *is* a God, I know He will be looking after us. This is no different from any other race. It's quick, but this track is built for this type of racing."

"I know." Mabel sighed and laid her head on Remington's shoulder. "Please, just be safe out there, Rem."

The pre-race festivities were well underway by the time Remington emerged from the hauler dressed in his driving suit, the sun now beating down on the track. Mabel, Jersey, and Lionel stood by Remington's car, which displayed a custom Northwest Tribute paint scheme. The hot orange and yellow were artfully blended to reflect a sunset and of course, Flux's new Mandarin Energy Liquor. It was a perfect venue to unveil their new product as Remington was practically the tagline for the entire event. "Come see Remington Mason tackle the newest super-speedway in the country! Welcome IndyCar!" Remington even captured the pole position, adding to the hype.

"You are already the star of the show. You might as well go out there and win the darn race," Chet said, joining the small group on pit lane as two US Forest Service smoke jumpers parachuted into the venue. "Seriously kid, I see your face everywhere I look. The banners, the newspaper, the website — it's like you own the place."

"You just wait until I get on the track, boss. Then I really will own this place."

"I knew I hired the right kid. Get out there and get it done, Rem. Bring one home for the team."

Remington's crew made some final adjustments to the car as everyone stood for the national anthem in the sold-out inaugural crowd, an impressive sight from both sides of the fence. The crowd roared as the last words were sung. Remington tossed his hat to one of the crewmen and embraced Mabel for a quick kiss.

"Please be careful out there, Rem."

"Don't worry babe. I got this," Remington said as he turned to Lionel. "Love you Pop. See you in a couple hours." Remington bumped fists with the rest of the crew and jumped in the cockpit to begin to focus on the race and melding himself with his car. The quicker he could become one with his machine, the quicker he could get up to speed on the track and begin hitting his marks. Remington was just about to close his visor and eliminate the outside world when Jersey leaned into the cockpit, her black hair covering his gloved hands. "Your dad wants to pray with you. Is that okay? He was too polite to bug you, but I could tell he really wanted to."

"Right now? Can't he do it from the pits?" Remington could see his father standing behind Jersey looking over the field of cars staggered down the front straightaway. His dad straightened his glasses and pulled up his loose jeans as he stepped back to allow the bustling crews to pass by. Remington instantly felt bad.

"Send him over, but please hurry. I have to focus." Jersey flashed Remington a smile and quickly went to retrieve Lionel, who leaned in close to his son.

"Hey, thanks for wanting to pray for me," Remington said from beneath his helmet.

"I just didn't want to bother you. I know how you have your routine." Remington closed his eyes as his father squeezed his hand. "Dear Jesus, we are so grateful for all that you have blessed us with. We thank you for dying on the cross to give us a life of freedom, purpose, and above all, an eternal life with you. Thank you for my boy and the man he has become. Thank you for giving him the opportunity to live out his dreams, for placing him right here in this very seat. Father God, protect my boy and grant him victory today as he performs in front of thousands, but for an audience of One. I am grateful for the chance to be here. Thank you, God. Amen." Remington, Lionel, and Jersey simultaneously opened their eyes.

"Thank you, Pop. I really appreciate that."

"I love you son. Go get 'em." Jersey helped Lionel to his feet as he gave his son three pats on the helmet, something he had done since the day Rem started racing. Today, it provided Remington a sense of focus as his mind flashed back to his early days racing quarter midgets in the Northwest. He was ready. Jersey mouthed the words "thank you" from the pit wall and flashed him another smile. He gave her a thumbs up.

A rap song began to blare through the loud speakers as Russel Wilson, quarterback of the Seattle Seahawks, was handed a microphone to deliver the command to start the engines. "What's up, Seattle? Are you ready for IndyCar in the Northwest!" The crowd went wild as a few diehard football fans waved their Hawks flags from the grandstands.

"Drivers, hear me out! On the count of three, these fans and I are going to bring this place to life. Are you ready? One, two, three. Drivers, start your engines!" Remington's motor rumbled to life as his crew members quickly jumped over the pit wall, leaving nothing but the pace car between him and turn one. It was race day.

Mabel climbed atop the pit box just as the pace car was getting ready to pull off the track. She tucked her skirt under her legs as Craig handed her a radio headset so she could listen in to Remington and the crew.

"Green, green, green," Remington's spotter said as the starter waved the flag, setting the field free like a pack of wild horses. Remington quickly shifted through all six of his gears as he roared down the front stretch in front of the packed grandstands. The picnic areas between turns one and two were a blur as he approached 200 miles an hour coming out of the second turn and rocketed down the backstretch side by side with Tony Kanaan. Normally the field would have been strung out as they entered turn number three, but the drivers were still two wide and nose to tail as they tore through turns three and four, climbing to 220 miles an hour. Remington placed his right front wheel virtually on the side pod of the ten car to try and catch a small draft that would propel him to the lead as the first lap quickly came to a close. It worked. Remington was scored as the leader after round one of 200.

Most of the crowd were still on their feet as the pack of drivers raced lap ten. A handful of cars were starting to distance themselves from each other as set-ups and tire wear began to meddle with handling, but the top eight were still wheel-to-wheel as they jockeyed for position, inches from the wall and each other.

Approaching the end of the front stretch, Remington got the "all clear" from his spotter and dove toward the apex of turn one. Without warning, sparks showered from a puff of smoke near the back of Remington's car as he flashed into the corner. He could feel the backend of his car trying to pry itself from the racing surface and hurl him into the outside wall. He fought to maintain control as the other cars swallowed up his wounded Flux car, darting in all directions to avert disaster.

"We touched!" Remington shouted over the radio. "He cut my right rear with his wing." Just as quickly as the two cars made contact, Remington found himself a straightaway behind the field but in a relatively damage-free race car.

"Box this lap and we will get you fixed," Craig said as he readied his crew for an unplanned pit stop. Mabel slammed her water bottle on top of the pit box; the stop would most likely shatter all chances of Remington winning the race. The sentiment was echoed in the Flux suite as Chet Buckner stood watching the live broadcast while Lionel and Jersey sat shaking their heads. But as the field roared into turn 3 and completely evaporated from Remington's sight, a string of yellow lights flashed along the catch fence. The Flux suite erupted in a loud cheer — a caution flag might have just spared their race.

"We got a caution for debris, Rem. Kanaan's front wing is on the track. Lucky break."

Remington slid to a stop in his pit box with nothing but the rim on the right rear. The air jack quickly elevated the car as his crew attended to his chassis like doctors to an ER patient.

"We'll come back in later for fuel," Craig said. "We can't let the field get back around to you. We will be at the back either way. Go, go, go!"

As Remington felt the car hit the ground, he put it in gear and exited his pit box, careful not to exceed the slow pit lane speed limit. He popped out in front of the field, spared the potentially fatal wound of going a lap down. He caught up to the rear of the pack and waited for the pits to reopen before joining the orchestrated ballet of cars and crews dancing their way through pit lane to service their machines. An eight-second pit stop gained Remington two positions before even going back to racing, a break considering that five laps before he was on the ragged edge of hitting the wall and potentially taking out an entire field of race cars. The Flux crew was in high spirits once again.

As soon as the green flag dropped, Remington began climbing back to the front of the field, maneuvering through five of the slower cars. By the time he reached the fifteenth position, he could feel the tires fading as he made increasingly daring passes on the outside of the sweeping turns. The green track was incredibly abrasive following the morning's rainstorm that had washed all the rubber off the racing surface, and Remington's Firestone tires were being eaten alive every turn he made through the outer reaches of the corner. The now single-file string of cars showed he was not the only one struggling with the issue.

Remington pulled in line, knowing not to push any further beyond the limit. He would have to count down the laps until his next pit stop, only chancing a pass to capitalize on the mistake of another driver. Every lap turned by the field of cars was laying down a valuable layer of rubber that would allow him to be more aggressive through the final stages of the race. His patience would play to his favor as the race wore on.

By the time Craig called Remington to the pits, he was barely able to maintain control of the car at speed, and threads were beginning to expose themselves on his right front tire. The fifty-five mile per hour pit lane speed offered a welcome reprieve this time around, and another flawless pit stop cycled Remington back into the race in thirteenth position after all the cars in the field had made their stops for tires and fuel. After a couple laps, Remington had warmed his tires and found that his patience had served him well. His car was lightning fast. It was time to get back to the front.

As Remington once again drove into turn one, his mirrored visor gave him the illusion he had driven into a dark tunnel. The shadows that enveloped the corner made it nearly impossible to see. As he exited turn two, Remington noticed the clouds that had built over the backstretch, seemingly out of nowhere. Menacing clouds at that.

"Rem, we got a threat of rain. We have been watching the radar but it blew in a lot quicker than anyone thought it would. It's time to push it. This race may get cut short."

"Are we halfway yet?"

"Yes. Just crossed halfway. Per IndyCar rules, this thing is over if the red flag comes out for rain."

"I'm on it."

Any patience Remington had evaporated. All the competitors seemed to have received the same message at once. Drivers instantly started making moves in places they had not been before, and the field of cars resembled a nose-to-tail LA rush hour within a few laps. The margins for error were razor thin, but that was what racing drivers lived for.

The turbulent air off the cars ripped through the pack, pinning drivers' heads to their seats and bouncing the cars side to side. Donuts began to appear on side pods as the field continued to build momentum. All Remington could see from his thirteenth-place position was a wall of gear boxes blocking his way to the front. There was only one way to advance: take the high line and make it three wide. Remington gathered himself on the front straight — he would have to be going substantially faster than the two cars on the inside line to make a pass around the longer, outside radius of the turn.

As the other cars eased off the gas pedal and clung to the inside of turn number one, Remington buried his foot in the throttle and placed his right side tires inches from the outside wall. Instantly, his car felt as if it were floating. Marbles littered his visor as he skated through turn one on the verge of control. The green track early in the race had produced a war zone of marble mines ready to destroy any car that placed a wheel in them.

"Come on; come on!" he grunted to himself as he slid through the turn.

"Remington Mason is in the marbles!" the announcer said as the crowd gasped. "He made it! He made it! How did he hold onto that car? A phenomenal piece of driving from Remington Mason in the Flux Energy machine. With rain threatening, these drivers are not wasting a second trying to get to the front of this field. Hold onto your seats, this race is heating up."

Remington calmed his raging pulse as he ripped a tear-off from his visor going down the back stretch. He would have to repeat what he had just done to clear the marbles off the high line in turns three and four before he could get enough speed to start making passes. He took another deep breath and drove into the marble field, hoping the aerodynamic ground effects on his car would suck them from the racing surface and give him just enough room to make a pass in the laps to come.

Mabel cringed, her red nails digging into the back of the seat on the pit box as she realized what Remington was doing. She strained to see turn four, hoping her fiancé's orange car would reappear in the middle of the field, in one piece. Mabel saw him rocket out of turn number four and down the front straightaway. Craig shook his head and breathed a sigh of relief, knowing better than to jump on the radio and caution his young driver.

The clouds darkened around the raceway as the drivers continued trying to pick up positions. No one else was brave enough to attempt to follow Remington to the outside of the track. As the front straight blurred by once again, Remington smiled under his helmet knowing he was about to begin taking positions no other driver could. He found nothing but metal between his Puma racing shoe and the foot cradle of his car as he shot into turn one at a blazing rate of speed. Just as he thought, the cars on the inside began fading in his rearview as he tore through the corner.

The seas parted once again between the field and the outside retaining wall as Remington approached turn three, leaving him alone at the top of the track, in perfect position to make up a few more spots.

As Remington shot to the outside of the turn, a storm of fire and sparks reflected in his visor, eerily lighting the dark sky near the front of the field. Remington's instincts pleaded with his mind to slam on the brakes, but he kept his foot glued to the throttle. In an instant, his decision was made for him. He was driving through whatever melee was unfurling in his path. With rain materializing, the first driver to emerge unscathed might be the one standing in victory lane. Now was Remington's chance.

Fans covered their heads and shied away from the catch fence as cars viciously hit the wall, mangled parts exploding into the sky. Mabel covered her mouth with both hands as she watched carnage erupt. All she hoped was to see Remington's orange car emerge from the alarming cloud of smoke and flame blanketing the exit of turn four. Winning had become secondary.

As Remington approached the apex of the turn, the smoke and junkyard of wrecked cars made it impossible to see. "Stay high; stay high!" Remington's spotter shouted as he quickly bore down on the epicenter of the wreck, still at full throttle. Remington could see gravity beginning to overcome the forces that had unforgivingly mangled the wrecked cars and pull them down the banked track and out of his path. It was what he had hoped for, what he was depending on.

As Remington dove into the vale of gray smoke, he could faintly see the yellow caution lights lining the fence as they flashed through the debris and smoldering oil. Their glow revealed an unobstructed path through the tempest raging around him. His nerves did not fail him as he once more ensured his throttle was on the floor. If he could time it right, he could avoid any cars that might still have enough momentum to crash into the outside wall of the track. He tucked his head further down in the cockpit as debris ripped by within inches of his helmet.

Lionel felt helpless as he watched the wreck unfold in front of his son. "Clear a path for him. Please Lord." Jersey echoed a similar prayer in her mind as Chet cut loose a slew of expletives. The rest of the suite remained silent.

Craig Doucet leaned over the top of the pit box intently waiting for his driver to emerge while fans leapt to their feet and pointed toward the wreck. Even the track announcer was silent as cars continued to disintegrate on the racing surface.

Remington plunged his car deeper into the gauntlet of smoke and shrapnel, that even at 215 mph, seemed endless. Without warning, a shadow stealthily slipped into the corner of Remington's vision. Its sudden manifestation startled him. He instantly let off the throttle. The black car appeared out of nowhere, careening from somewhere near the bottom of the track and squarely into his path. Remington snapped his steering wheel to the right in hopes of planting his car into the wall instead of directly into the wounded machine now blocking all hope of emerging from the wreck. He waited for his car to turn, but it was too late.

Another explosion of carbon fiber chunks rocketed from the cloud of smoke — they were orange. The impact to the rear of the black car stunned Remington, knocking the wind from his body as the nose of his car evaporated, sending a shower of sparks and carbon fiber into his helmet. By the time he was able to lift his head from the initial impact, he realized he was airborne. His car had been launched skyward as he hit the rear wheels of the car in front of him.

A roar arose from the crowd as they saw what was left of the orange number seven car appear above the cloud of smoke. Remington tucked in self-preservation as he felt weightlessness take his being. He could only see glimpses of the sky, track, and catch fence as G-forces ripped his head from side to side. Remington felt he could escape serious injury as long as his car did not hit the catch fence upside down or nose first, but all he could do was hold on. For once, he had no control of his car.

Remington could sense he was edging closer and closer to the catch fence. He braced for the impact as his left rear tire clipped the racing surface. The brief contact with the pavement rotated his car toward the fence, nose first. The Flux car smashed into the catch fence, twisting and turning in a tangle of shredded metal. The back half of the car ripped away from the cockpit, severed oil and fuel lines spewing flames across the track. Remington's protective tub slid to a halt on its side at the entrance to pit road. The smell of hot metal and burnt plastic blew through pit lane as the destroyed cars ground to a halt and those that survived slowly picked their way through the detritus.

"Remington, you okay bud?" Craig's voice cracked as he radioed his driver. "Remington, can you hear me?"

Nothing.

"It's okay. His radio may have been damaged." He did his best to reassure Mabel and the crew as they gathered around hoping for word on their driver's condition.

"Please say something, Rem," Mabel pleaded as Craig wrapped his arm around her and pulled her close. "Anything!"

The track medic peered out the window of the safety truck as they approached Remington's car, hoping to see his visor pop up, the sign a driver gives to medics and fans that they are okay. Remington's remained closed. The truck screeched to a halt, just feet from where Remington lay upside down in what was left of his race car. The medic jumped out of the truck before it had even come to a complete stop. Remington's arms hung limp in the cockpit. The medic could see broken bones and got no response from the driver. The cockpit of the race car had been severely damaged and deep cuts and scratches ran through Remington's helmet. Calm and efficient, the medic signaled for the helicopter and went about stabilizing her patient.

Lionel's heart throbbed inside his chest. He fought the urge to break down. His many years as a neurosurgeon were the only thing keeping him in his right mind. The rest of the suite sat stunned as the screen showed more safety personnel cautiously approaching Remington's overturned car. Chet Buckner had turned a ghostly white and sat quietly in the corner. Many of his guests had already left the suite to give those closest to the team some privacy. Jersey sat in shock and immediately resorted to praying, her head bowed at one of the tables overlooking the track. Lionel walked to where she was sitting. The two joined hands and began praying together.

The other drivers had since climbed from their destroyed cars, shaking their heads as the ambulance escorted them past the spot where Remington was still being extracted. They all knew it could just as easily have been them, the sting of reality setting in as one of their own lay unconscious in a mangled race car.

Brody Compton was the first driver to emerge from the infield care center after his mandatory check-up. A group of reporters leaned over the fence trying to get a word from him as his wife wrapped her arms around him in tears. "I knew I had a bad feeling about this race." Brody gently rubbed her back and looked her in the eyes as he tried to console her. The broadcast team gave them a moment before somberly approaching for an interview.

"Brody, that was a horrific wreck. First of all, are you okay?"

"Yeah, I am fine. I just hate this for all the fans who came out to support us. We had a great race going."

"Any idea what happened?"

"Honestly, no. I was running on the outside right behind the leaders and it looked like something may have broken on the two car and sent him up the track. From that point, it was complete carnage. The next thing I knew I was bouncing off the outside wall. It all happened so fast. Really, no clue. I just hope everyone is okay."

Mabel shook uncontrollably, her hair soaking wet from the rainstorm that had now unleashed itself in full force. Chet Buckner jumped up from his seat and wrapped his jacket around her as he ushered her into the suite.

While no one knew exactly what to say, Lionel gently squeezed Mabel's hand and began to speak. "I don't know any more about Rem's medical condition than you do, Mabel. What I do know is that Remington is a fighter, and that is the most important thing right now. He has overcome a lot of obstacles and I know that if God gives him the chance, he will do the same with this one, all right? I know the wreck looked scary, but until we know more, let's all be strong and pray for him." Mabel nodded and wiped her eyes.

Craig Doucet watched the TV race broadcast for any word on the condition of his driver. The crew busied themselves organizing race parts and tools as they silently awaited the same news.

The heavy-rock inspired theme song that played as the race broadcast returned from commercial didn't fit the somber mood that had been cast over the speedway. The TV announcers did their best to sound positive as they returned to the air. "Thanks for staying with us as we bring you the inaugural Seattle Grand Prix. As you are probably aware, the race has been concluded after rain officially ended the event just past the halfway point. Minutes before the rain began to fall, there was a terrifying crash. We will show you the wreck, but please be aware it is a violent incident. Before we do, we have an official from the infield care center to give us an update on the condition of driver, Remington Mason, who was involved in the crash in the number seven Flux Energy entry. Dr. Bradley, what do you know at this time?"

"All I can tell you is that Remington Mason has been airlifted to Harborview Medical Center for emergency treatment. He was unresponsive when medics arrived at his car and has not regained consciousness at this point." The doctor looked down at his notes. "The medics took every precaution extracting him from the car and were able to get him to the hospital within thirty minutes. The biggest concerns at this point are head trauma and other internal injuries. That is all the information I have at this time."

"Dr. Bradley, thank you for the update."

Mark's wife Joanne pushed open the side door of the barn. The radio crackled and the cat rolled over and stretched in hopes of getting its belly rubbed. "Mark?" Joanne searched for her husband. "Are you in here?" The cat stalked her along the edge of the bench seat.

"Where is your dad you silly cat?" Joanne checked the back room before she noticed his tackle box was missing.

"Fishing? Mouser, you need to hold him more accountable. He said he was going to mow the lawn after the race was over." The cat playfully batted at her hand as she pulled away and headed toward the pond on the edge of their property.

It was a warm, humid Indiana spring day and Joanne began to sweat as she approached the pond. She could see a bobber floating in the water. "Mark?" She waited for a response. "His hearing has never been the same since he started working on those cars," she mumbled as she took a few more steps to see around the big sycamore tree that shaded the pond. Her husband sat at the end of the rickety dock on the pickle barrel that had served as his perch for years. She hollered his name again. Still, nothing. She stepped carefully over the boards that had begun to separate as the dock settled into the muddy bottom. She put her hand on her husband's back.

"Are you okay, honey?"

Mark couldn't hold it in any longer. He slid down the side of the pickle barrel as he began to sob. Joanne eased her way down next to him. Dirt ran down his cheeks as he wiped his eyes with the hand he had just used to bait his hook. Joanne cleaned his face with her apron.

"What's wrong, Mark?" She ran her fingers through his gray hair.

He breathed in with short staccato breaths before gathering his composure. "It's Remington. He was in an accident. It doesn't look good." The bobber at the end of Mark's line went unnoticed as it was tugged under the murky water.

CHAPTER 17

Check In, Check Out

THE BELLHOP PLACED THE BAGS in the corner of Lionel's room, and Lionel slipped him a five dollar bill. He washed his face and put on a clean shirt before grabbing his room key and heading straight back to the lobby. Jersey was waiting. The two left the hotel and walked across the street to the hospital, where they were greeted by an entourage of reporters and news teams standing in the rain. Jersey quickly ushered Lionel through the tunnel of microphones being shoved at them before stepping back outside to address the media.

"We will give you an update as soon as we know something ourselves. Thank you for your understanding of Mr. Mason's privacy at this time. That's all I have for now."

A representative from the hospital showed Lionel and Jersey to a conference room where Chet and the rest of the team had gathered, awaiting news on Remington's condition. Craig Doucet paced the room as he stirred powdered creamer into his cup of coffee. A couple of the crewmen quietly chatted in the corner, but for the most part, the room was silent and somber.

Chet greeted Jersey and Lionel and pulled chairs out for them. He looked defeated as he began to speak. "Mr. Mason, I'm so sorry. Based on what I am feeling right now, I cannot fathom what you are going through. I never would have put your son in a car had I known this would happen." Chet shook his head, glancing out the window at the Seattle skyline, only partially visible through the sheets of rain. "Damnit, I know this can happen in this sport, but not to us — not to Remington. I am so sorry, Lionel."

"Chet, you don't need to apologize. You gave my son the chance to do something he'd wanted to do since he was a child." The gentle smile on Lionel's face caught Chet off guard. "My son strapped into that car today knowing very well what could happen to him and he did it anyway. Long ago, we discussed the dangers inherent in this sport, and we both accepted them. Even in this moment, I still accept them. And beyond that, I believe God can work miracles. Maybe not in ways we feel they should be worked, but I trust Him with my son's life right now." Lionel gently squeezed Chet's shoulder until the two made eye contact. "It will be all right."

The evening dragged on with no word of Remington's condition. He had been in surgery since moments after the helicopter had landed on the roof. Many of the crew had since returned to the track and only a handful still waited in the conference room.

"Has anyone seen Mabel?" Jersey asked, suddenly aware of her absence.

"I dropped her by the hotel on my way here," Chet said. He straightened up in his chair. "She said she was going to catch a taxi after she put on dry clothes." Jersey pulled up her number and tried to give her a call. There was no answer.

"I should probably go check on her." Jersey glanced at her watch. "It has been almost nine hours since we left the track. Can you call me if you hear anything while I am gone?" Lionel nodded.

The taxi dropped Jersey off in front of the boutique hotel where Mabel and Remington had been staying. She introduced herself to the staff, showed them her Flux Racing credentials, and asked them to place a call to Mabel's room. Still no answer. After a few more moments of explanation about Mabel's condition after the wreck, the hotel staff agreed to allow Jersey to check the room.

The manager of the hotel knocked on the door. "Ms. Foster, this is Michael, the manager here at the hotel. We were asked to check on you. Is it all right if I come in?" He put his ear to the door. He looked at Jersey and shook his head. He slipped in his keycard and slowly opened the door for Jersey.

"Mabel? It's Jersey. Are you here?" She stepped into the room to find it completely made up. "That's strange. Chet said he dropped her off here around 7:30 last night. It doesn't look like anyone has been here." The manager turned on a few more lights. Only Remington's belongings were there. "I wonder if I passed her on the way here and she is heading to the hospital?"

A lamp shone from the other room of the suite. Nothing looked out of place. Jersey was about to flick the light switch off when something on the night stand caught her eye. At first glance, she thought it was a hotel notepad, but next to the bedside lamp was an envelope. On the front were the words "To Remington Mason, care of Flux Energy Racing Team." Jersey felt something solid tucked in the corner of the envelope. She opened it carefully. Mabel's diamond engagement ring slid into her palm as she unfolded a handwritten letter.

"My Dearest Remington,

I hope by now someone has found this and either read it for you or given it to you to read. After your wreck, I went back to our hotel room and I was paralyzed with sadness. I didn't know what to do. After hearing you were unresponsive, I guess I was afraid to see you like that. We had everything going for us. We were finding success at every turn. I was so in love and I wanted it to stay that way. I wanted the good parts without this, without what happened today. I know that is all probably unrealistic, and I accept that people are going to call me weak, faithless, whatever, for this decision, but it is one I have to make. I love you, and I thought I could handle the dark side of racing if it ever happened, but I can't and I am sorry. This isn't what I signed up for. I won't risk it again. My plane departs to Long Beach in an hour. I would give anything to check onto it with you. I should have known that falling in love with a race driver would never work out. I hate it had to end like this. I wish you nothing but the best, Remington, and hope you continue doing what you love. I am so sorry.

With love,
Mabel Foster"

Jersey's taxi rolled to a stop at a red light. She laid her head on the window and listened to the early-morning rain pelt the cab. Her cheek felt cool where it touched the glass. This was the first time she had been alone since the wreck, nearly eleven hours before. She had been so busy helping Lionel with logistics, she had not yet afforded her own mind the chance to process the day's events.

Tears flooded her eyes. The image of her driver, her friend, lying upside down in his mangled race car haunted her mind. Somehow, she was able to wrestle the images away and replace them with the day they first met on the beach. Remington had been so full of passion and life. Now he was tethered to both by God's grace.

"Miss," said the taxi driver, looking in the rearview mirror. He handed her a box of tissues.

"Thank you. I am so sorry. This has been a tough day."

"It is okay, Miss," he said. "You are with the Flux Racing Team?"

"Yes."

"I am so sorry about what happened today. I grew up watching races in Mexico with my grandfather. I am a huge fan. I had to work today, but I was listening on the radio. I will be praying for you and your driver." They pulled into the hospital parking area.

"Thank you. That is so kind. I have been doing a lot of praying myself." Jersey collected her cab fare as the driver put the car in park and came around to open her door. She handed it to him as she stepped out of the car. He politely declined as he gave her a hug.

"This one is on me, Miss. You go take care of your driver." Rain bounced off the roof of the taxi as it pulled away.

As Jersey walked down the hallway back to the conference room, she noticed a team of doctors and nurses filing into the room ahead of her. She hurried down the hall to join them.

"Mr. Mason, I am Dr. Randy Belkamp. I am the lead neurosurgeon on your son's case. I understand you are a neurosurgeon yourself?" Lionel nodded. "Very good. That'll help. I would like to introduce you to Dr. Samantha Crowder. She is the lead orthopedic surgeon taking care of your son. Now, is it all right if the rest of the team stays in the room while we talk?"

"Of course. They have all been waiting to hear an update."

"Very well. I want to start out with the bad news. Remington is in a coma. He experienced massive head trauma in the wreck, but I do expect him to heal from the impact to his head. We will keep a close eye on swelling in his brain, but are hopeful for a full recovery."

The doctor looked at the floor as he cleared his throat. "Unfortunately, his spine did not fare as well. He has fractures in his vertebrae that appear to have damaged his spinal cord. We have pinned them and done our best to repair the damage. At this point, it is too early to determine a prognosis. As you would understand, Dr. Mason, there is a possibility he could be paralyzed from the damage."

Dr. Belkamp looked Lionel in the eye. "The brain is a very complex organ, and even though we see minimal damage on the MRI, it still has to choose to wake up. We will do our best to take care of Remington. He was a hell of a race car driver." Lionel shook the surgical team's hands and thanked them for their efforts. There was not a dry eye in the room. Lionel did the only thing he knew how to do at that moment. He began to pray out loud.

"Father God. We know Remington is in your hands. You created every last fiber of his being. You created him from nothing, and we know you can repair him too if it is your will. Please be with the doctors as they manage his care, and give my son the will to fight from deep within himself. Fight is something he has never lacked, but he needs it more than ever right now. And God, please be with the people in this room. I know they love Remington. Give us all the strength to persevere and trust you in this difficult time. I love you Lord. Amen."

CHAPTER 18

Dreams

REMINGTON COULD NOT ESCAPE. The links of the catch fence ricocheted off of his helmet, stripping it of paint. The sound penetrated through his body like he was inside a tin can with a firecracker. What was left of the front of the car planted itself into the fence post. His legs cracked and contorted with the impact, the broken bones sending a shockwave through his entire body. Before his brain could even register the pain, his helmet hit the same post with obliterating force.

"Don't back off. The track is clear. Don't back off. The track is clear." The words kept running through Remington's mind as if he still had a chance to make it through the wreck. "Don't back off." Over and over again he experienced the terror of the moment, unable to escape.

Jersey had given Lionel a break to grab a coffee and get cleaned up at the hotel. It had been nearly two days since the wreck, and one of them had been at Remington's bedside at all times. Jersey and Lionel had waded through the darkest hours of the tragedy together. It was a blessing in the midst of destruction. Jersey was unwavering in her support of Remington, and Lionel found it quite remarkable.

Lionel handed Jersey a latte as he checked back into his post beside Remington. "Thanks for taking a shift. I needed to get cleaned up."

"You're welcome. I used my time to pray."

"Thank you, Jersey. It's hard looking at my son lying here. He looks like he is in perfect peace. I don't know what is going on in his mind, but I hope it is just that — peaceful."

"Don't back off. Don't back off." Remington could not break free from the dream that continually punished him, that made it look as if he were home free and then thrashed his body with a metal fence. "Don't back off." The weightlessness, the track, the wall, the catch fence — all once again ready to devour him.

"Did you see that?" Jersey asked, sitting forward in her chair, trying not to spill her coffee.

"See what?" Lionel asked.

"His eyelids just moved!"

"Are you sure?"

"I'm positive."

The fencing began to shred the top of his helmet once again. The noise of the fence disintegrating his car was so loud he winced as the car sailed toward it. Remington knew what was next. He did everything he could to break free from this nightmare before hitting the post once again and starting the cycle over. As the nose of the car hit, Remington shuddered and with a supernatural effort, shied away from the post in his mind.

"There it was again! Did you see it this time?"

"I saw it. I think he is trying to wake up. Call the nurse."

The room was quickly flooded with a barrage of medical personnel. Jersey and Lionel were escorted out and forced to wait once again for news on Remington's condition. They did not have to wait long. The on-call neurosurgeon came to them within minutes.

"Remington is awake," he said as he sat beside Lionel and Jersey. "Something must have stimulated his mind enough to wake him from the coma. A lot of the science around this type of head injury is inexplicable, but regardless, it is good news he is awake. I want to warn you that he is unable to speak and is most likely suffering from severe memory loss. He is still unaware of his surroundings and probably does not remember anything leading up to the wreck." Any relief Lionel and Jersey had received from the news quickly dissipated. "It will just be a matter of time before we see how much he recovers. We don't want to push him too hard at this point. But I think it would be good for him to see you."

The lights in the hospital room were blinding as Remington opened his eyes. Fuzzy images of people buzzed about, checking his body and adjusting the tubes and wires making their way from his arms and mouth. The repetitive wreck spiraled to the back of his mind as he attempted to focus. Afraid he might slip back into the nightmare, he fought the weight of his eyelids, trying to determine his surroundings. As hard as he tried, he could not find respite from the white noise echoing in his head. He strained for clarity: just a single clear thought. Where he was, who he was . . . he felt trapped. The heart monitor beside his bed showed a rapidly climbing rate as he wrestled to free himself. The physician quickly administered a sedative. Remington felt himself relax; clarity still eluded his mind.

The blurry figures in his room must have finished whatever they were doing and had left as quickly as they had come. He looked about the room in a continued search for clues as to his new actuality. Something squeezed his hand. He slowly moved his eyes to the other side of his bed, unable to turn his splinted neck. Two of the blurry figures had returned and stood beside him. As the figure continued to squeeze his hand, he realized for the first time that he was hearing something. The other figures had come and gone with no sound, but this was different.

"Remington. It's your dad; can you hear me? I'm here for you. I have Jersey here with me as well. Can you hear me?" Remington focused even harder as the figure continued to talk and squeeze his hand. Lionel and Jersey watched as he blankly stared at them. He appeared lost. As they watched him struggle, they feared the worst, that they may never get him back, that this existence would become his new reality — their new reality.

Lionel brushed the hair from his son's eyes, hoping for any sign that he knew who he was. Remington looked the same, but the shell staring back at him was not his son. Tears began pouring down Lionel's face. "God, spare him. Please spare my son! You knit him together in his mother's womb. You created him and know him better than any doctor. You know what is going on inside his body and his mind. Please heal him, God, even if it is just his mind. If I could trade places with him, I would. Please, Jesus. Please." Jersey put her hand on Lionel's shoulder as he prayed, dabbing her eyes with a tissue. "If it is your will that he be healed, I ask it would happen. I love you, son."

A warm feeling filtered through Remington's body as he listened to the muffled words from the figure next to him. Though he couldn't decipher their meaning, they were comforting. Something had welled up inside of him, trying to break him free from the shackles that obliterated any clear thoughts.

He was on the cusp of coherence but could not scale the other side. Remington fought with what little energy he had to keep from slipping back into the dark abyss from which he had temporarily emerged. Further and further he tumbled, grasping at fleeting thoughts, until he could no longer hold his eyes open. Once again, darkness overwhelmed him.

As Lionel watched, he could feel the struggle raging inside his son. What hope had arisen was swallowed with the closing of Remington's eyes.

Lionel's thoughts turned to the future, with hope and faith that God could heal his son — that He *would* heal his son. Lionel grabbed the pen and notepad he brought from the hotel and began hashing out a list. It wouldn't be easy to get Remington to Montana, but Lionel knew it would be the best place for him to heal. His son's final moments could be on the life support machine that beeped rhythmically from behind the hospital bed, but Lionel refused to let this thought rule his mind as his pen raced feverishly back and forth across the paper.

- Refurbish Remington's bedroom with a hospital bed and equipment
- Convert the TV room to a rehab room
- Make the home wheelchair-accessible
- Put together a shopping list re: what the nutritionist said he needs to gain back his weight
- Hook up the TV in his bedroom
- Schedule visits from his teammates
- Have church schedule a prayer service for him
- Have Pastor Traeger come visit

The list went on and on as Lionel thought through every detail. He couldn't sit idle while his son fought for life — he had to fight alongside him. It was time to take a trip home to prepare for what he hoped to be the battle ahead.

Jersey helped Lionel unload his bags in the drop-off zone at SEATAC airport.

"I'll be back in a couple of weeks," Lionel said. "Thank you for staying with Remington. Call me with any updates."

"It's the least I can do. I'll let you know right away if there is any change in his condition." Lionel gave Jersey a hug, grabbed his bags, and entered the terminal.

Jersey felt like Harborview Medical Center, room 620, had become her second home as she checked her makeup over the sink in the corner of Remington's room. She had just re-dipped her mascara brush when something caught her eye in the mirror. She quickly turned to Remington's bed, only to find him resting quietly. After watching him for a couple of minutes, she went back to applying her makeup in the mirror. There it was again. At first, it was only slight twitches under Remington's eyelids, but the movements continued to build until his head began to turn. Jersey grabbed his hand.

"Come back to us, Rem. C'mon. You can do this." She squeezed his hand harder, and his eyes opened. Remington slowly glanced around the room until his gaze met Jersey's at the side of his bed. It was not the same blank gaze from a week earlier. This time, she could see the man behind the eyes staring back at her.

"Remington, can you hear me?" To her amazement, Remington squeezed her hand and tried to mumble some words. She quickly pushed the nurse-call button clipped to Remington's pillow.

"You know it's me, don't you?" Once again, Remington squeezed her hand and managed a slight nod. "Oh, praise God! You *are* coming back." Jersey hurried to the hallway to see if the nurse was on her way. They nearly collided in the doorway.

"He is awake and he recognized me. He even squeezed my hand!"

"All right, that *is* great news," the nurse said as she approached the bed. "Let me page Dr. Belkamp and I'll get some vitals while we wait." Jersey stood in the corner of the room, overwhelmed with joy as the nurse tried to communicate with Remington.

"His vitals are stabilizing." As the nurse hovered around Remington's bed, Remington never took his eyes off of Jersey. "I think he likes you, Ms. Antonelli. He hasn't taken his eyes off you since I came in." They both noticed a fragile smile on Remington's face. "These are very encouraging signs. But let's not get ahead of ourselves. The doctor can give us a better idea of what's next."

Jersey paced through the hospital cafeteria, unable to contain her excitement as she dialed Lionel's number in Montana.

"Hello?"

"Lionel, it is —" Before Jersey could even introduce herself, she was overcome by emotion, and began to sob.

"Jersey, is that you? Is everything all right?"

"Yes, yes it's me. I am so sorry." She wiped her eyes and sniffled.

"What's going on? Is Remington — is he — is he all right?"

The rattling of plates in the cafeteria momentarily came to a halt as the cafe employees watched Jersey fight to capture her composure. "Lionel, Remington is awake. He recognized me. He squeezed my hand and tried to smile. The doctors say he still has a long way to go, but I can't help but be excited about what I saw in that room today — we may have him back, Lionel." The smile that emerged on Jersey's face seemed to ensure the staff in the cafe that everything was okay. The clattering of dishes slowly began again as Jersey ended her call.

CHAPTER *19*

Long Road

REMINGTON COUGHED AND GAGGED as the endotracheal tube slipped from his airway.

"I know; I know," Dr. Belkamp said as he handed the tube to a nurse. "Trust me, you will be a lot more comfortable with this out." The nurse suctioned the secretions that had collected in Remington's mouth. "I am also going to start you on a little heavier dose of pain medication now that you are awake. You may begin to notice some pain that you haven't felt before." Remington gave the doctor a slight nod, already well aware of that pain in his head and neck. Surprisingly, the pain in his legs did not appear to be too bad, even though he could now see they had both been severely injured.

The pain medication felt icy as it tore through his veins. He winced as the nurse finished squeezing the syringe. Almost immediately, he could feel the ache in his head and back begin to subside.

Jersey pulled up her seat by Remington's bed and wrapped his hand in both of hers. "Does that help?" she asked. Remington nodded. "I know it is probably miserable for now, but you are a fighter, Rem. You will heal. I just know it." He gave another half smile. "Your father ran home to Montana to take care of some things. But he is on the first plane back to see you."

Lionel took a deep breath in the hallway before entering the ICU to see his son. He gently knocked out of habit from his days as a surgeon and entered the room. Remington was asleep. Lionel sat next to him and folded his hands. He had been praying for a few minutes when he heard a shaky, broken voice.

"Love you, Dad."

Lionel lifted his bowed head and made eye contact with his son for the first time since the day of the wreck. Tears flooded his vision. "I love you too, son."

Remington struggled to form another sentence, as if he were learning to speak for the first time. There were long pauses as he desperately searched for words, and then mouthed them. "I . . . will . . . be . . . okay . . . Dad." Lionel dragged his flannel sleeve across his wet eyes. He could only muster a nod. "Don't . . . worry . . . me . . . no . . . about."

Lionel could see Remington was frustrated by the search for the final word of his jumbled sentence. "Don't worry about you?" Lionel said, trying to help.

Remington nodded and did his best to smile. "I'm . . . a . . . a . . . fight." Remington tried to raise his fists like a boxer.

Lionel chuckled as he blew his nose. "I know you are, Rem. I know you are. We will get through this together."

"Mmm . . . Mmm." Without his son even completing the word, Lionel knew the question being gasped from between his son's cracked lips. He had hoped for more time to prepare. "Mabel?"

Lionel simply shook his head. Remington gave a slight nod and looked away. The expression on Lionel's face told him all he needed to know. And then some.

"I'm so sorry, Rem." Remington squeezed his father's hand and closed his eyes.

The next few weeks showed minimal, but promising signs of improvement in Remington's condition. He could form complete sentences with much less effort, and he was becoming more mobile in bed. But Remington was also beginning to fully grasp the fact that Mabel had left him. *She doesn't even know if I survived. That's it? That is goodbye?* He was devastated.

"I know you probably don't want to hear this, Rem," Lionel said while the physical therapist exercised Remington's arms, "but you need someone who will stay with you no matter what. Mabel's gone, and I know that hurts, but you have a whole slough of people here pulling for you and sticking right with you."

"I know, Dad." Remington groaned with pain as the therapist rotated his arm above his head. "I just don't want to hear it right now. I need to deal with it on my own, try to get healthy again."

"Fair enough. I just want you to know we are here for you."

"All right, Remington," the therapist said. "One more exercise and then I am going to have Dr. Belkamp join us so we can do a couple of tests on your legs. Does that sound okay?"

"Whatever you say."

Dr. Belkamp patted Lionel on the back as he entered Remington's room and began washing his hands. Out of respect, Lionel and Jersey moved into the hallway to give Dr. Belkamp and his team room as they began their examination of Remington's legs.

"Hello, Remington. It sounds like you have been making some great progress with physical therapy," Dr. Belkamp said.

"I guess. It feels like I have a long way to go. One day at a time, right doc?"

"That's right, Rem. One day at a time." Dr. Belkamp finished washing his hands. "I want to do some tests on your legs today, Remington. We noticed a couple of things on the latest X-ray of your back that concern us a little."

"What do you mean?"

"It looks like your spine is not regenerating the way it should be at this point. Your back and neck suffered massive injuries in the wreck. Fortunately, the fractures to your vertebrae didn't sever your spinal cord, but the trauma shocked your spine."

Remington felt like he had just been punched in the stomach. "What the hell, doc? Is that why I can't feel my legs? I thought it was because of the casts."

"That is our concern, Remington. After we conduct these tests, we'll know more."

A few minutes later, angry shouts tumbled from Remington's room and echoed through the neuro-trauma unit. They quickly melted to sobs. Dr. Belkamp gently closed the door behind him as he stepped into the hall.

"Can we talk in my office? Jersey, you are welcome to come along if it is okay with Mr. Mason." Lionel nodded. They walked in silence to his office. "Please, have a seat." Dr. Belkamp stood in the corner of the room, half sitting on the window ledge overlooking Seattle. "Listen, this is not easy to say, but

I want to get it done so you can go back to Remington. We caught some abnormalities on his X-rays and MRIs from earlier in the week. His spinal cord is not regenerating the way it should be. We were able to confirm today that Remington has suffered a complete spinal cord injury. I'm sorry to have to tell you this, but Remington has suffered total paralysis from the waist down. If past cases tell us anything about this type of injury, it is that the odds he will walk again are small." Lionel buried his head in his hands. Jersey quietly wrapped him in her arms. "I am so sorry. You may stay in my office as long as you need to."

Lionel pushed open the door to Remington's room while Jersey waited in the hall. His son's eyes were marred with tears and reflected a hollow despair Lionel had never seen before. His son had always been full of life and passion. The man staring back at him now was a different person. Never again would he race. Never again would he walk. Remington would be giving up the seat of his dreams and instead, be unceremoniously relegated to a wheelchair, a seat born of catastrophe, of loss, and of despair.

Before Lionel had a chance to say anything, Remington broke the sullen quiet that draped the room. "I wish I would have died in that car."

"What are you talking about, Rem?"

"What don't you get? I wish I had died in that car."

"Son, no, that is not what you wish." Lionel fought for words.

"Don't tell *me* what I wish. You are *not* the one stuck in a bed you can't get out of. You see, look, they don't work!" Remington gritted his teeth and tried with everything in him to move his legs. "Damnit! You see that? *They don't move!* So don't tell me what I want. I want to be dead in that car. At the track, where I belong. Not lying in this bed thinking about spending the rest of my life in a wheelchair."

"I am so sorry, son. I am so sorry." Lionel tried to grab his son's hand but Remington jerked it away.

"I need some space. And don't let Jersey come back in here. Ever. I don't want her around anymore. No one needs to see me like this. Please, get the hell out!" Lionel gently shut the door behind him. Jersey was waiting in the hall. Lionel could tell by the look on her face that she had heard everything.

CHAPTER 20

Montana

LIONEL WAVED FROM THE FRONT PORCH as the medical team pulled away. It was already seven o'clock in the evening. The entire day was consumed with movers and construction personnel weaving through his home. Remington's bedroom was converted and the rehab equipment moved in. The doors were all widened, the ramp to the front porch complete. Lionel had always believed Montana was simply good for the soul in and of itself. The medical equipment was a necessary extra. He knew how difficult the next few months and probably years would be, but that didn't matter. Remington's life had changed, and so had his.

Remington had been in the hospital for nearly five and a half months when at last, he received word from Dr. Belkamp that he was able to go home for further rehabilitation and rest. The walls of the hospital had closed in around him, had pressed so hard that everything he cared about had been lost. Remington had always been one of the most calm, cool, and collected drivers on the circuit. Now, anxiety plagued him, sucking rest from his body and mind. If he could just get one good night of sleep . . .

Remington participated in his rehab, but barely. Never before had he felt so trapped by the limitations of his own body and increasingly, his own mind. He was uncertain how much of it was lingering physical damage from the wreck, and how much was the anger, fear, and depression that had placed its cold grip on his life over the months in bed.

After a quick stop at security, the ambulance drove onto the tarmac. Remington could see the Flux Energy Liquor jet out the small window. Before, the sight of the jet had filled him with adrenaline in anticipation of his next race. Today he felt nothing. If anything, the jet was a grim reminder of what he had lost, what had been ripped from him in the most violent, unforgiving way.

Remington was greeted by the flight staff as he sat helplessly in his wheelchair at the bottom of the stairs, the first reminder of how difficult life would be from here on. The ambulance crew and a male flight attendant hoisted Remington up the stairs and through the cabin door. He groaned in pain as they gently lowered his body onto the luxurious leather chair. The pain paled in comparison to the humiliation he felt in having to be lifted into his seat.

"Is that comfortable, Mr. Mason?" asked the paramedic who had helped carry him to his seat.

"Yeah, that's fine."

"All right. Make sure you keep buckled in during the flight. That might seem obvious, but sometimes the basics take some getting used to with your new condition." Remington winced as he used his arms to reposition himself in the chair and nodded as he buckled his belt.

"Can I get you anything before we take off?" a member of the flight crew asked. "Mr. Buckner had the plane stocked with drinks and a ton of food. He thought you would probably be ready for some real food after being in that hospital for so long."

"No, thank you. I don't have much of an appetite these days."

"Let me know if you change your mind. We have about a two-hour flight to Missoula. I'm happy to get you anything you might need." *That's precisely the point,* Rem thought. *If I need anything, somebody has to get it for me.*

The inversion tucked around Mount Rainier made it look like an island in a billowing sea of clouds. The sunrise kept the west side of the mountain in complete darkness as the plane leveled out. In the midst of a beauty he once adored, all Remington could focus on was how bad the reflection of the sun off the snow made his head hurt. He slammed his window shade closed and washed another oxycodone down his throat. He was asleep before the mountain disappeared from view.

Lionel watched the tiny puffs of smoke roll from the tires of the private jet as it touched down on the runway. He had always been thrilled to pick his son up from the airport. It brought back so many good memories. But this time was different. Sure, he was excited to have his son home, but he had no delusions about the hard road ahead.

The aircraft marshals guided the plane to a halt outside the aviation office before signaling Lionel to bring his truck out to the plane. He parked his F-250 next to the jet on the tarmac. He boarded the plane, gingerly got down on one knee next to Remington's seat, and hugged him. "Welcome home, son."

Remington blinked, still groggy from the effects of the opioid. He rubbed his temples. "Thanks, Dad." Remington's voice was weak and raspy. "I was ready to get out of that damn hospital."

"I've got you here with me now. There is no better place to heal than good old Montana. Let's get you off this plane." Members of the aviation team picked Remington up and set him gently in the front seat of the Ford truck. They spread a blanket over his legs and wished him a successful recovery.

"Are you hungry, Rem? I thought we could stop and grab a bite at that place we like on the way out of town. The one we always stopped at after we fished the Clark Fork."

"That sounds good, Pop. I could probably stand to eat something." Lionel eased the truck in gear and pulled off the tarmac.

The waitress brought out the hot biscuits with honey the restaurant was famous for. "You used to love these when you were a kid," Lionel said.

"Still do." Remington plopped a splotch of butter on the steaming biscuit and topped it with honey.

"I will always remember your mom going through an entire pack of wet wipes cleaning butter and honey off you. I would let the Lab lick you once we got back to the truck just to make sure she didn't miss anything." Lionel chuckled. "I'm glad to have you back."

"I'm glad to be back, but can you spare me the jog down memory lane?" Remington motioned to his legs. "Right now I need to fix my mind. I need time. I need space."

Lionel sagged in his chair. "Whatever helps you get better. I hope your past can be a place of refuge and solace in the not-too-distant future."

Lionel signed the check and rolled Remington to the front door. The hostess held the door open for them. She recognized Remington.

"Aren't you that race car driver? Didn't you, well . . . weren't you the one guy?" Remington could tell she was unsure of what to say.

"It's all right," Remington said. "I know, it's not how you saw me on TV." There was an awkward pause as the hostess stared at him, unsure how to proceed. Remington suddenly felt agitated. "*Say something!*" he shouted. "*Speak your mind!*" The lobby of the restaurant fell silent. "I'm sorry. Damnit." Remington shook his head, embarrassed by his outburst. "Please forgive me. Let's go, Dad."

"We have it from here," Lionel said. "Thanks." The young hostess quickly hurried back inside.

Lionel positioned Remington's wheelchair next to the running board of his F-250. He was careful not to set the parking break on the chair so he could slide it out and get more leverage once he had Remington in his arms. With one foot already on the running board, Lionel got behind Remington, tucked his arms under his son's and on the count of three, lifted with all the strength his aged body could muster. He elevated him enough to where Remington could grab the jam of the door and help pull with what little strength he had.

Lionel hunched over to catch his breath as Remington pulled his legs the rest of the way into the pickup. Lionel shut Remington's door, folded the wheelchair, and put it in the bed of the truck before limping around to the other side and pulling himself into the driver's seat. They rode in silence for a few minutes. Lionel was the first to speak. "I understand how hard this is for you, Rem. If there's —"

He was quickly interrupted. "Do you really, Dad? I don't think you do understand. You're not the one with these useless, numb legs, constantly reminding you of who you used to be. The one that has to depend on everyone for literally *every damn thing*. I don't think you *do* understand."

Lionel slammed the brakes on his truck and veered off on a dirt road alongside the highway.

"What the hell are you doing?" Remington asked.

Lionel shoved the truck into park and turned to face his son. "Listen to me, Remington. Maybe I don't understand what *exactly* you are going through, but I do know I love you, and it grieves my heart to see you go through this. But I will walk through hell for you before I let this beat you. Before I let it beat us." Remington had rarely seen this explosive side of his father. "I am *not* going to sit around and feel sorry for myself. In fact, I'm not even going to feel sorry for *you*. We have had a chance to cry, and to think this thing through, and trust me, I have done plenty of both. Okay, you might not ever strap into a race car again, but that doesn't mean you can't have a great life. I watched you fight with everything in you to get to where you wanted to go in racing. This can't be any different. You *have* to fight, Remington. There is no other option. I'm not going to let you lose your life just because you lost your legs." Gravel pelted the wheel wells of the Ford as Lionel accelerated back onto the highway. Remington sat silently, a stunned look on his face.

Lionel pointed the F-250 down the dirt road toward home and could see the lights of his log house through the trees. Remington had long since succumbed to another self-administered serving of pain killers.

Lionel felt a tremendous sense of sadness and loss well up in him as he saw his son sleeping against the truck window with Flathead Lake framing the small hobby ranch behind him. He and Rem had hunted the fence rows for pheasant in the nip of the early fall and built duck blinds along the edge of the lake. They trolled for trout and swam in the heat of the summer when they were not on the road, racing. Remington and his friends bucked hay bales and raced four wheelers through the pastures. Lionel had bought the small ranch when he first started as a neurosurgeon in Montana. It was a great place to raise a family. Now it was just the two of them, but shared memories still lingered in the warm evening breeze. Lionel stopped a hundred yards short of the house.

"Rem. Wake up. We're home." Remington groaned and slowly wiped his eyes. "I need to tell you something before we get up to the house, and I don't want you to get mad. I figure we better settle it here."

"What now?" Remington looked out his window at the lake. "It can't be any worse than anything I've already been through."

"You know good and well that I am too old to take care of you alone."

"What is that supposed to mean?" A stubborn look appeared on Remington's face.

"It means having to lift you and help you do your rehab and drive you to appointments. It's too much for me — and I'll need some help." Lionel paused for a moment as he nodded toward the house. "Jersey offered to come help me out. I accepted the offer. She's waiting for us inside."

An ominous silence filled the cab. Lionel put the truck in gear and slowly started down the driveway.

Chapter 21

Settling In

"Lionel, I should just leave," Jersey said. "Let me grab my things and get packed up. This was a bad idea."

Lionel limped over to where Jersey sat at the kitchen table. He pulled out the chair next to her, slowly lowered himself down, and grabbed her hand. "Listen, Jersey. I know Remington is mad, but he is mad at me, not you. We knew there was a chance he would react this way. We talked about it back in Seattle."

"*Mad?* He threw a *phone* at the wall. I think he was a little more than mad. I just don't want to cause him any more stress than what he is already going through."

"Remington will come through this. He is still trying to get his mind back, and the medications he is on are affecting his personality right now," Lionel said. "Agitation is common after a head injury. He is getting used to a new way of life. Remington has always been the first to take on a challenge, to jump up and help someone — he was born independent. He can't jump up anymore, and he needs time to adjust." Jersey looked like she wasn't buying any of it. "Jersey, you've been a rock in my life the past few months." Lionel shook his head as he looked around the room. "I need you. Please, stay with us."

The look in Lionel's eyes was the same look that caused her to come to Montana in the first place. Lionel was right. He needed her, and maybe Remington would some day as well. She was willing to stay and find out.

"I'll stay — for now," Jersey said.

Lionel exhaled with relief. "Oh Jersey, you are a blessing. Thank you."

"On one condition: if my presence ever becomes a hindrance to Remington's recovery, I will leave."

Lionel embraced Jersey. "We have a deal."

Jersey had just poured a second cup of coffee when she heard something hit the floor in Remington's room just off the kitchen. Coffee sloshed onto the old wooden table as she slopped the cup down and ran toward his room. She stopped to knock. "Remington, are you okay?" She cracked the door just enough to see Remington trying to pull himself off the floor into his wheelchair. She quickly entered.

"Damnit, I'm fine. Don't come any closer." Jersey stopped at the foot of his bed. "I don't have any pants on." He continued to wrestle with the comforter as it slipped off the bed. Jersey grabbed it to give him some resistance.

"Remington, I don't mind. I can come — "

Remington cut her short as he struggled to catch his breath. "Please don't. This is humiliating. And it's exactly why I didn't want you here. I'm fine. Please just go." She backed out of the room and quietly closed the door.

"Is he all right?" Lionel asked as he limped down the stairs.

"He's fine. He tried to get into his chair by himself and missed."

"It's way too early for him to be trying that. It's a good thing we don't have a race car around here. He would probably try and crawl into that too. Do I need to go help him?"

"It might be best to let this one go."

Lionel had just set the coffee pot back on the burner when Remington's bedroom door opened. Remington rolled out and headed toward them.

"I guess I owe you both an apology for last night. And probably this morning, too." He paused for a second as he set the brakes on his wheelchair. "But first, can somebody help me pull my damn pants up?" The three of them laughed, the first time since the wreck.

For the next two weeks, Remington's progress impressed his doctors. He was adjusting to his new situation at home and was even beginning to appreciate Jersey being around to help.

Jersey walked into the kitchen with a bundle of checkered flag balloons. Lionel was trying to figure out how to shove a plate of raw hamburgers into an already-overflowing refrigerator. "Do you think he is ready for this?" Jersey asked, anchoring the balloons to the table.

"I think he is. It will be good for him to see the team. And they have been dying to see him."

"Either way, we will find out soon," Jersey said. "I just got a call from Chet, and they are only about thirty minutes out."

"I better go check on Rem, make sure he is ready." Lionel dried his hands and disappeared into Remington's bathroom.

The water dripped across the floor as Lionel pressed the button on the wall. The lift hummed as it raised Remington's nude frame over the edge of the tub and to his chair, where Lionel had already placed two towels, one for his legs and one for his upper body. It was a routine they had down.

"Thanks, Dad. If you can just help me with some pants, I can do the rest." Lionel groaned as he got down on one knee and started the underwear over his son's feet. Once they were to his knees, Remington lifted his body from the chair so Lionel could cover him. They repeated the process with pants. Lionel slowly pulled himself to his feet and kissed his son on the head.

"Once you get dressed, come on out to the deck. I have something I want to show you. I threw a shirt on the bed for you."

"Sounds good. I'll be out in a few."

Remington wriggled himself into the flannel shirt before heading to the mirror in his room. He took a minute to examine his face and arms. A shell of the man he used to be stared back at him. His arms had shrunk, and the dark circles under his eyes made his face look sunken. He shrugged and applied some pomade to his wavy hair. It was one of the few things he could still control about his appearance. He gave the right wheel on his chair a solid push to spin himself toward the door. He paused as he rolled past the small bottle. "Why not? It will just make me smell good." He grabbed the cologne off his dresser and gave his neck a couple of sprays. "Dad and Jersey will wonder what has gotten into me, trying to be all fancy." He recapped the cologne and left his bedroom.

"Dad? Jersey?"

"On the deck. Come on out," Lionel said.

Chet Buckner had already started drying his eyes when he saw Remington roll around the corner. It was futile. He burst into tears while the rest of Remington's race team yelled, "Surprise!" Chet looked startled by the person sitting in the chair in front of him. Remington's chiseled figure had been swallowed up and replaced with skin draped over bone. The strong hands that once gripped a steering wheel were frail and fragile-looking, and his shoulders poked through his flannel.

The rest of the team rushed to hug their driver. They surrounded him as if he had just won the Indianapolis 500. It was a victory that their driver was alive. Chet tried to dry his eyes a second time as he caught Remington staring his way while the crew told Rem how they could hop up his wheelchair a little. For a driver of Remington's caliber, the standard chair simply would not do. Remington laughed, enjoying the company. Lionel and Jersey breathed a sigh of relief.

"Oh no — here comes the boss. Now what did I do wrong?" Craig Doucet said as Chet approached the crew, still huddled around Remington.

"Very funny, Craig. Let me have a moment with the kid."

Craig slapped Remington on the back. "See ya in a bit *kid*. Don't let him tell you what to do."

Chet took a seat on the porch swing next to Remington's wheelchair. He cleared his throat as he searched for words.

"Good to see you too, boss," Remington said.

Chet's voice cracked as he began to speak. "I'm — " he cleared his throat again. "I'm so sorry, Remington. I am so sorry this happened — to you." He shook his head, unable to look Remington in the eye. "I have not been able to forgive myself for putting you in that car. I just can't help but think I could have said no two years ago when you presented yourself in the boardroom at our headquarters. If I had, you wouldn't be in this . . . this damn seat." He kicked the wheel of Remington's chair.

"Hey, look at me Chet." Remington hit Chet's forearm with the back of his hand. "*Look* at me. *You* didn't put me in that car. Yeah, you gave me the platform to do what I love, but whether it was you or someone else sponsoring me, I would have been in a car. Somewhere, somehow, I would have been racing, and this could have happened in anyone's car. Or on anyone's team. It was my choice. Hell, I would do it again. So please, Chet, move on man. It is not your fault."

Chet grabbed Remington's shoulder and finally looked him in the eyes. "I'm so glad you are alive." He embraced Remington. "Hey, this kid needs a beer." Chet vigorously signaled for assistance. Remington's right-rear tire changer dug his arm into the Yeti cooler on the corner of the deck and fished out an ice-cold round top. "Hey doc, this guy allowed to drink yet?"

Lionel gave Chet a thumbs up from behind the grill. "He's off his meds, and you all came to celebrate with him. I think a beer at this point is fair game." A loud cheer erupted from the crew. They were a team once again, and Remington was the man of the hour.

The leaves in the aspen groves dawned their changing colors and October breathed a new nip into the air. The fly rods were put away, the duck blinds nearly complete, and the rifles and shotguns cleaned for the season ahead. The archery hunters were already in the woods while the occasional fishing boat drifted by on the lake, trolling for trout. The humming of the jet skis and the shouts of kids swimming were packed away until next summer. On the ranch, the cattle were brought in from higher ground, and the occasional high-school football player bucked hay for a little extra cash on the weekend.

Remington passed the time on the corner of the deck, watching the changing of the seasons from his wheelchair. Other than Jersey occasionally pushing him down to the dock to cast a line for smallmouth, he was a helpless bystander watching his life from an otherworldly perspective. Remington's mind continued to heal, but pain still ravaged his back and neck. Sometimes he even welcomed it as a distraction.

Despite the pain, Remington's doctors said he was progressing well. "But toward what?" he thought. They would pat him on the back and tell him great work. "What am I working *toward*? No pain? A clear mind? Regardless, I am going to be stuck in this chair for the rest of my life. What the hell are they talking about?"

A squeeze on his arm broke him from his thoughts. "Hey Rem, can I get you some hot tea or coffee? It is freezing out here." Remington declined as Jersey pulled the Hudson Bay blanket tight around herself and grabbed a chair next to him on the deck. "I find it amazing that the sunset can be that bright, and it can still be so cold here!"

"God has an interesting way of working things out I guess," Remington said. "I'm learning that every day."

"As long as you are learning, right?"

Remington smiled and shook his head. "How do you do it?"

"Do what?"

"You're so optimistic. Seriously, do you *ever* have a bad day? Even when I wouldn't acknowledge your existence, you still treated me like I was a king. I just don't get how you do it." Jersey laughed and pulled her legs up on the chair, tucking her pink, wool socks under the blanket to hide them from the cool breeze on the porch. Her long, black hair fell in waves over the multi-colored blanket she was cuddling into, and her blue eyes flickered as she watched the sun sink behind the trees. Remington couldn't take his eyes off her. Her face radiated in the fading light. He had been so involved with Mabel, he had forgotten just how stunning she was.

The moment ripped him back in time to the first day they had met on the beach in Florida. Despite his head injury, Remington recalled it like it was yesterday. She splashed him in the surf as she attempted to steal back her innertube. Her body was perfectly sculpted in an orange bikini and her teeth almost blinding behind her red lipstick. Jax dunked him under a wave and all he could think about was getting to the surface to see this beautiful woman again. The night ended with nothing more than a fond goodbye as he dropped her off at her place in Miami. At the time, he thought he would never see her again — and now she was sitting next to him on a porch in Montana.

"Hey you!" Jersey snapped her fingers. "Where did you go?"

"I'm sorry. Just got lost looking at that sunset for a minute."

"Sure you did. Is that why you were staring at me?"

"I was?"

Jersey flashed a smile. "Anyway. You asked how I stay so positive and I was going to tell you before you disappeared. You really want to know?"

"Honestly, can we just watch the sunset and enjoy this moment?"

"Of course we can."

They watched the stars slowly replace every ray of light in the Montana sky. Lionel smiled as he looked on from the kitchen window. He could sense it. He could almost hear it. He had prayed for it. It was hope, and he could see it on the horizon.

CHAPTER 22

Lost

THE FOUNTAIN GURGLED in the hospital waiting room, trickling over a sculpture of rainbow trout and river rocks. Remington remembered when the fountain was donated to the hospital. Lionel was the keynote speaker at the dedication and started his talk by casting a fly into the fountain. Everyone got a good laugh when he hooked a cupcake, and nearly the caterer, on his back cast.

"Mr. Mason?" The nurse scanned the waiting room as Remington unlocked his brakes and slowly rolled out from behind the fountain. "There you are. Doctor is ready to see you." She held the door open for him as he wheeled himself into the exam room. "I'm going to get your vitals and then get Dr. Dillinger in to do your exam." Remington felt the blood rush back into his arm as the pressure cuff relinquished its grasp. The nurse made notes in his electronic medical record, a process he had become all too familiar with. "All right Remington, I'll get Dr. Dillinger."

Remington thought about what he would tell Dr. Dillinger. He *was* feeling better physically, but something unnamable still haunted him. As much as he tried to stay positive, a dark cloud had rolled in to shade his heart and mind. He had always been able to eliminate doubt, fear, distraction, or whatever it was that clamored for his attention. It was the quality that made him such a good driver.

But this was different. He'd gain moments or even days of clarity only to find the storm rolling over him once again. He had to tell Dr. Dillinger something, but what would he say? That he was a fraction of the man he used to be? That once, he could drive a car at 230 mph without a hint of distraction in his mind, and now he had trouble staying focused enough to brush his teeth? That his every moment was riddled with panic, fear, and doubt? Three gentle knocks pulled him back into the exam room.

"Mr. Remington Mason. How's my favorite race driver doing?"

"Hey, Doc. I'm doing as well as can be expected. How about yourself?"

"I'm all right. You would appreciate this. I just took my bird dog out this past weekend to get her used to seeing ducks again, with the season coming on. Good thing I did. We walked up to the pond and the first thing that dog did was bolt and jump in after a raft of coots floating on the bay. It took me thirty minutes to get her back to shore. At least now I know I have a lot of work to do before opening day. She *is* a good dog, but still a pup at heart."

Remington chuckled. "I remember when we were training Pepper. For the first couple of seasons, he scared more ducks than he retrieved, but he finally came around. He's getting old now, but Pepper is the best bird dog I have ever seen. I could drop a duck two feet from his face, and he would wait for me to tell him to fetch it before he moved an inch. There's hope yet for your pup."

"I'll keep that in mind as I watch her send all my ducks away this season."

"Look on the bright side — you won't spend as much on shells." The two got a good laugh as Dr. Dillinger pulled up Remington's shirt to listen to his lungs.

"Looking at your notes here, Rem, you seem to be doing pretty well. I see we took you off your pain medication after your last visit. How's that been going?"

Remington's pain had been manageable, but the second Dr. Dillinger mentioned the medication, Remington had a physiological response. His neck relaxed and felt as if warm water were trickling down his back, soothing every muscle in its path. The more he thought of the relief the oxycodone had brought him, the more he relaxed. Maybe a few extra pills would help his mind settle?

"You know, Doc, my pain has been building up again. I don't want to get to be like one of the dopers you probably have to deal with all the time, but it would be nice to have some on hand for when it gets unmanageable."

"Rem, you had massive trauma, and it's hard to predict pain in a patient with your type of injuries. I'll send a prescription down to the pharmacy. Make sure you keep pushing hard with your therapy. The more we can get you conditioned, the quicker we can knock your pain back and get you off those things for good."

"You got it, Doc."

Jersey passed Remington a menu as she took a sip of hot tea. "Do you guys want to split a large pizza?" Lionel and Remington both nodded. As they waited for their food, a few people from the community came over to wish Remington well. He was polite and took time to talk, but moments like this were also the reason he avoided going to town. He wanted people to remember Remington the race driver, not Remington the paraplegic.

Four of the people who stopped by were from Lionel's church, including the pastor, Treager Nielson. He shook Lionel's hand and gave Jersey a hug before moving his way around the table to Remington. "How are you doing, Remington? I don't get to see you too often."

"I'm doing all right Pastor Nielson. Things are taking some getting used to, but I am hanging in there. I'm lucky to have these two around." He nodded toward Lionel and Jersey.

"They're a good pair to stick close to," Pastor Nielson said. "Well, I just wanted to say hello, Rem. I think I see your pizza coming up, but before I go, would you mind if I prayed for you? I can pre-bless your food."

"I guess so. Sure. I'd appreciate that, pastor." Remington always thought it felt awkward to be prayed for in public, but figured it would be more awkward to decline.

Traeger put his hand on Remington's shoulder. "Father God, thank you so much for the chance to see Remington here today. I feel so fortunate to have watched this young man grow up racing cars and winning every step of the way. You truly blessed him with phenomenal talent, Lord. I know it brought a lot of joy to a lot of people, including his father."

Jersey opened her eyes and looked at Remington as Pastor Nielson continued to pray. She couldn't contain her smile. Jersey believed in prayer, in the impact it could have. She knew first hand. Jersey was 12 years old when her father packed his bags and moved away in hopes of saving his faltering career as a race driver. Racing had started out as a family sport for the Antonellis, but when her dad had a run of bad luck, and podium finishes became sparse, his sponsors started to bail. Family money became tight, and instead of turning to Jersey and his wife for support, he turned to drinking — lots of drinking. He told them he was going to meet with a group of investors in San Francisco that had a plan for getting him back in a car. The money never came, he permanently traded his driver's seat, and family, for a barstool. They never saw him again.

Jersey was shattered. Her father used to stroll through pit lanes around the country with Jersey on his shoulders, showing her off to his fellow competitors, promising she would one day be "kicking their tail" in a race car. When she was ten, he even bought her a go-kart to start her own racing career, but when he spent their last dime, her car got parked in the corner of their garage, never to race again. While her friends continued to race karts with their families every Saturday afternoon, Jersey felt like she had become a spectator in life.

It wasn't until a year after her dad left that a friend invited her to a party her church was having on the beach. That night, after a short sermon, the youth pastor asked if anyone wanted to know Jesus. Out of a lonely desperation, Jersey slipped out of her seat and went to the edge of the ocean where the pastor was praying with some other kids who had walked up with her. With her toes curled in the sand and the tide lapping at her ankles, she said a short prayer and made a pledge to give her life over to the Lord.

It all seemed a little mystical at the time, but as she learned more about a God she didn't even know existed, she felt Him help patch the holes her father had left in her life. She opened her heart to love, and as she healed, life felt worth living again. There were still moments when her father's absence stung her, but now she had a God, a heavenly Father, who loved her and would never leave her.

Pastor Nielson continued: "So God, while Remington may find himself in a seat he did not choose, I pray that you would continue to heal him physically, emotionally, and spiritually and use his new life to show others that courage is more than just strapping on a helmet and going fast. Courage sometimes shines the brightest through adversity. I believe it was Samuel Chand who once said, 'The amount of pain we are willing to endure sets the limits of our effectiveness.' God, take the same courage Remington once had in a race car and apply it to the seat in which he now sits. There are a lot of people out there who could still benefit from his courage. Amen."

"Thanks pastor. I appreciate that. I just hope I can live up to everything you just said."

"You will, Remington. You will."

Lionel finished a final slice of pizza and paid the tab. They piled into the truck and started the drive back to the ranch. "Look, Rem, I know it's hard on you when you go into town, but Jersey and I would love to have you join us for church tomorrow if you feel up for it. It might be good for you to get out more. Plus, like pastor said, you are an inspiration to people."

"That will all fade with time, and pretty soon I'll just be the cripple around town. I'm better off just laying low and letting it blow over."

"If nothing else, Rem, just come to be with us," Jersey said, giving him a longing look. Remington was fine with them going, but more than ever, he felt as if there was not a God, and if there was, He was too far away to do him any good. Most Christians he met were no different from anyone else. They talked the talk, but did all the same sinful stuff as everyone else.

"Look, I need to fight through this on my own. Not with a bunch of hypocrites who are just going to say, 'Everything will be all right. God will make a way.' Most of those people have no *idea* what it's like to live in this chair. Sometimes God *doesn't* make a way. I just don't want to hear it." They drove the next few miles in silence before Lionel finally turned on the radio, dismissing them all from the awkward encounter.

Jersey looked stunning in her gray sweater dress and black boots. It was a modest dress for church, but Remington could easily see the lines of her body through the sweater. He reminded himself not to stare. Her long, wavy hair was pulled over her shoulder as she came to say goodbye. "Can I get you anything before we head to church, Rem?"

"No, I'm good. Thanks though." Her floral perfume lingered as she grabbed her Bible and handbag off the table and headed to the door. Lionel shuffled down the stairs wearing his finest flannel shirt and a bolo tie.

"We'll see you in a couple of hours," Jersey said. "And we'll bring something back for lunch. Bye, Rem."

"You look . . . " Remington mumbled the last word under his breath.

Jersey turned around smiling. "Did you say something, Rem?" He shook his head. "Okay, bye." She closed the door behind her.

A small flock of crows sprung up from the driveway as they left. "*What* is your problem!" Remington punched his lifeless legs in frustration. "You *used* to drive IndyCars and now you can't even tell a girl she looks beautiful? You are worthless. What would she even say in return? You look great too? Or at least, what's left of you?" The energy he used to be able to disperse through working out, or even going for a walk, now built inside him with no outlet, a dam trying to hold back an ocean of frustration.

The wheel on his chair caught the doorframe as he shoved himself into his bedroom. He pushed hard to propel himself forward once again, ripping the trim from the frame. He yelled a string of expletives as it tore loose, ran it over on the way to his closet, paused, and stared for a moment before plunging his hand into the far corner.

The relief was already tingling on the back of his neck when he heard the pills rattling inside his old racing trophy. Remington pulled out a bottle of oxycodone he'd been hiding. Popping two of them into his mouth, he tossed clothes aside as he rummaged deeper into the closet until he found the bottle of whisky, rolled up inside a black and white checkered blanket his mother had knit for him when he was a child. The cork came free from the bottle and he washed the pills down with a single shot. Never before had he taken the two together, but it was what he needed to clear his mind. The cork squeaked as he replugged the whisky and threw the blanket back in the closet. It caught on the brake of his wheelchair. As he angrily tried to tear it loose, he noticed the other side of the blanket. Remington had forgotten long ago that a number of the squares were stitched with scriptures his mom had prayed for him as a child.

He uncorked the bottle again and took another slug. It burned as it raced down his throat. "I'm glad you are not here to see me like this, Mom." He dried his eyes and folded the blanket, setting it on the corner of the bed as he wheeled himself to the bathroom. He placed the bottle of whisky and the pills on the edge of the tub and leaned in to start the water. He slowly peeled his shirt off and examined his body in front of the mirror, taking sips of the dark whisky. The storm in his mind was beginning to abate. He ran his hand over the stretch marks on his arms where the atrophy had eaten them away. His face was gaunt and his hair oily and limp. He felt no emotion as the tears began to well up and pour from his eyes. He checked the water level in the tub: full.

Water sloshed over the sides as he slid into the bath; it was scalding hot. He grimaced and gritted his teeth as he held himself up with the straps from his mechanical lift until the water cooled down. He felt nothing on his legs as he watched them turn red under the searing water.

He lowered himself once again as a cool stream found its way through the tub. The debris in his mind cleared as the warm water increased the blood flow through his body, speeding the alcohol and opium to his brain. He sank deeper into the tub until just his mouth and nose were above the water. He could hear nothing but the sound of the tub filling and his own heart beating. Everything finally seemed to make sense.

Once again he traced the scars and bumps on his frail, submerged frame as he thought about Jersey — the most beautiful girl he had ever seen. He followed the trail of scar tissue down his left arm. She was the most caring woman he had ever known. His hand stopped over his left pec where his heart used to pound whenever she entered the room. She had always believed in him.

He finally reached his genitals floating limp in the water. Even if he could somehow persuade her to love his broken frame, he could never be intimate with her. He could never have a family. It would never be a normal relationship.

The further he sank into the tub, the less he felt of anything. He pinched his legs, hoping to feel *something*, even pain, but all he felt was the weight of the burden he would always be to his father. His young fans would be shocked to see him now, a grim reminder of why their parents didn't want them to race cars, and why he was no longer their hero. His breathing became labored as the water continued to rise. Just a few more inches and it would trickle to his lungs until they were full. It had all become so clear. He had even failed himself by giving up. Maybe the warm water of the tub would wash away his sins and failures. It was time to go.

Jersey helped Lionel up the front steps of the cabin, where ice had formed the night before. "I'll get some salt on that in a bit, Lionel. Let's find Rem and eat before the food gets cold."

"Sounds good. It got frigid last night. This will start the ducks moving." Jersey set the takeout Chinese food on the table and called for Remington as she took off her winter parka and scarf. There was no answer. The heels of her boots clicked on the wood floor as she walked over to his closed bedroom door and gently knocked.

"Remington?" She pushed the door aside and heard the water running in the bathroom. She walked over to Remington's bed and picked up the checkered flag quilt folded on the corner. She smiled as she unfolded the blanket. "What a precious gift," she thought as she set it back down.

"Rem, are you back there?" Down the short hall, toward the bathroom, she could still hear the tub running. She took a few steps and realized she was walking in a pool of water. She ran the last few steps to the small bathroom and threw open the door. Water rushed over the side of the tub, but Remington was nowhere to be found. She breathed a sigh of relief at the sight of the empty tub.

It was short-lived. The pill bottle bobbed under the faucet as she turned off the water. She plucked it from the tub and scanned the label. OXYCODONE. The bottle was empty. "What have you done, Remington?" she pleaded under her breath. Then she saw the whisky bottle sticking out from a pile of his clothes on the floor. She yelled for Lionel as she raced from the bathroom.

"What's wrong? Is Rem all right?"

"I can't find him!"

"What do you mean you can't find him?"

"The water is overflowing in the tub and he isn't in his room. I found this floating in his bath and a bottle of whisky on the floor." She handed the pill bottle to Lionel.

"We have to find him fast."

Jersey ran back to Remington's room to look for clues to his whereabouts. She noticed the trim had been dislodged from the door, and she leaned in closer to investigate. As she observed the damage, the light coming in hit the hardwood floor in the entryway just enough to highlight a set of wet tire tracks heading toward the front door.

"Lionel!" Jersey grabbed her coat as she opened the front door. "I think he's outside."

"Go! Go! I'll catch up. We have to find him *fast*." Jersey slammed the door behind her. Tears welled up in her eyes as she ran through the yard, looking for anything that might lead her to Remington.

Small patches of sun did nothing to warm the gray day as Jersey's search came up empty. In desperation, she turned to the trail that weaved from the home and through a stand of ponderosa pine to a point overlooking the lake. A wooden bench on the edge of the cliff marked the end of the trail. It had been a place of romance, worship, and inspiration for years. It was one of her favorite places on the Mason ranch, and Remington's too. *Maybe he just needed some fresh air and clarity,* she thought as she sprinted along the path, shouting his name over the roar of the waves pounding on the shore below. She had to summon the courage to glance toward the jagged rocks at the base of the cliff, praying she would not see a mangled wheelchair. She ran harder as she approached the end of the point where the path leveled out and gave way to the view of the Mission Mountains.

It appeared out of nowhere: Remington's wheelchair. Jersey slid to a halt on the path, unable to catch what little breath was left in her stinging lungs. The chair was tipped on its side next to the trail, a few feet from one of the sheer cliffs plummeting to the lake below.

Jersey apprehensively approached the chair, fearful of what she might find. A hand protruded from under the overturned chair. A final step revealed Remington's frail body, nude on the frozen ground. He shook uncontrollably; his lips were dark blue. Jersey threw the wheelchair back onto the trail, took off her coat, and placed it over Remington. She sat in the dirt behind him and gently lifted his upper body off the ground until it was propped up against her own. She wrapped him in her arms and yelled for Lionel. Remington coughed and spat as he continued to quiver in her embrace. His voice gurgled as he tried to speak.

"Shh . . . shhh." Jersey held him even closer, willing her warmth into him.

Remington coughed as saliva ran from the corners of his mouth. He stuttered the only words he could. "I am so sorry." He began to sob uncontrollably. Jersey put her cheek on his, their tears mixing as they ran down Remington's face.

"It's okay. I'm here." She rocked him as she looked over her shoulder for Lionel. She was startled when Remington yelled over the sound of the waves.

"I am so sorry!" He sobbed even louder. "I am so sorry!"

Lionel came up the trail, winded and panting. "We have to get him loaded in the chair," he said. He fought to catch his breath. "He needs to get to the hospital right now so they can pump his stomach." Steam covered Lionel's spectacles and ice crystals framed the corners of his mustache. Although shaken at the sight of his son, Lionel's medical training kicked in as he instructed Jersey. "We get him in the chair and you get him back as quickly as you can. I'll catch up."

They hoisted Remington's body from the cold ground and planted him back in his wheelchair. Lionel took off his jacket and draped it over his son's legs, and immediately collapsed to the ground. Jersey tried to help him up.

"You have to go." Lionel held his hand up and motioned toward the house. "Please, go. I'll be all right in a minute."

Lionel heard gravel crunch under the tires as Jersey sped down the dirt road to the main highway. He got on all fours, crawled to a stump a few feet away, and propped himself up. He had to get back. Digging into his slim reserves, he used the stump to pull himself to his feet and haltingly made his way back to the house.

CHAPTER 23

Cash

LIONEL AND JERSEY woke to a blizzard on Christmas morning. The wind whistled by the windows, framed by piles of snow as whitecaps majestically rolled across the lake.

Jersey wore red long johns when she greeted Lionel in the upstairs hallway. "Merry Christmas, Lionel."

"Merry Christmas, Jersey. Some storm out there, huh?"

"I love it. Somehow I find it calming. We never had anything like this growing up in Florida. This is the white Christmas I always dreamed of and only saw in movies."

Lionel chuckled. "Wait until March. You'll miss Florida."

They walked down the stairs together and passed by Remington's room. It was quiet and dark. As they rounded the corner to the kitchen, they were greeted by plates of steaming hotcakes, fluffy eggs, and sausage links. Bubbles made their way through the foam at the top of the mimosas, and hot biscuits were waiting to be covered with the homemade apple butter from the Mason jar sitting next to them. The blue and white speckled kettle on top of the wood stove whistled, their mugs already primed with creamer.

"Sit, please. I didn't think you two were *ever* going to wake up." Remington wheeled around the corner of the table and pulled Jersey's chair out for her.

"Remington, this is unbelievable. It's only seven. What time did you wake up?"

"No matter! What's important is that you two are finally awake. Merry Christmas by the way."

"This is amazing," Lionel said. "Can I help you with anything?" Remington controlled his chair with one hand as he moved around the table and filled their mugs with coffee.

"Not a thing, Pop. It feels good to be able to do something for you two for once."

Lionel and Jersey filled their plates as they sipped their mimosas and coffee. It took them a moment to realize Remington was staring at them as they tore into their breakfasts.

"You all right, Rem?" Jersey asked through a mouthful of pancake and syrup.

"I just thought being Christmas morning and all, we might say a little prayer."

"Oh my gosh! Remington, you are so right. I had this food in front of me and — I don't know. I just couldn't resist. Would you like to pray?"

"I would really like it if one of you did," Rem said. Jersey deferred to Lionel and they bowed their heads in prayer, thanking God for the meaning of Christmas, the delicious food, and in particular, that Remington was sitting across the table from them. Two months earlier, Remington's life hung in the balance at the local hospital. He was resuscitated three times in the emergency room. Yet, against all odds, here he was celebrating Christmas. They all had plenty to be grateful for.

Lionel had cut the Christmas tree a couple weeks earlier in the hills overlooking the ranch. The aromatic pine scent hung throughout the room. Jersey spent hours decorating it. After breakfast, they basked in the living room, sipping coffee and admiring the lights weaving in and out of the waxy, green needles. They fought for the energy to start exchanging gifts, unwilling to let the moment together pass them by.

Lionel made the first move as the wood in the stove settled, signaling for another log. "Anyone need a refill on coffee?"

"I think we are both good, Dad."

"Then let's open gifts!"

Presents were exchanged with joy, but an unspoken gratitude for the greatest gift warmed the room, made the lights twinkle a little brighter, and the fire crackle a little louder: Remington was alive.

"So, your dad and I got you one more thing, Rem," Jersey said. Lionel grabbed the small bag from behind the tree. He handed it to Jersey. "We are so grateful that you are here with us. This place would be so . . . so empty without you, Rem. We know you're still trying to find your new purpose and passion in life, and we thought this might help."

Remington ruffled through the bag until he found the small card nestled near the bottom. "What's this?"

Jersey barely gave Remington time to open the card before she jumped in to explain. "Okay, Rem, I have to tell you. I have been really excited to give you this."

Jersey looked so cute in her red long johns and the scruffy flannel shirt she wore for pajamas. The cardboard invitation sat static in Remington's hand as he watched her sparkle with delight. Whatever the gift was, it had already been worth it. His cheeks felt warm as she scooted closer to the edge of the couch and grabbed his hand. She smiled.

"I met this guy at church a couple of months ago. His name is Chris Cash. He is from Australia and is a complete surfer dude. I mean, his hair, his clothes . . . the way he talks. The guy belongs in a VW van at the beach." Jersey acted like she was surfing a wave. "Anyway, back to your gift. On top of being a cool guy, Chris is a pro wakeboarder and just moved to Flathead Lake to start a wakeboarding camp for kids. He owns a bunch of gyms on the West Coast that specialize in training extreme athletes. Your dad and I thought he might be willing to work with you at his gym." Jersey gave Lionel an expectant glance. "I hope it's okay, but we asked him, and he said he would love to work with you. He even followed your racing career, Rem. So we bought you a membership to his gym."

Rem turned the gym membership over in his hands. "You know, not that long ago, I would have said no to this." He tapped the plastic card on the handle of his chair. "But I guess I owe you both something for what I put you through, and I am in need of a new hobby. I'm willing to give it a shot. Plus, Chris does sound like a pretty cool dude if he is anything like what you just described."

Jersey pumped a fist before wrapping her arms around Remington.

The diesel fumes from Lionel's truck filled Remington's nostrils as his dad pulled away. He wheeled himself toward the front door of the Phoenix Gym. He wasn't thrilled to be there, but after what he told them on Christmas morning, he figured he owed his father and Jersey the courtesy of at least trying. And they were right — he needed to find something that would fire him up again the way racing did. Remington's gloved hand was about to grab the front door handle when it slowly opened. Snow swirled through the gap.

"Hello there, mate. You must be Remington?" Remington nodded and stuck out his hand. "Chris Cash. Pleasure to meet you, bro." Chris was wearing board shorts, and his shredded arms and chest more than filled out his shirt. The wings of the Phoenix bird in the gym logo strained to span the width of Chris's chest, and his curly blonde hair hung almost to his shoulders from a backward trucker cap. Jersey was right: Chris Cash was a surfer dude.

"Come on in, man. Welcome to my gym." The lobby was full of pictures and memorabilia from Chris's exploits around the world: sky diving, bungee jumping, snowboarding the Swiss Alps. His professional wakeboarding trophies lined a lobby that was decorated to look like a busted-up abandoned building. Fake electrical wires dangled from crumbling bricks and graffiti art of Scriptures and motivational sayings were sprayed on the floor and walls. Chris led him through a metal door with a skull and crossbones prohibiting entry. Someone had slapped a biohazard sticker on the doorframe for good measure. The doorway opened to an expansive, state-of-the-art gym that carried through the theme of the abandoned building. Weight racks sat in front of piles of rubble with cracked mirrors behind them, and lights flickered above the brick alcoves that housed the bench presses. Remington had never seen anything remotely like it.

"Remington, I'm glad you decided to show up, mate. Your father and Jersey talked with me at church awhile back, and they were so full of hope. Look, I don't know if you are here for them, or yourself, or both, but I'm glad you showed up."

"Thanks Chris. I appreciate that. I was sitting outside your front door thinking this was a bad idea. In all honesty, there was a split second before you opened the door that I thought about rolling down to the coffee shop. Too darn cold." Chris laughed. "But now that I'm here, let's see what we can do. I have no idea how you are going to work out a guy with useless legs, but that's your problem."

Chris rubbed his hands together as a mischievous grin spread across his face. "Oh, you just wait."

Remington tossed his gym bag in a locker and wheeled himself back out to meet Chris.

"There you are! Hey, if you don't mind, one of the first things I do with clients is snag a picture of them. I like them to be able to look back and see the progress they are making. You cool with that?"

"Of course. Should I flex these bones?" Chris had trouble holding the camera still as Remington pointed to his withered bicep.

"All right, three, two, one." Remington's clothes hung on him like a shirt on a wire hanger in a closet.

"You want to take a look?" Chris held up the camera.

"I'm good. I have a mirror at home. It's pathetic."

Chris pulled out his iPhone. He tapped "play" and rock music shook the walls of the gym. "If you think the view is pathetic, then let's do something about it."

Remington clung to the rim of the garbage can as he purged a day's worth of caloric intake. His body had not been challenged like this in months — maybe ever.

"You all right there, mate? I told you we would change what you saw in the mirror."

"I didn't think we'd start tonight." Remington dry heaved over the garbage can. "And I didn't know your idea of change involved puking into the trash like some teenaged drunk."

"Trust me, bro. We are going to get your body running like a scalded wallaby. This will be good for you, my friend." Remington stuck his fist out as he wiped vomit from his mouth with the back of his other hand. Chris reluctantly returned the knucks.

"I'm in, Chris. I'm in," Remington said as he spit into the garbage can. "I want this. I will get better. I promise."

Remington threw on his hoodie and gloves before going out to meet Lionel in the parking lot. Chris was tidying up the gym for the night when Remington rolled out of the locker room.

"Chris, out of curiosity, where did you come up with the name for this place? You live in Phoenix or something?"

"You really want to know? If so, you get the whole story. That's the only way I tell it . . . from ugly start to finish."

"Give it to me," Rem said. "Well, within reason." He checked his watch. "Dad will be here in ten to pick me up."

"No time to waste then." Chris plunged into his story. "In case you couldn't tell by my accent, I grew up in Australia."

"Really?" Remington smirked. "That's what Aussies sound like?"

"Ah, smart guy, huh?" Chris continued. "Australia's where I first got into extreme sports, but that wasn't always my thing. I never knew my dad, and my mom gave me up for adoption when I was three months old. I was taken in by a great family, but I think my real parents instilled a little of the devil in me. When I was 17, I moved to Melbourne, and I got into drugs. Drugs and girls. I slept with every hot girl I could, and usually after ingesting, shooting, or snorting whatever mind-altering substance I could find. I'll spare you the gory details, but it messed me up bad. Real bad. In fact, there is no reason I should even be alive."

"Damn, I'm sorry Chris."

"Apologies unnecessary, my man. I didn't know it then, but those times laid the foundation for everything you see here, and a whole lot more. My adopted family never gave up on me, even though I put them through hell. Almost broke up their marriage."

Chris continued racking some loose free-weights. "I was about to start my senior year of *high* school, pun intended, and on the first day of school I met this unbelievably hot chick who was new to our school. An exchange student. I bet my friends $50 dollars I could sleep with her before the first week of school was up. So one day, absolutely stoned out of my gourd, I asked her if she wanted to chill with me after school out at Kerford Road, the local beach hangout. I honestly was so high I wasn't even sure of what I asked her. I was ready to cough up the fifty bucks to my friends . . . after selling fifty bucks worth of hash, of course. The crazy thing is, bro, she said yes. And it changed my life."

Remington was stunned at Chris' willingness to divulge details most people would bury for the sake of their image. "So here you are trying to hook up with this girl and she ends up taking you wakeboarding?" Remington asked. "Sounds like a sweet date. I thought you were going to say she made you do one of those wine and art classes where you get drunk and draw a sunset. You can drink at, like, ten years old in Australia, right?"

"Yeah, actually, Fosters is sold in the baby food aisle at the market. Grows us into men real quick down under." Chris had replayed the day over in his mind hundreds of times. A cocky, drunken high school dare had introduced him to the sport he would one day master as a professional. Some would call it a stroke of good luck. Chris called it Providence, or at least after that day he did.

Chris wrapped a towel around his neck as he sat on the end of a bench and continued his story. "I made an absolute fool of myself behind the boat. I still remember all those girls laughing at me. You have to start somewhere, right?" Chris snapped Remington's chair with his towel. "I have put in some work behind the boat since then, but shredding for the first time wasn't what changed me that day. It's what happened next."

Remington could sense the gravity of what Chris was about to say. Whatever happened must have had an impact. After all, he was sitting in a former drug-addict's gym surrounded by all of his pro wakeboarding trophies . . . dozens of them.

"By the end of that night, I had given my heart to Jesus. I was trying to sleep with this girl and instead she tells me about Jesus? I mean, really mate? God has a funny way of working, Rem," Chris said. "At the time, I wasn't even sure what giving my heart to Jesus meant, dude. All I knew was I woke up that next morning a different Aussie. I came up with a plan for the rest of my life, a new course. I became the boarder that was excited to tell people about Jesus."

"And what about the gym?" Remington asked.

"Oh yeah! The gym." Chris's words now sizzled. He paced in front of the weight racks telling Remington how his wakeboaring career thrust him into a position as a role model, and onto a platform with a powerful opportunity to impact people. Chris embraced his new mantle, started extreme sports camps for youth, and ultimately developed Phoenix Gyms.

"Phoenix just resonated with me, man." Chris pounded his fist into his palms. "It's what I had to call it. It was symbolic of my own rise from the ashes and how God can bring us through trial, build us into something we never dreamed we could be. I had to share that message." Chris looked around his gym and finally back at Remington. "Plus, the bird logo is super sick, bro."

Chris flicked the lights off in the gym and locked the front door. "See you tomorrow, Rem?"

"Yeah, see you tomorrow. Thanks, Chris." Remington wheeled himself to the parking lot with an energy he had not felt in over a year. It wasn't being back in the driver's seat, but whatever it was, it felt good.

CHAPTER *24*

Redemption

REMINGTON SAT WITH A TOWEL wrapped around his waist in front of the mirror, his body still wet from the bath. He carefully studied himself, as if for the first time. Over the past year, he had become well acquainted with the apparition taunting him at every glance, steadily chipping away at his dignity. But this time was different. An image of familiarity flickered in the bathroom light. He could once again see veins running along his biceps, and his collar bones no longer jutted from his skin. He gently traced his fingers over the line dividing his abdominal muscles. His face had filled back in, and his hair was no longer thin and oily. Remington saw something he had given up hope of seeing again . . . himself.

Remington ran a comb through his hair and took one more look in the mirror. Chris was right. His hard work at Phoenix had paid off physically, but the mental gains were what surprised Remington the most. It seemed like each physical rep also tore away at the mental barriers that had stacked up in his mind since the wreck. Rep for rep they fell, the seemingly impenetrable barricades replaced with clarity and peace. He hoped one more was about to fall.

Remington respected Chris's outlook on life. It had changed his own and was one of the reasons he had accepted his invitation. Remington had not been to a Bible study since grade school, but Chris had shown Remington a new way of practicing Christianity: an authentic, less religious way, and it was appealing. He wasn't sure he was ready to fully embrace religion again, but it certainly wouldn't hurt to see what it was all about. Plus, Chris and the guys at the gym wouldn't let him live it down if he didn't show. He was part of the group now.

Remington was unsure when his own skewed view of faith had taken hold in his life. He assumed it must have been a gradual process of spiritual neglect that he severed entirely when his mother died. But after seeing how Chris lived his faith, rather than just talking about it, he began to see that his father and Jersey lived out their lives like this as well. He had just been too self-absorbed to notice. What he *did* know, was that they cared. Did they want him to have a relationship with God? Absolutely, but they never forced him to accept their spirituality. They just showed up, day after day, and took care of him. Remington was embarrassed he hadn't recognized it earlier, that it took them introducing him to Chris to see what they had been doing all along. It was time for change. Remington smiled at himself as he grabbed the Bible off of his dresser and headed for the bedroom door.

Remington wheeled himself into the conference room at Phoenix, or at least what Chris referred to as the conference room. The small room overlooking the gym had a completely functioning telephone booth with a loudspeaker Chris used to take his business calls, and the room was decorated with couches, recliners, and coffee tables fashioned from used wakeboards. Most inviting was the espresso machine steaming away in the corner. Chris held the occasional meeting in the room but mostly, it was where he chilled out.

"Two espresso shots or four, Rem?" Chris yelled from where he stood manning his espresso machine. Pat, Bo, and Austin jumped up to greet Remington as he entered the room.

"Make if four, bud," Remington replied as he hugged his new friends one-by-one. "Been a long day."

Chris slumped down on the couch next to where Remington had parked his chair. His feet made a thud when he propped them up on the coffee table and handed Rem his drink. "Welcome to the study, mate. Quad shot vanilla latte on the house!"

Remington sucked the foam off the top of the latte. "Shoot, this is pretty good for being free."

Remington never had liked to talk about his feelings, but there was something safe about this room and the four other guys lounging around it. As they sipped their coffees and laughed, a genuineness permeated the conversation that instantly put Remington at ease. He had been in some stuffy, legalistic church groups before. This was different, far different.

"All right, mates! Let's get this show on the road. What do you say?" Chris asked as he tossed his phone on the couch. The guys all reached for their Bibles. "I had something else planned to chat about tonight, but I was reading my Bible earlier and ran into this Scripture. It really stuck out to me and I wanted to share it with you. See where it takes the conversation."

Chris thumbed through his Bible until he found the page he was looking for. "The scripture is 1 Timothy 4, verse 8, and it says, '*For physical training is of some value, but godliness has value for all things, holding promise for both the present life and the life to come.*'" Chris paused and marked the page he was reading with his coffee stirrer. "I was thinking as I read this how much emphasis we all put on physical training for appearance, and to help us be better athletes, but the thing that really got me, was that who we are and what we do goes way beyond the shells of our bodies. Our culture is all about appearance, but I don't feel we can fully be ourselves, who we were created to be, until we better understand this concept of godliness. If godliness truly has value for all things and holds the promise for both the present and the life to come, we have to understand what that means, here and now, in our lives."

Austin quickly chimed in. "I feel you, man. If godliness really has that much value, which I believe it does, what are we missing by not fully living for God? We may be holding back some of our chips, not going all in." Remington listened intently as Pat and Bo weighed in on the scripture.

"It's one thing to sit here and talk this out," Chris said. "But I thought it would be pretty rad to take it to the next level and set some goals, put a plan in place to develop this godliness in our own lives. We push each other to be better athletes every time we hit the gym, but why not push each other in this too?"

Remington was intrigued by the concept of pushing each other spiritually. It was not something he had ever considered. Push each other as athletes, as competitors? Of course. That made sense. But spiritually? Remington had always had friends, but there was something special about these guys. They were not afraid to be vulnerable, to be real with each other. They bonded at a level beyond superficial friendship. They could talk football and wakeboarding, even the stock market, but they could also talk from the heart about life and relationships. It brought them together as a team, like no team Remington had ever been a part of.

Chris grabbed a notebook and started jotting down everyone's goals as they went around the room. "If you don't write it down, it'll never happen," Chris warned as he feverishly took notes. Austin and Bo made goals to work on their godliness by better loving and serving their wives. Pat vowed to find ways to incorporate God more into his small business, and to spend time every day reading his Bible. "Remington, how about you? Any thoughts on a goal?"

Remington suddenly felt awkward as he fumbled for some sort of goal he could share. Inside he didn't feel ready, or even worthy, of taking steps like the other guys. He felt he needed to pay his spiritual dues first, whatever that meant. Ask forgiveness? Go to confession? He started talking before he had fully formulated an idea. "You know, what I really need is a goal to help rebuild my courage to simply live my life. To keep me motivated to be here with you guys. To live this life we are talking about now outside of this gym. I need something exciting down the road to keep this, whatever it is we have here, going." Remington looked around the room hoping something, anything, would spark an idea. "So, I want to take up wakesurfing this summer." Remington immediately realized the hilarity of his decision considering his physical condition. It was all that came to mind. But, to Remington's surprise, the guys let out a raucous cheer. He played it off. "I know I can't do it in the traditional sense, but I figured if I could lengthen the rope and hit the curl of the wave a little further from the back deck, I could probably belly-surf it. I know little kids do this type of stuff all the time, but for me, this would be a big step, something to keep me going."

Chris got up from the sofa and wrapped his arms around Remington. "Bro, that is the best goal I have heard. Don't worry, we'll help you figure out how to keep from drowning." His friends rallied around him. Bo even promised to design a special board for him in his shop. "You see this?" Chris said as he slapped his notebook. "It's in ink. This goal is official. Case closed!"

Chris said a quick prayer before they dispersed for the evening and promised he would email each of them their goals and notes from the discussion. As Pat, Bo, and Austin bantered their way to the front door, Remington held back until they had disappeared.

"Hey Chris, can I talk to you for a minute?" Remington asked.

"Of course, Rem. What's up, man?"

" I guess I feel a little convicted, or something."

"How so, mate?"

"I wasn't all that honest in our group tonight."

"What do you mean?"

"The wakesurfing thing? I pretty much pulled that out of the air on the fly, just to have a goal. To fit in I guess. For what it's worth, after I said it, I was . . . I am, serious about it."

"Then what's the big deal, bro? I think it is an awesome goal for you."

"You're too kind, Chris. It's a good goal to keep me motivated, but I guess it isn't the biggest step I want to take. There's something more."

"Mate, you can have as many goals as you like. You'll just put the rest of us to shame, but you can handle more than one."

Remington ran his hand through his hair. "These guys, this gym, you, are the best things that have happened to me since my wreck. After my mom died, I was sure there wasn't any such thing as a God. The cancer was so far along by the time they caught it, treatment wasn't even an option. I was trying to get my career going in IndyCar while I finished college, and Dad was all alone here in Montana." Remington paused to gather himself.

"It just seemed like a lot and I didn't feel God in any of it. To make it more confusing, things were going great. I didn't feel I needed God. Looking back, I see it was a foolish way of thinking. I was messing a lot of stuff up." Remington tapped the cover of his Bible. "Then there was the wreck. After that, whatever flicker of spirituality remained in my life, I made a point to snuff out. I wanted nothing to do with it. It got so bad, Chris, that every time the poor hospital chaplain came to visit me, I pretended I was sleeping. I know, what a jerk move. Don't judge."

"Dude, you were in a coma," Chris said. "Must have been pretty easy to fake the whole sleeping thing."

Remington laughed. "I tried to take my own life and that was the last straw. I knew I had to change. I tell you all this to let you know that I am easing back into this whole God thing."

"Rem, the only thing that matters is that God knows your heart." Chris smiled. "We love you no matter what — and so does God. He always did. The whole time. I get that you messed up. I was there too, but look what God has done with my life. Don't worry about how spiritual you feel. Just keep doing what you are doing. A relationship with God is lived out in public, but it is also something that is just between you and God." Chris slung his arm over the back of the couch. "So what's this other goal you wanted to work on?"

"Oh yes, the other goal." Remington looked nervous. "There's one other person, besides my dad, who helped pull me through this last year. Without her, I wouldn't have made it. I would be dead, no question. I can never repay her for all she has done."

"Some people just do things out of the kindness of their heart and never expect to be paid back, Rem."

"I know, but this is different. She's been there for me for so long, and I have never recognized her for what she did for me. I was so messed up, by the wreck and everything else that seemed to be going wrong in my life, all I could think about was myself: how much pain I was in, how much I had lost, how *my* future had been taken from me. But she — she . . . "

Chris held up his hands to stop Remington. "Mate, you are in love with Jersey."

"What?" Remington asked. "What are you talking about?"

"Bro, come on. I know you better than this. Are you kidding me? I wish you could see the way you look at her."

"When have you seen me —"

"Rem, I was sitting there, across the aisle, at church last week and I tried to get your attention for half the service. You just kept staring right at her. Plain as day my man. I mean, she *is* gorgeous."

"It's that obvious?"

"Uh, yeah. It's that obvious. You should ask her out. Is that what all this is about?"

"I guess I took the round about way of getting there, but yeah, it is." Remington let out a deep breath. "I have these feelings for her, Chris, and I have no clue how to handle them, or what to do with them. She's the most beautiful girl I have ever seen. She is funny and kind — it doesn't get any better. She's perfect, man." Chris listened as Remington continued to share his feelings. "I was a complete asshole after my wreck. I told her to go the hell back to Florida. She moved here to help my dad take care of me and that is how I greeted her. Look at me, Chris." Remington gestured toward his legs. "On top of all that, *I am paraplegic. No* way a woman like her would ever fall for me. And even if she did, I could never have kids or, you know, keep her happy in that way. It's just not meant to be — but damn, I wish it was." Remington started to choke up. "It's just not in the cards. I don't even want to bring any of this up with her, because I already know the answer. I'm sorry I even mentioned it, Chris. Now that I say it out loud it sounds even more ridiculous." Remington unlocked his hand brake and wheeled himself toward the door.

"Whoa, hang on there, boss. You can't dump all that on me and not expect me to at least say something."

"Forget it, Chris. I'm sorry I brought it up." Remington pushed the door open.

"Nope," Chris said as he jumped in front of the door. "You aren't getting off that easy. Remember when you wanted to quit during your first workout with me? I pushed you until you puked all over my bathroom. I held your legs while you did an extra thirty tricep dips. What in the world makes you think I'm going to leave you now? Not push you a little?"

Remington let the door close. "Fine. Let's hear it."

"You have to see these feelings through, mate. They'll eat you alive if you don't. You need to ask her out. I'd suggest you try and get her number, but she lives at your house." Remington shook his head at Chris's attempt at humor. "I think this is an important step for you to work through these feelings, to continue your healing, Rem. Regardless of the outcome, I think it may be about more than just your feelings. Remember the story about Peter walking on the water from the Bible?"

"Yeah, I recall," Remington said. "Jesus calls Peter onto the water and like any normal person, he gets out there and sinks. Exactly what I feel like is going to happen if I talk to Jersey. I'll sink."

"Partially right," Chris said. "You're missing the point though. The part you mentioned about Peter being like any human?"

Remington rolled himself back into the conference room.

"Peter was. He was just like you, man. A regular old dude. He was one heck of a fisherman, but other than that, just like you and me. What set Peter apart was his faith." Chris sat on the arm of the couch next to Remington. "Jesus was right out there on the water calling to Peter, sitting in his perfectly good boat. Out of nowhere, Peter gets the brilliant idea to say, 'Lord, if it is you, tell me to come to you on the water.' Who does that? Especially in the middle of a storm. Well, Peter did. Maybe he thought Jesus wouldn't answer him or something, but Jesus tells him to come. Peter was probably like, 'Oh man, I didn't think he would actually say to do it. I got all my fishing buddies here watching me. I have to now.'" Remington smiled as he watched Chris tell his story. "Peter does it. He gets out of the boat and with his eyes on Jesus, he actually walks on the water! But then, he notices the waves raging around him and he instantly begins to sink the moment he takes his eyes off Jesus."

"I know the feeling," Remington said.

Chris patted his leg. "This is where it gets good, mate. In a moment of panic, Peter musters the faith to yell, 'Lord, save me!' Jesus plunges his hand into the water and rescues Peter. You see where I am going with this, Rem?" Remington nodded. "Peter is *you,* man. Peter is me."

By this time, Chris was pacing wildly through the room. "We all get stuck in boats that feel comfortable, but Jesus doesn't call us to comfort. He calls us out onto the water where adventure is! Right now, you are comfortable not asking Jersey on a date. Comfortable not stepping out and challenging yourself. But that's not what we're called to. Jesus beckons us to more, to be bold and courageous, to *get out on that water.*" Chris stopped pacing and knelt down in front of Remington's chair. "Peter sank and we may do the same sometimes, Rem. But, the key is to keep those eyes on Jesus once you are in the water, once you take that first, courageous step in faith. It won't be easy, but Jesus will be right there. All you have to do is call out to Him. I can't tell you how Jersey will respond, if she will say yes to a date, but I *can* promise you will never know God at work in your life unless you get out of the boat."

Remington took a moment to let Chris's words work their way through his mind. "Chris, this is all very encouraging . . . I just don't think I can do it. This chair —"

"Stop with the chair!" Chris all but shouted. "You're pointing to the waves while you're still in the boat, mate. You have to give that girl some credit. She is an amazing woman. If she is into you, I can guarantee you she is looking way past that chair and into your heart."

"Looking into my heart?" Remington chuckled at Chris's comment. "That's worse than the chair. I appreciate the vote of confidence, but I highly doubt she thinks I have a good heart. Sleeping with my girlfriend, partying with celebrities at race events . . . let's be real here. She was my PR rep. Her job was to help me cover that stuff up."

"Remington, you have to let it go. The shame and guilt will eat away at your future. God offers us grace, a fresh start. You have to embrace His new plans for you. Jersey can see the same good in you that everyone else can. You may have been struggling with some things, but God was still using you. You had a glow, man."

Remington smiled. "Like a pregnancy glow?"

Chris sprayed the sip of water he had just taken all over the couch. "Yeah, but a dude version!"

"Is that a compliment?"

Chris looked Remington in the eyes. "No, what I mean is that you are *really* hard on yourself. Jersey says you were the most generous driver on the circuit. You would always stop for a picture or sign for a young fan. You were kind, and you cared. That goes a long way. You made more of a difference than you realize. I'm telling you, God was using you whether you knew it or not. Jersey saw that. I see that. You need to ask that girl out."

"One more question?"

"Shoot."

"You think Jesus will make a way for me to roll on water instead? Because otherwise, this wheelchair will sink like a rock."

CHAPTER 25

New Life

THE STEAM WAND made a sucking sound as it swirled the heated milk into a froth. The coffee grinder whirred in the background, and an acoustic guitar drifted through the mingled conversations. Jersey had her surfing sweatshirt pulled up, her straight black hair pouring out each side of the hood. She looked at Remington, her hands enveloping a warm latte.

"Thank you for the coffee, Rem. This place is great."

Remington's heart raced. He could not believe that the nerves he once controlled so effectively in the cockpit of a race car now ravaged his body, and there was nothing he could do to reel them in.

Remington cleared his throat and began to speak. "Jersey, I —" He was overcome with emotion as he mulled the words and feelings he wanted to convey. He could feel a lump in his throat and hot tears boiling up behind his eyes.

Jersey reached across the table and squeezed his hand. "Are you okay, Rem?"

He nodded and cleared his throat again. "There's something I want to share with you, Jersey."

Jersey's smile gave Remington a much-needed boost of courage. He started again. "I want to thank you and apologize all at once. Since we met three years ago, you have been there for me. You worked so many long hours and late nights to promote my racing career. You kept me focused when I was distracted. You built my name in IndyCar racing. You even tried to teach me about giving back, and unfortunately, I just wasn't ready to listen."

Jersey tried to object, but Remington held his hand up and stopped her. "I'm sorry I didn't acknowledge you for all you did for me. And then, my wreck." Remington choked down the lump in his throat. "I don't know how I can ever repay you for everything you did for my father. When I was in a coma, you helped him through the worst of it. You gave up everything to come here and help me. You left your job, your family, your home — all of it, to take care of me. And the way I repaid you? I yelled and said I didn't want you around, and I tried to take my own life. I am so, so sorry, but I am also so grateful. Thank you, Jersey."

Remington nervously tapped the lid of his latte. "I know I am not as spiritual as you and Dad, but I have been doing a Bible study on the life of Jesus with Chris and the guys at Phoenix. I have never met anyone who exhibits the qualities of Jesus like you, Jersey. You humbly serve and give no matter what the cost. You're selfless."

Jersey was beginning to blush, as if the heat had left her coffee and gone right to her cheeks. "I know this is a lot and I'm probably rambling, but I had to get this off my chest and let you know how grateful I am."

Remington paused. "There is something else." He fought the urge to stall. If he couldn't find a way to say it now, he feared he may never.

"I have feelings for you, Jersey." The words came more suddenly than he had expected, and with a wave of embarrassment. He shook his head as he looked down at the table. "Look, I don't expect you to share the same feelings. I'm stuck in this chair for the rest of my life. I could never expect you to fall for someone like me. You already know what it's like to care for me. I would be a burden and you need someone who can take care of you. Not the other way around. I just had to tell you . . . tell you I've fallen in love with you."

Remington felt a strange sense of relief. His mind was clear and a peace had quelled his nerves. He had said everything he wanted to say. "Anyway, thanks for hearing me out. You ready to go?"

Jersey gave him a puzzled look as he began to dig for his wallet in his jacket pocket. It took him a second to notice.

"You okay?" he asked.

"Don't you care how *I* feel about everything you just said?" Jersey asked matter-of-factly.

Remington was so relieved to unload his burden, he forgot that Jersey might have something to say too. Her question pulled him back to the moment and sent his heart racing. He was not sure he was ready to hear her response. Jersey reached across the table and took his hand into hers once again. He breathed a sigh of relief.

"Remington, thank you for sharing your heart with me," she said. "I've never heard you open up like that before. It means a lot, and by the way, you are forgiven." Jersey rubbed the back of Remington's hand with her thumb. "And as for what you said about your feelings for me . . . " Remington felt sick with anticipation as Jersey's other hand joined his. "I have them for you too, Rem."

A numbness slowly poured its way through Remington's body. He could hear his heartbeat pounding in his ears. He fought to stay focused as Jersey continued to talk. "I have cared for you since the day we met in Miami, Rem," Jersey said. "I never would have let my feelings interfere with our professional relationship — or with you and Mabel, for that matter — but they were *always* there. I just hoped someday there would be a chance for us to get together. After your accident, I prayed so hard for your recovery, but selfishly, I also prayed you might have feelings for me someday. It just took a while for our paths to merge, but I'm glad they finally did."

Remington was overwhelmed. "You can love me like *this*?" Remington pointed at his lifeless lap. "I am going to be in this chair the rest of my life. I mean, if we *were* to ever get married, I can't even . . . even . . ."

"Rem, I love you no matter what. If that is God's plan for us, we will figure it out. You are incredibly handsome, and you're strong, even on four wheels. Have you looked in the mirror lately?"

"Chris has been pushing me pretty hard I guess."

"It's not your body I love, anyway. I am in love with your heart, your determination. And this new-found faith has been rekindled in your life. Not many people bounce back from the type of tragedy you went through."

"Thank you, Jersey. I am not all the way back, but thank you for taking a chance on me. If you are willing to give me a shot, I promise I will give you my all."

"After all we just discussed? Of course I'm willing to give it a shot. I've been waiting for this moment, Rem. Wondered if it would ever come, but yes . . . yes, I am willing!"

The front door of the Phoenix Gym burst open. Remington rolled in like his wheelchair was a tank and propelled himself straight to the gym's sound system and plugged in his iPhone. DJ Khaled poured through the speakers. *All I do is win, win, win no matter what!* Remington grabbed two dumbbells and repped them until the veins in his biceps bulged. A grin filled his face the entire time.

"What got into *him*?" Chris asked.

"I don't know, but I like it," Austin said. "I'm joining him." Chris and Bo grabbed dumbbells too and started half dancing, half lifting alongside Remington until they were all winded. Finally, Remington hit pause on his iPhone.

"Wow, mate, that was a good pump! I'm going to add that to my regime of workout classes," Chris said. "Dumbell dance class. Even has a nice ring to it. What got into you?" Chris paused for a moment before it dawned on him. "Wait, wait, wait — you talked to her, didn't you?" Remington's grin got even bigger. He didn't have to say a word.

"Did we miss something here?" Bo asked.

Chris looked at Remington. "You mind if I tell them?" Remington shook his head. "After you all left last week, Remington said he wanted to step it up a little with his goal. Come to find out, he has had feelings for Jersey for quite some time now but didn't know how to tell her. Anyway, we chatted for a bit, and in one week, he goes on and full-on asks her out. My mate Remington wasn't faffing around!"

Remington felt as if he had somehow broken from the cramped confines of his chair. That he had destroyed a mental and spiritual barrier. Remington sensed the green flag was waving on the rest of his life. *Go, go, go!*

The moment carried a striking resemblance to Remington's high school prom. He was meticulously dressed, not one lock of hair out of place as he sat waiting in the living room for his date. His composed look belied his nerves, his sweaty palms the only indication his heart was racing.

Remington heard Jersey's bedroom door open upstairs. He glanced at Lionel, smiling back at him from the kitchen table. He cleared his throat as Jersey reached the top of the stairs holding a pair of bright red heels that matched her lipstick. The black cocktail dress swayed as she glided down the staircase. She walked straight across the room and kissed him on the cheek. Her perfume made his head spin.

She smiled as she tucked her hair behind her ear. "You look so handsome, Rem. I can't wait for our date night."

Remington was still reeling from Jersey's entrance and the lingering scent of her perfume. It finally occurred to him he should probably say something. "You look absolutely stunning." Rem shook his head in disbelief. "Remind me, how did I get lucky enough to land a date with you?"

The sound of tires on the gravel echoed through the open window that was ushering the first warm breeze of spring into the house. "Who's here?" Jersey pulled the curtain back to look out the living room window.

"That's our ride," Remington said with a mysterious smile.

"That's a limo!"

"That's right. You guys have had to chauffeur me everywhere. It's time I finally handle the transportation. You ready?"

Remington grabbed two champagne glasses from the mini bar in the back of the limo and filled them with sparkling cranberry juice as their driver pulled onto the main road. Remington raised his glass in a toast. "Here's to the most beautiful woman I have ever seen, and to the most beautiful heart I have ever known. And thank you for saying yes to this date."

Jersey slowly leaned into Remington, her blue eyes fixed on his. Her warm lips reminded him of a thick, warm honey that slowly poured through his entire body as they kissed. "Thanks for finally asking me out," Jersey said.

"Had I known this would happen, I would have asked a whole lot sooner."

Jersey gave him a playful punch in the ribs. "Drink your cider." Ignoring her order, he lifted her chin and kissed her again.

The candlelight ricocheted off gentle ripples as they lapped at the shoreline beside the patio of the quaint Italian restaurant. Remington positioned himself behind Jersey's chair and did his best to seat her before rolling to the other side of the table. The propane heaters kicked in just the right amount of warmth as the sun lazily melted into the hills over the western bank of Flathead Lake.

Remington and Jersey filled the air with conversation, their waiter a phantom, occasionally appearing on the fringe of their own little world. They spoke about racing, travel, dreams, passions, and about Remington's new-found interest in God.

"This looks so yummy." Jersey rubbed her hands together as she examined her plate of lobster-stuffed ravioli. "Your salmon Alfredo looks good too, Rem." Remington looked distracted. "Is your food okay, Rem?"

Remington put his napkin on his lap. "Yeah, it's good. I was just . . ." He paused. "This isn't something I do too often and I am probably no good at it, especially in public, but would you mind if I blessed our food?"

"I would be honored, Rem," Jersey said.

"All right. Cool. Well, here goes then. Dear God . . ."

Remington's hand met Jersey's in the middle of the table. They locked fingers as he started to pray. His heart was pounding in his chest and his mouth felt dry. He wondered if the couple at the table next to them were watching him pray. He opened his eyes long enough to glance at Jersey. Her eyes were closed and she was smiling. He must have been doing something right.

"I thank you so much for this day. Thank you for allowing me to be here. To be alive. I thought my life was over after my wreck, but there is no place I'd rather be than right here, sitting across from this amazing woman you brought into my life. I am undeserving of her, and I am certainly undeserving of your grace, but I thank you for both. Jersey means the world to me, Lord. Please guide us as we continue to get to know each other and bless our evening together. I love you, God. Amen."

Remington opened his eyes and quickly scanned the room. No one was looking his way except an older couple who smiled and nodded when Remington made eye contact with them. Jersey's hand still squeezing his brought his attention back to their table. The tears that had collected under her blue eyes and the smile on her face said enough . . . he had done just fine.

Remington grabbed a couple of Starlight mints as he and Jersey left the busy restaurant. They politely smiled and waved as people wished them well. Remington's story had been covered in the local papers, the small town cheering him to recovery.

Their limousine was waiting out front, but Remington asked the limo driver to give them some time, and he rolled off toward the lake. "Jump on."

"What do you mean, jump on?" Jersey asked with a puzzled look. "On your wheelchair?"

"I know you are all dressed up, but have a seat on my lap. I want to show you something." Jersey tucked her dress under her legs and put her arm around Remington's neck as she gently sat on his lap.

"Hang on tight."

"What are we *doing*? You are making me nervous, Remington."

"Don't worry about it. You just went on a date with a race driver. I appreciate a good rush. I know you do too." Remington propelled the wheelchair toward the long ramp leading down to the pier.

"Hang on!" The chair continued to gain speed as Jersey let out a scream. "Here we go!" They raced down the ramp and past the docked boats toward the last few feet of the pier. Remington pulled the brakes and they slid to a stop under the last street lamp, winded and laughing.

"See, that wasn't so bad. I told you to trust me. I have to get my rush wherever I can find it these days."

"Yeah, but you don't have to drag me along." Jersey wrapped both her arms around his neck. "Thank you for bringing me down here, Rem." Jersey's lips were warm as they pressed against his in the chilly air. It was the only warmth they needed.

It was easy to tell that summer was on the way. The boat traffic steadily increased on the lake and reached its pre-summer pinnacle as anglers took to the water for the traditional Memorial Day Mac Fishing Tournament. It was a big hit with the locals and even drew some out-of-state anglers, but for the Mason family, it was, and always had been, race weekend.

"Hey, Rem. What do you think about this?" Jersey asked.

"I'd hang it a couple inches higher." Jersey stretched as she placed the checkered streamer over the mantel in the living room. Remington watched as the small of her back emerged from under her flannel shirt.

"Remington, I know you are watching."

"Watching what? That looks perfect, babe."

"Which? My butt or the streamer?"

"Both. Should Dad and I start putting the food out?"

Jersey gave him a wink as she climbed down the step ladder. "I think so. Everyone should be here in about thirty minutes."

The house was meticulously decorated. The kitchen was designed as a pit wall for "refueling" with an assortment of drinks and food, and the living room resembled the Indianapolis Motor Speedway Museum. Pictures of Remington's racing career and trophies were scattered about and checkered flag banners and streamers hung everywhere. The IndyCar season was already well underway, but this would be the first race Remington had watched since the accident. The Indianapolis 500 had always been a tradition in the Mason household, and this year would be no different.

A few months before, he would have felt bitter even talking about racing, but Remington was excited about the 500. The sense of peace he'd acquired in light of his new reality allowed him to love things he thought he might never love again and opened his mind to all sorts of new possibilities. He credited it all to what he had learned going to church with Jersey and from hanging out with Chris and the guys at Phoenix. He embraced his fresh perspective.

The church used to seem so self-serving, petty, even silly: a place where people who needed confidence went to build each other up and sing happy songs. He was coming to realize it was much more. There was life in the church and genuine people who actually cared. The relationships he had built there gave him hope and purpose.

Lionel turned the crock pot to low as everyone gathered in the living room. "Back Home Again in Indiana" filtered in among the conversations in the kitchen, and Chris Cash took on the task of recording everyone's picks for the race, putting their five-dollar bid in the pot.

"I can't believe you used to do this, Rem," Pat said. "This is incredible. Weren't you nervous beyond belief before you raced the 500?"

"Absolutely, but that's a major part of racing: learning to control your nerves. I got pretty decent at it over the years. You sort of channel your nerves and fear and use them to motivate you, rather than letting them run wild in your mind." Remington noticed Jersey smiling at him from across the room as he talked. It made him feel like he was once again the Remington she had fallen in love with . . . strong, confident, and passionate.

"The one thing I regret is not walking with the Lord at the time. Not that I was worried about getting hurt, although maybe I should have been, but I wasted an opportunity to show a lot of people God's love. I always encouraged people to pursue their passions, chase their dreams, but without the Lord, all of that is pretty empty in the end. I think you have taught me that better than anyone, Chris."

Chris set the stack of money he had collected on the mantel. "Thanks, mate. Once we start living for God, it's never too late to reach people. You have overcome some horrific challenges, Rem, and to think about the impact your story could have on people's lives — it's powerful."

Jersey sat on Remington's lap and wrapped her arms around his neck. "I second that. You inspire me every day." Remington pulled her close as he watched the cars circle the Speedway, counting down the laps. Surprisingly, he didn't miss being behind the wheel, the smell of the methanol, or the roar of the fans. Jersey on his lap and a room full of friends and family brought a joy to Remington he had never anticipated. One he would not trade.

The white flag flashed in front of the twenty-seven drivers still in the race. It had been a fierce battle, and the final lap was proving no different as the leaders approached the third turn two-wide, neither driver giving an inch. Everyone in the living room leaned forward in their chairs: all except one. Remington had been glued to the TV the entire race, but as he sat behind the couch observing his friends watch the final lap of the Indianapolis 500, he found himself relishing their excitement.

It did not seem all that long ago that he sat in the same room as a child, filled with awe for the first time as cars screamed by on the television. He would never forget. It was the moment he first felt the gravitational pull that automobile racing would have on his life.

Feelings of old welled up inside him as he watched his friends, but something was different. Remington knew he would never climb into a race car again, yet his emotions were hard to contain, his heart racing as the field of cars roared into turn four for the final time. Remington adjusted his wheelchair to get a better view of the TV. As the checkered flag flew in front of the field, Remington captured a victory of his own. The feelings he wrestled with throughout the race had given way to clarity, to understanding. His reward was not a victor's wreath or the Borg Warner Trophy, but a renewed purpose.

Remington's inherent love of car racing did not die the day it nearly snatched his life. It simply changed. The wheelchair he sat in was not what defined him. The seat he used to dream of careened down the straightaways of legendary racetracks at 230 miles an hour and drew thousands of cheers; his new seat barely moved, and drew the occasional, uncomfortable look of sympathy. But what Remington now understood was that both seats, both stories, could be used to inspire, build hope, and demonstrate God's love. It was his second chance, and he was ready.

CHAPTER 26

A Proposal

"**YOU HAVE TO CLOSE YOUR EYES!** I told you, no peeking," Jersey said.

Remington allowed Jersey to push him with his hands over his eyes. "Race drivers never trust anyone else to steer for them."

"You have to trust me. I read this in a book."

"In a book? What book?" Remington could smell popcorn and cotton candy as his wheelchair bounced over the sill in the doorway.

"Almost there. Okay, open!"

The disco ball and flashing lights caught Remington off guard, although the 80's music blaring when they came through the door should have given him an idea. "Rollerskating? You know that I am —"

"I know. You will probably never let me plan date night again." Remington was nervous as Jersey finished tying on her skates and playfully pushed him onto the roller rink, the other skaters waltzing by them at full speed. "I was reading your book about one of your heroes. The guy who was the famous midget car racer."

"Mel Kenyon."

"Yeah, Mel. I thought it was so sweet when he took his wife to the roller rink and pushed her in her wheelchair. I figured it would be a way for me to keep my balance, and to make you go fast."

"You are so sweet." Remington reached back and squeezed Jersey's hand. "Thank you for this. I'm sure Mel would be proud."

Remington could feel Jersey gaining confidence, and speed, as she weaved in and out of the other skaters. Her turns got quicker and quicker. Remington's smile grew as he heard the tires on his wheelchair begin squealing through the turns. "Faster, faster," Remington yelled as other skaters drew even with his chair ready to race, or at least he imagined. "We can win this, Jersey!"

"Easy for you to say," Jersey panted as she tried to keep pace. "Your motor weighs a hundred and ten pounds. Any faster and we might take out one of these poor kids."

By the time Jersey ran out of gas, the two of them had the entire roller rink cheering them on. Each skater the duo passed sent the other patrons into a roar of approval. They posed for pictures with the other skaters, and signed the occasional autograph. Remington even came close to winning the limbo competition with Jersey in tow. He had to settle for second as the handles on his wheelchair couldn't get as low as he could. After a celebratory lap around the rink, they pitted for ice cream.

"Thanks again for this date," Rem said. "This was a blast."

Jersey licked a drip of ice cream from the side of her cone. "Did you see the way those people responded to you out there? That was like your rookie season all over again — and I wasn't even doing PR."

"Oh trust me, you do PR for me every time we go out. It's not every day a guy like me gets a girl as hot as you pushing him in a wheelchair at the roller rink."

"Please. As if you need me to get attention."

"Sure helps. My very own super model."

Jersey flicked her hair back and gave her best runway pose. "Why, thank you. Seriously though, Rem, people really look up to you. Have you thought any more about starting some sort of ministry? When we talked after the 500, you were pretty excited about finding a way to share your story and give back."

Remington talked through the frozen chunk of cookie dough he found in his next bite of ice cream. "I *have* thought about it — a lot. I have been praying about it too. I really want to work with young drivers, to coach them: professionally, personally, and above all, spiritually. Like a personal trainer. I have even started putting together a business proposal for it."

"Remington, that is amazing."

"Like you said, it hit me that day watching the 500 and gnawed on me until I had to do something with it. I still have a lot of logistics to get figured out, but it's a start. One thing I am really struggling with is how to find a good marketing and PR person to help me get this thing up and running. You know anybody who might be interested?"

Jersey crossed her arms and put her finger over her mouth as if she were deep in thought. "I think I might know someone."

"Good. Let her know she can start right away."

The garage doors that formed the back wall of the Phoenix Gym were open, the early July breeze adding the sweet smell of lilacs to the scent of hard work. The clink of barbells and weights being re-racked blended in with the music echoing through the gym. Jersey glistened with sweat as the incline on the treadmill gained elevation, and Remington and Chris tackled a dumbbell workout in the next room.

"Come on! One more rep, one more." Chris snatched the dumbbells from Remington. "Great work, mate."

"Thanks for the motivation, brother."

"You got it," Chris said. "Hey, you remember a while back when all the guys picked a goal they wanted to work on at Bible study?"

"Of course. I'll never forget. The fruition of my goal is right there in the purple yoga pants on the treadmill. You think I would forget that?"

Chris nodded in agreement. "I guess you wouldn't. But I think you're forgetting the other half of your commitment."

"How so?"

"If my memory serves me well, you made a goal to take up wakesurfing. My MasterCraft surf boat is in the water and it is time you pay the piper." Chris let out an evil laugh that echoed through his gym.

"You think I forgot about that?" Rem said as he started curling a set of dumbbells. "You think I am just lifting these things for fun?"

"I thought it was for the girl."

"It's for both, my friend." Rem gave Chris a wink in the mirror. "You name the dock and the time, and I am there."

"This weekend. My house. Bring Jersey and your courage. I already have your board."

"It's on!"

By the time Jersey and Remington pulled up to the dock at Chris's house, the temperature was approaching ninety — not warm enough to take the sting out of a mountain lake in early July, but it was a start. Chris and a few friends were already at the dock in their board shorts testing out the water in a highly contested match of "king of the dock." Chris's wife seemed to be getting the worst end of the deal, yelling as he threw her into the chilly water. Chris waved when he saw Remington at the top of the stairs and grabbed Bo to help carry him down to the boat.

"What's up, brother? You made it." Chris high-fived Remington and gave Jersey a hug. "The water is actually getting pretty nice. Just ask my wife down there. That's her, shivering, wrapped up in that beach towel on the back of the boat."

Remington slapped Chris on the shoulder as he and Bo carefully picked him up in his chair. "You ready for this, or what?" Chris asked.

"Of course I am," Rem said as they set him down on the dock. "I think."

"Hey, before we head out, we wanted to give you something. The boys and I put our heads together and made you something special." Chris jumped in the boat while Jersey greeted the other women. He came rumbling back with a new wakesurf board, painted the same color as Remington's old race car and sporting a bold number seven with his signature beneath it. The board had been fashioned to accommodate Remington's condition. They had lengthened the board and added a strap to hold his legs and waist.

"We designed and built this board just for you, Rem." Chris said. "I think it will be exactly what you need to start your wakesurfing career off right."

Remington examined the thoughtful work his friends had put into the board's design and creation. "This is amazing. Thank you so much. You are all too good to me." Remington rolled through the group, hugging each of them, one at a time.

"Let's go see if that thing works," Chris said. The women jumped into the boat as Chris started the blowers and cranked up the music that echoed across the lake. Pat and Austin eased Remington over the gunwale as Jersey shed her swimsuit cover and laid out a towel next to Remington. Her skin was hot as she cuddled up to him, extending her long legs across the back bench. He wrapped his arms around her and put his face next to hers. Remington felt complete with Jersey in his arms.

The boat gurgled to life as Chris kicked it in gear and slipped away from the dock. A breeze rustled Jersey's hair as they headed toward the small chain of islands off the end of the point. The water was a sheet of glass, ideal for wakeboarding and surfing. Chris put the boat in neutral and let it glide to a stop.

"All right, Rem, jump in!"

"Wait. What? Me?" Remington had never been afraid to try something new. After all he had been through, wakesurfing seemed like nothing. But nerves crawled up his spine as Chris threw him a lifejacket.

"You know anyone else named Rem out here?" Chris climbed up the side of the boat and began unstrapping Remington's new board from the tower.

"I want someone else to at least warm the wake up for me."

"Warm the wake up? It's going to be cold no matter what!" Chris put the strap back over Remington's board and pointed to Bo, as he sat straddling the bow.

"Wake warming duty. Better swim, Bo." Chris threw Bo's board into the water. It slapped the surface and skimmed away from the boat. Bo jumped to his feet, ditched his shirt, and threw on a life jacket in one fluid motion as his board continued toward the island. He ran across the deck and sailor-dove off the stern before starting a frantic swim to catch up with his board.

Chris tossed him the rope. "Whenever you're ready."

"I was ready the second I hit this freezing water. Go!" Chris hammered the throttle and Bo immediately popped up and began surfing the enormous wave that billowed to life behind the boat. Remington was stunned by the size. With all the water ballast loaded to one side, the boat produced a perfectly curled wave for surfing. Before long, Bo had tossed the rope back in and used nothing but the wall of the wave to keep his momentum.

Remington gave Jersey an ominous look. "Don't expect me to do anything like that," he said. "I'll be holding onto that rope for dear life."

The sun continued to warm everyone as they took turns behind the boat in the chilly water. Chris pulled himself back onto the surf deck after an impressive display of aerial tricks and began unstrapping his bindings. "You ready or what, Rem? I'll get that ballast switched back over and we can get you behind the boat."

"I hate to follow that, but I think I am ready. The only aerials you might see are me getting tossed by that giant wave." Remington pictured himself riding up the curl of the wave on his stomach, unable to stop and launching into the air before getting swallowed by the wake. "Any chance we can do a little less ballast for my run?"

"What's that, mate?" Chris said. "I can't hear you over all that water pouring into the tanks."

"Very funny, Chris; very funny," Remington said as he cinched up his life jacket. "Should I wear two of these?"

They eased Remington onto the deck where Chris was waiting with the board. "You know I have an advantage over you guys in these conditions, right?"

"What do you mean?" Chris asked.

"I only have to feel this frigid water with half of my body." Chris and Austin strapped Remington's legs and torso to the board while Jersey snapped photos on her phone. Chris went over how the quick release strap system worked, in case Remington got stuck in the water upside down. All he had to do was pull a handle and he would pop to the surface. Pat and Austin jumped in the water and helped ease Remington off the surf deck and into the lake. They swam alongside him until he got a feel for the balance of his new board. Chris went over some final instructions and wished him good luck.

"All right, Rem," Chris said. "This is what we trained for. You let me know when you want to go. We'll start nice and easy and build you up to the wave." Remington saw Jersey standing in her hot orange bikini cheering him on from the back of the boat. Her smile dispelled any nerves he was feeling. He squeezed the handle as Chris eased the boat forward, removing the slack from the line. The smell of the boat fuel and exhaust reminded Remington of his race car. And just as the first green flag lap consumes a good driver's nerves and replaces them with an unwavering concentration, the cold sting of the water was erased by a similar focus as the boat began to gain speed. Never before had he balanced so much with only his upper body. It didn't take him long to get the hang of it.

He gave Chris a thumbs-up, and he gently bumped the throttle. Remington could see the lip of the wave beginning to form next to him. Water splashed from the crest of the curl, dousing his eyes as he leaned into the trough. The boat continued to pick up speed. Jersey yelled encouragement from the back of the boat. He inched himself closer to the wave. Chris squeezed the throttle. The wave now towered next to Remington, blocking his view of the far side of the boat. He gave the rope one more tug and suddenly he felt the wave hurl him forward. There was no longer any tension on the handle, and slack quickly built up in the rope. Not knowing how to react, he gave the handle a toss toward the stern. Bo quickly pulled it in.

"He's doing it — he's surfing! First try! Keep going, Rem!" Remington leaned his body toward the wave. The board cut through the water and immediately sucked him up the side of the wall of water. He leaned away from the wake, instantly dropping himself two feet back to the trough of the curl. His chin bounced off the board as Jersey and the other onlookers gasped. Remington wiped the water from his eyes and prepared to try again, this time with a little gentler cut. The next thing he knew he was slicing back and forth, up and down the wave. He used his hands to help guide the board and used his abdominal strength to speed up and slow down as he entered and exited the sweet spot of the wave. The spray off the back of the boat caused rainbows as he zipped through the water. Jersey looked him in the eyes. Remington felt alive.

The boat came to a gentle stop as Remington glided to the side. Jersey jumped into the water to celebrate his impressive accomplishment. She swam to where he floated, still strapped to his board. She pulled herself onto the front of the surfboard and kissed him. Remington had never felt so loved, so supported. And he had never loved anyone else the way he loved Jersey.

The sun glowed orange in the western sky, showering shades of pink and purple on the mountains as the last remaining rays of the day shone between the pine trees. Everyone had traded bikinis and board shorts for hoodies and sweats as Chris plucked out a worship song on his guitar.

Remington cuddled with Jersey as they listened to Chris play and watched the sun slowly fall behind the islands. As perfect as the moment seemed, Remington could not relax. "Jersey, I feel like I need to say something. To *do* something."

"What's that? Are you okay?" Jersey looked concerned.

"I want to get baptized."

Jersey turned to Remington. "Rem, that is so amazing." She planted a kiss on his cheek. "I am so excited for you. That is such a huge decision. We will have to tell Pastor Nielson at church this weekend."

"No, I want to do it right now." He nodded toward the water.

"Right now?"

"Yep, right now," Rem said. "I mean, look at this. There is no place more memorable and no group of people I love more. Why put it off any longer?"

"Then I'm in," Jersey said as she jumped to her feet, startling the rest of the group. "Remington wants to get baptized!"

"Remington, that's incredible, mate," Chris said as he sat down his guitar. "As soon as we get back to town, we can — "

"No, like right *now* he wants to get baptized." Remington was already taking off his shirt. Jersey pointed at him. "See? *Right now.*"

Chris jumped into action. "Then let's make this happen! Bo, you grab a towel, and Austin, help me get Rem down to the back. We are getting our bro, Remington, baptized."

Everyone crowded around Remington as he lay on the edge of the surf deck. He could feel the cool water lapping at his shoulders through the slats in the deck.

"Jersey, would you like to pray for Remington?" asked Chris, as he held Remington's head in the palm of his hand.

Jersey nodded. She choked up as she grabbed Remington's hands and began to pray. "Father God, thank you so much for Rem. I love him and am so grateful to be a part of his life. I thank you that he is here with us." Jersey wiped away a tear with the sleeve of her hoodie as she took a moment to collect her thoughts. "It was not that long ago I feared I was going to lose him, but we are about to watch him take the final step of committing his life to you. Thank you, God. Thank you for this beautiful evening in your creation, a reminder of your love and how powerful you are. We thank you for your love, your grace, and your promise of eternal life." Jersey smiled at Remington as Chris prepared to lower his head into the water. "Remington, do you believe that Jesus is God and that he died on the cross for our sins to give us eternal life and freedom?"

"I do."

"Then we baptize you in the name of the Father, the Son, and the Holy Spirit." Remington's life raced through his mind as the quiet depths of the lake reached up to envelop him. He could only hear the muffled sound of the waves lapping against the boat and feel Chris's strong hand supporting his head. An indescribable peace encompassed his heart and soul. He could feel the regrets of his past slipping away and the promises of a new future invigorating his heart. Guilt had been traded for hope, emptiness for faith. Remington had become the man he always wanted to be, the man God intended him to be.

The sun spilled its last light on the water as Remington broke the surface, greeted by the open arms of Jersey and Chris. The stars above seemed to be signaling an addition to the Kingdom of God as they crawled over the Mission Mountains and peered down on the scene below. It was the perfect end to a perfect day, and the dawn of a life renewed.

The papers were strewn across the wooden table in the back room of the coffee shop. Remington pored over them as the baristas behind the counter poured coffee.

"What do you think about this one? STM. Seat Time Motorsports."

Jersey thought for a moment before responding. "I like it. It's symbolic of your story and the transition you have made in your life from one seat to another. As a marketing person, I think the STM stylizes well too. I can picture it on our very own line of competition clothing."

"All right, STM it is then. I'll finalize the business plan with that name and we can make this thing official. I feel so blessed I get to embark on this adventure with you."

Jersey organized documents on the table as Remington signed the final page of their business plan. Word had gotten out about their plans, and they had already received inquiries about when they would be open for business. Calls came from families with young racers already cutting their teeth on quarter-midget and go-kart tracks, looking for a competitive edge to propel their sons or daughters to the next level. Before slipping the plan into its envelope, Remington read their mission statement again. *Seat Time Ministries, equipping young racers for the track, the boardroom, and a life of purpose.*

October always dropped the green flag on winter with a coating of snow capping the higher peaks in the Mission Mountains. From there, winter slowly worked its way down to the valley floor until the first dusting of snow gently sifted in amongst the homes. For many locals, it was their cue to head south, like the migrating ducks and geese from the north-country. Jersey was certainly no snowbird and would be returning in three weeks, but her bags were packed for Miami. She was excited to see her mother and kick off the official Seat Time Ministries promotional tour in South Florida.

Jersey jumped onto Remington's bed and rested her head on his chest. "I'm going to miss you so much, Rem."

Remington gently ran his fingers through her hair. "I'm going to miss you too. It will be good for you to see your mom though."

"I know it will. It has been too long. She can't wait to hear more about STM. Every time I talk to her, she asks if we thought of this or that. She actually has some great ideas."

"Write them down, and let's use them," Remington said. "Hey, I was thinking, before you leave, I could take you on a date. Would you have some time tomorrow night?"

"Of course I have time. What else would I be doing?" She patted his chest. "What time, handsome?"

"Meet in the living room at eight?"

"Eight o'clock it is." She kissed him and headed upstairs.

It was no surprise, Jersey looked stunning. Yet there Remington sat, breathless, as Jersey entered the room in her tight bluejeans, cardigan sweater, and knee-high brown leather boots.

"You look gorgeous, Jersey," Remington said. Jersey tossed her lightly-curled hair over her shoulder and batted her long eyelashes. The nip from the October air suddenly turned warm inside Remington. "I could sit here all night and just take this moment in, but are you ready to go?"

"I'm always ready. Where are we going?" Jersey opened the door and pushed Remington down the ramp to the driveway. "No limo this time?"

"Don't need one. I've got something better."

"What? Me driving?"

Remington rolled his eyes at her. "Nope. Our ride will be here in a bit, if you must know. I thought we could take a quick stroll down to the dock in the meantime."

"Really? It is freezing out here, Rem." Jersey blew into her cupped hands for warmth.

"I know. Just a quick walk."

"Whatever you say." Jersey eased Remington down the path to the dock. "Wow, it is a beautiful night. I didn't realize how clear it was. I see why you wanted to come down," Jersey said. "May I sit on your lap?" Remington patted his leg. Jersey burrowed into him as they both stared at the sky.

"If you stay out here late enough, it looks like the Big Dipper takes a scoop right out of the lake," Remington said. "And Orion stands right there on top of Haystack Mountain." Remington pointed toward the other side of the bay.

"What is the really bright one off the end of the point?" Jersey asked. "It almost looks like it's on the water." A blinding light suddenly rounded the corner of the point.

"What is that?" Jersey asked again.

"No idea, but it looks like it is heading this way. Pretty sure we can rule it out as a constellation." It took a minute for Jersey to make out the white Christmas lights draped over the boat. Remington watched her face as it approached the dock.

"Remington, it's Chris!" Remington just smiled as he watched Jersey put two and two together.

"Ahoy there, mates!" Chris chimed out. "Request permission to enter the harbor."

"Ahoy," Remington yelled. "Hard to starboard, Mr. Murdoch! It's not an iceberg, it's my dock!" Chris slid the boat to a perfect landing next to the dock and stuck out his hand. He was dressed in a captain's outfit and had even grown out a mustache.

"Madam, may I?" Jersey accepted Chris's hand and climbed aboard the wakeboarding boat. White Christmas lights hung from the tower, and a perfectly set table had been laid near the back of the boat. Burners kept the food warm, and a propane heater pumped warmth onto the deck. Pillows and blankets were strewn across the bench seat.

"Welcome aboard the Ti-tiny-tanic, lady and gentleman. Tonight, you can call me Captain Chris. I will be your tour guide, captain, waiter, and whatever else you may need. I can assure you, there are no icebergs in our path this evening." He covered his passengers with one of the blankets. "All you need to do is sit back and relax. Champagne for the lady?"

"Why, yes please." Chris poured Jersey a glass of bubbly with a white napkin draped over his arm.

"And you, Sir?"

"Of course, Captain Chris."

Chris returned to the driver's seat, kicked the boat in gear, and pulled away from the dock. He gently bumped up the throttle as he pointed the bow toward the center of the lake.

"Remington, this is beautiful," Jersey said. "You are so sweet. This is the best date I have ever been on. I could not ask for a better man."

"I could not ask for a better woman. Planning dates is easy when a guy is with someone like you."

After two glasses of Champagne and twenty minutes of cruising, Captain Chris put the boat in neutral and killed the engines. They could see their breath dissipate in front of them and hear the occasional wave caress the side of the boat.

"Sir. Madam. May I interest you in a Caesar salad?"

"Please, Captain Chris," Jersey exclaimed, playing along in a British accent.

The salad was followed by a three-course meal: chipotle apricot glazed salmon, garlic mashed potatoes, honey smoked green beans, and a delicious Oregon pinot noir.

"I am stuffed," Jersey said. "I feel like I just indulged at a three-star Michelin restaurant. Thank you so much, Remington. And what a phenomenal job, Captain Chris. Am I supposed to tip him?" Remington shook his head. "Well, I am forever indebted to you for this beautiful voyage, and of course, for keeping us afloat."

"Miss Antonelli, please do not wish the night away. We are only beginning," Chris said as he pulled a silver plater from under the dash. "Chocolate hazelnut mousse, anyone?"

"Captain Chris — how did you know?" Jersey asked. "Chocolate mousse is my favorite. You must be well-connected."

"Would the two of you like to turn up the romance a notch and have dessert under the stars?" Chris asked with a grin.

"I'm always good to turn up the romance a notch," Remington replied. "Jersey?" She quickly agreed through a mouthful of mousse.

"Very well. Let me know if you need anything else." Chris gave Remington a subtle wink as he turned off the Christmas lights.

Jersey took another bite of mousse and snuggled closer to Remington. "This is so amazing, Rem. And so thoughtful. Thank you for planning all of this. Captain Chris is a nice touch."

"You're welcome, babe." Remington kissed her on the temple. " I'm going to miss you over the next few weeks."

"I'm going to miss you too. Now all I will be able to think about while I am gone is this romantic evening and how much I want to be home with you. I will remember this night for the rest of my life."

Remington quickly dug through his pocket until he felt the jagged edge of the diamond ring. "You really think you will remember this date for the rest of your life?"

"Of course I will. The boat, the stars, the food — I will always cherish this, Rem."

Chris slipped his hand over the light switch on the dash of his boat in anticipation. "Captain Chris, I may need those lights. Just dropped mousse on my pants." Chris readied his camera and prepared to flick the switch.

"Yes sir, Mr. Mason. Right away."

Remington had gently slipped to the floor of the boat and propped himself on top of his legs. Chris cued the lights perfectly. Remington had the ring in his hand as he balanced himself on the edge of the seat. Jersey quickly reached to help him up when she noticed him on the floor. He grabbed her hand.

"Jersey Antonelli, you changed my life. Somehow, you found a way to love me. I may not know why or how, but I do know it is real. I love you with all of my heart, with every fiber of my being. Will you marry me?"

Remington could see tears welling up in Jersey's eyes. He had rarely seen her cry, but these were tears of joy. Maybe it was the warm look in her eyes, or her gentle smile, but Remington already knew her answer. It was just a slight nod at first, but the resounding yes that followed was worth the wait. He was getting married.

CHAPTER 27

Bells and Bagpipes

REMINGTON AND JERSEY sat reviewing the stack of applications. The response to their initial marketing campaign for Seat Time Ministries had gone well. They had already filled two-thirds of their available openings for the first summer of training.

"This kills me to think we may have to turn some of these kids down," Jersey said as she pulled her feet under a blanket and picked up another admissions packet. "I wish we could add a few more slots to the roster just in case. All these young drivers deserve an opportunity."

"The success of your first promo tour in Florida is what sent this thing into high gear," Remington said. "I'm glad we decided to send you back down for another round. You will have the final slots filled in no time."

"And what else?" Jersey asked.

"Oh yeah," Remington responded. "There was some store or something down there you wanted to see. An old pawn shop or something, wasn't it?" He left her dangling. She playfully slapped his hand in disapproval.

"I could just get married in these pajamas," Jersey said as she tugged at the sleeve of her pink nightshirt. "Would you be okay with that? Save some money."

"You look hot in that. Why not?" Jersey rolled her eyes. "On second thought, your mom would kill us both if you got married in PJ's. I guess you better go ahead and check out that fancy bridal store you've been talking about. Not to mention, I think your mom is pretty excited about helping you pick out a dress."

"Speaking of my trip," Jersey said as she heaved her suitcase onto the couch in the living room. "I need to finish packing. Throw me those sweats if you don't mind."

"Sweats? It is ninety degrees in Miami today."

"Yeah. And it's thirty-three degrees here. I'll wear them over my shorts on the plane."

"Good call. I will keep talking to vendors while you are gone too. Are you sure you are good with a winter wedding? If nothing else, being New Year's Eve and all, I won't forget our anniversary." Jersey leapt onto Remington's lap and put him in a harmless head lock.

"You better *not* forget our anniversary — no matter what day it is."

"Point taken."

"I'm going to miss you, Rem. I'm glad this trip is a little shorter."

"Me too, babe."

Remington eased himself into his chair from the back seat of Lionel's truck.

"I'll wait here," Lionel said. Remington thanked him as he piled Jersey's bags onto his lap and wheeled them through the automatic door into the airport.

"There are advantages to not being able to feel your legs. You pack pretty heavy."

Jersey smiled and gave Remington a longing look. "I'm going to miss you, Rem."

"I will miss you too, but I'll see you in two weeks. It will fly by, and you will come home with a wedding dress. One step closer to becoming my bride."

Remington waited in the lobby until Jersey looked back at him from the other side of the security checkpoint. She blew him a kiss and entered the terminal. Remington gave her a final wave as she disappeared from sight.

Lionel was sound asleep by the time Remington got back to the truck. He knocked on the window.

"Darn it, I'm sorry, Rem. Must have dosed off," Lionel said as he opened his door and carefully shuffled over the hard-packed snow to the other side of the truck. "Did you get Jersey all sent off?"

"I did, Pop. Thanks for driving us down here." Lionel groaned as he pushed Remington into the cab.

"No trouble at all. I would do anything for you two. You know that."

"I know, Dad. Want to grab some breakfast before we head back?"

"Good idea. Our old fly fishing spot?"

"I can taste those buttered biscuits and honey already."

Remington and Lionel had just unfolded the napkin covering a warm mound of fresh biscuits when a young waitress approached their table. "I'm sorry to interrupt you two, and pardon me if this is personal, but I have to say, you look amazing, Remington. You have come a long way since you and your father were in here the last time. It's great to see you."

"Thanks. I really appreciate that. I wish I could say things got better right away, but it took some time. I'm getting there." She smiled and filled their coffees.

"So, Rem. I wanted to run something by you," Lionel said as he stirred cream into his coffee. "I was driving by the church last week on my way to take some hay out to Blailock's farm for a nativity scene they are building in their yard. There were a bunch of cones set up in the church parking lot and an old beat-up van parked sideways in a few of the spaces. I was curious, so I pulled over to watch. After a few minutes I saw a young woman and a boy come out from behind the van with an old quarter midget. The beat-up car had to be thirty years old. There were holes in the fiberglass, and the tires had threads showing through. I could tell the car was this kid's pride and joy."

Crumbs tumbled to the table as Lionel took a bite of his biscuit. He continued his story. "The woman with him tightened a few bolts while the kid put on a hand-me-down race suit in the back of the van. The only new thing they had was a Remington Mason racing sticker on the kid's helmet. I don't think they had much money, and everything they *did* have was probably bought second hand, but the pride on that kid's face — reminded me of when you got your first quarter midget."

"I could tell the woman didn't know a whole lot about wrenching on cars. I could also tell she didn't want to let this boy down," Lionel said as he wiped his mustache and took another sip of his coffee. "After some more tinkering, the kid hops in his car and she gives him a running push start. The car spit and sputtered, put out a plume of dark smoke, but somehow started on the first try. It was close to freezing that day and I figured there was probably ice in the parking lot. Sure enough, he put the throttle down on that little car, turned left and skidded through pert' near the whole lot. Too bad too — he hopped a curb and bent the right front tie-rod." Lionel snapped a toothpick in half to illustrate his point. "The woman, probably his mother, leaned into the cockpit of the car to break the news that their day was over. The boy slouched back to the van, grabbed a dolly, and helped his mother load up the car."

Lionel raked the remains of his breakfast into a tidy pile on the edge of his plate. "As they were loading up their tools, I pulled in to chat with them. They probably thought I was there to kick them out. Anyway, I told them who I was. When I mentioned you were my son, that boy's face lit up. You were his favorite driver. The woman was his mother, and she told me he was bawling unconsolably the day you got in your wreck."

Remington listened intently as Lionel shoveled his last bite and kept talking. "This poor kid has wanted to race since he knew what racing was. Mom is single and works in the local market. They saved every penny they could to buy that car. Look, Rem, I know you have a lot going on right now, but I told them I would talk to you and see if you might be willing to meet up with this kid and give him a few pointers. Is that something you would do for your old man?"

"This is exactly why Seat Time was created, Dad," Remington said. He could hardly contain his excitement. "What's the kid's name?"

"Ricky. Ricky Coleman. His mom's name is Kate. It would mean the world to them, Rem. I have her number right here," Lionel said as he slid a folded piece of paper across the table. "Just in case you might need it."

Remington rolled into the pizza joint and scanned the room for Ricky and Kate Coleman. He didn't see anyone matching the description his father had given him. He asked for a table for three. Remington sipped a cup of hot tea as he watched the rain bounce off of the window. It would be snow by midnight.

As Remington squeezed another packet of honey into his tea, two dim figures caught his eye walking toward the pizzeria. At first, it looked as if they were going to pass by, but they darted into the restaurant and checked with the hostess. They were soaked. Remington watched as the hostess pointed them in his direction.

"Remington Mason?" the woman asked as she approached the table. Her blonde hair was matted and soaked as she removed her hood. "I am Kate Coleman. This is my son, Ricky." Ricky shivered as he stretched out his cold hand to Remington. Remington could hear Ricky's wet feet squishing in his tennis shoes as he scooted out from behind his mother.

"Ricky, it's a pleasure to meet you. Have a seat. Do you like hot chocolate?" Ricky nodded as he took off a dirty Seahawks jacket. A tear in the coat obscured the team logo, insulation popping out where the Hawk's head used to be. "We need to get you warmed up. Would you like coffee, Kate?" Remington signaled the waiter.

"That would be fine, thank you. I'm sorry we kept you waiting. We went to start up our van and it was dead. We weren't going to miss this for anything, so we made the walk down." Kate handed Ricky a Kleenex. He wiped the snot from his nose.

"How far did you have to walk?" Remington asked.

"Only a few miles. It wasn't bad."

"*Only* a few miles? In this weather? We'll give you a ride home later. This could very well be snow in the next couple of hours."

"Thanks." Kate stroked her son's wet, curly hair. "I think Ricky is in a little bit of shell shock that he gets to meet you. He was your biggest fan when you were in IndyCar." Ricky smiled as he stared across the table at Remington. Hot chocolate stained the corners of his mouth.

"I want to hear all about you, Ricky, but the important stuff first — what kind of pizza do you like?" Remington ordered an assortment of pizzas and salads so there would be plenty of leftovers to send home with Kate and Ricky.

"Now that we have that out of the way, tell me more about yourself, Ricky."

Ricky looked up at Kate. She nodded as if to give him permission to speak. "Well, I wanted to start racing when I was a little younger," Ricky said. "I had my car picked out and everything. But when my dad left, things got really tough. We didn't have much money and we were just getting by. Plus, Mom was always sad."

Kate's brown eyes collected pools of backed-up tears. Remington could see the hurt in them. "Yeah, it was really hard, wasn't it buddy," she said. She pulled Ricky close in the little booth. "But we are doing better. We are going to get you in a race car one way or another."

Remington watched as Kate embraced her son, doing her best to impart hope. Remington had once been filled with the same youthful zeal for racing as Ricky, was depleted, and recharged once again. He had lost, he had loved, and he had overcome. Now was his chance to share truth with them, what had carried him through — a peace and hope stemming from God.

When he was on the circuit, Remington did whatever he could to encourage his fans, to make their day at the track, but he never connected at the authentic level he was with Ricky and Kate. From bleacher seat to race seat, and then permanently onto the slick, black, leather seat of a wheelchair was not how Remington imagined a racing career in his youthful mind. Not even close. But as he watched a mother embrace her child in a small pizzeria, he realized he wouldn't trade a second of his journey. Everything he had gone through was preparing him for this moment.

Each slice of pizza was paired with a word of encouragement for the young mother and her son. The tears had disappeared along with the second round of hot chocolate, and the conversation had settled on the future. Remington could tell they were inspired by his story of redemption — his tangled, messy journey.

"I never knew it at the time, but God had a plan for my life all along," Remington said. "When I finally had the courage to submit to His will — and it took almost dying twice — the purpose of my life became a lot clearer. I believe that is why we are all here together now. Ricky, if I could give you one piece of advice, it would be to follow God with all your heart, and trust Him with your plans. He will do incredible things in your life." Ricky nodded, latching on to every word his hero spoke.

Remington signed the check and passed the boxes of leftovers to Kate.

"Remington, thank you so much for taking the time to meet with us," she said. "I can't tell you how much this means to both Ricky and me."

Lionel pulled into the parking lot in his truck. "You are welcome, Kate. We will be in touch. I promise. For now, let's get you and Ricky home safe and dry."

"You all right, Rem?"

Remington rummaged through the medicine cabinet in the kitchen.

"I'm good. I've had a headache all day today, but it's getting better. Thought I would try to kick it back with a couple of aspirin. Hey, thanks again for giving Ricky and Kate a ride home tonight. I couldn't believe they walked to the pizzeria." Remington pointed toward the window. "I told them it would be snowing by the time they got home, and I was right. I really appreciate you taking the time to set this up." Remington hugged Lionel. "Goodnight, Pop. I promised Jersey I would give her a call and let her know how it went. It's two hours later in Miami."

"I love you, son. Tell Jersey hello for me."

Jersey stretched her arm across the comforter until she located the vibrating cell phone. Her voice was groggy.

"Hello?"

"Hey angel, it's me. Did I wake you?"

"I was just taking a quick nap." She cleared her throat.

"You *did* tell me to call no matter how late it was."

"I would do anything at any time to hear your voice. How did it go?"

"In all honesty, other than asking you to marry me, I think it may have been the most rewarding thing I have ever done. They don't know it, but I think they helped me more than I did them. I just can't believe how inspiring it felt to let God use me in the life of someone else. I am so excited about Seat Time, and doing more of this work. Thank you for believing in me."

"I'm just grateful we get to do this together," Jersey said.

"Tomorrow is the big day, right? You are going to land a wedding dress?"

"I am so excited. I think mom is still in the other room poring over pictures of dresses. She may be more excited than I am. She can already hear the wedding bells." Jersey gave a small yelp of joy.

"Whatever dress you pick, you will be stunning. I know it is late there, so I will let you go. I'm pretty tuckered myself."

"I love you, Rem."

"I love you too, babe."

Remington turned off his bedside lamp and worked his way under his comforter. He laid his head on his cold pillowcase and smiled in the dark room. He whispered a short prayer thanking God for Ricky and Kate, and thanked God for his new life, his new seat, and his new mission. Amen.

The manager greeted Jersey and her entourage of friends at the door with mimosas.

"Welcome to Plumeria by the Sea Bridal. The store is exclusively yours for the next three hours. Our staff is here to take care of you and of course, find you the perfect wedding dress. Refills of mimosas as well as hors d'oeuvres can be found over by the register. Please, enjoy our boutique."

The assortment of handcrafted dresses were exquisitely displayed throughout the showroom. It felt more like they were in a museum of fine art than a bridal store. The women were having the time of their lives.

"Jersey, what about this dress?" One of her friends approached with the dress draped over her arm.

"Wow, it *is* beautiful. I may keep looking, though."

"Oh, come on! You at least have to try it on. For me. Please? There's a huge staff here. You may as well give them something to do besides refill our mimosas."

"Okay, you win," Jersey said. "I guess it is hard to tell if you like it until you see it on."

By the time Jersey had tried on the first dress, she emerged from behind the curtain to find each of her bridesmaids, and her mother, with a pick of their own. The joy it was bringing to them all was contagious. Even the staff of the boutique was joining in the fun.

Jersey had tried on a half-dozen dresses in search of the perfect one. She had eliminated her friends' choices systematically until she finally grabbed her mother's choice off the hanger. The boutique manager helped Jersey slip into the dress and made a few alterations in the dressing room.

The anxious group waited on the other side of the curtain. The store manager emerged with a grin and moved to the opposite side of the curtain. Her stilettos clicked as she scooted across the tile floor. She gave a subtle golf clap before she grabbed the curtain and pulled it back.

A collective gasp repeated through the boutique as Jersey stepped from the dressing room. Tears wet her mother's eyes. Apparently they were contagious. The store manager dabbed her eyes with a tissue as well.

After simply admiring her daughter for a moment, Jersey's mother rose from the white couch and embraced her. "Sweetheart, this is the one. You look stunning. I saw it the second we walked in the store and I knew this was the dress. Remington will love it."

"Well, now that you are all crying, I am going to get out of this thing so we can get lunch." Jersey was about to go back into the dressing room when one of her bridesmaids caught her attention.

"Jersey, your cell is ringing. Let me grab it for you." Her friend quickly dug through Jersey's purse until she found it. She handed the phone to Jersey.

"Hello?" An eerie silence followed. "Hello, anyone there?" Jersey was about to hang up when she heard Lionel's voice pierce the silence.

"Lionel, is that you? Are you all right?"

"It's me, Jersey." Lionel exhaled heavily. "I don't know how to explain this to you, so I am going to do it the only way I know how and just say it. I am here at the hospital. We lost Remington last night."

"What do you mean, we lost him?" Jersey turned and quickly slipped into the dressing room. She plugged her other ear in an attempt to hear Lionel more clearly, hoping she had somehow misunderstood.

"Remington passed away, Jersey. He had a hemorrhage in his brain. We tried so hard . . ." Lionel started sobbing. Jersey could hear medical staff in the background trying to console him. "We lost him, Jersey. We lost him."

Jersey's friends heard a thump behind the dressing room curtain and rushed in. Jersey was huddled in a corner, the beautiful dress scattered around her folded frame. She sat quietly, staring at the mirror as tears slowly pushed mascara down her cheeks onto the white dress. Her mother dropped to the floor and embraced her, stroking Jersey's hair.

"He's dead, Mom. Remington is dead."

Sunlight perforated the thick morning fog as bagpipes sullenly echoed through the quiet hills surrounding the cemetery. A few hearty orange and yellow leaves still clung to their branches, rustling in the breeze. Jersey and Lionel sat in the front row surrounded by friends and family. Chet Buckner sat speechless behind them with others from the racing community and the Flux team.

As Pastor Nielson concluded his eulogy, sun flooded the small cemetery. "Sometimes it seems that fog engulfs all that we do. We can't see beyond the pain, the hurt, or the brokenness. That was certainly the case in Remington's life after his wreck. Yet, as I stand here in front of you today and watch the sun burn away this fog, I am reminded of how God can do the same in our lives. The hurt, pain, and guilt that sometimes shroud our existence can be pushed back by the grace and love of Jesus Christ. We may not always see it through the struggles in front of us, but God's light is constantly chipping away at the walls that keep us from him, that keep us from true joy. And when we can open our hearts to the engulfing warmth of His love, we see life in an entirely different perspective."

Jersey dried her eyes as Pastor Nielson continued. "Remington was a glowing example of this. He came to the doorstep of death twice, before giving his life to the Lord. He went on to start a ministry with his fiancé and even though they have only begun, I can already see the impact Remington has made in the lives of so many, including my own. I know Jersey would say the same. As I thought about Remington and how I could best celebrate his incredible life today, one Scripture came to mind."

Pastor Nielson thumbed through his Bible until he found his place. "In First Corinthians Chapter 9, Verses 24 through 27, it says, 'Do you not know that in a race all the runners run, but only one gets the prize? Run in such a way as to get the prize. Everyone who competes in the games goes into strict training. They do it to get a crown that will not last, but we do it to get a crown that will last forever. Therefore I do not run like someone running aimlessly; I do not fight like a boxer beating the air. No, I strike a blow to my body and make it my slave so that after I have preached to others, I myself will not be disqualified for the prize.'"

Pastor Nielson gently closed his Bible. "I can stand before you today and tell you that Remington Mason lived this Scripture. From every ounce of himself that he poured out on the race track, to his love for God, and passion for helping others, Remington ran to get the prize. His body was beat. He was bruised and broken, yet he made the choice to follow God, rise above his circumstances, and inspire others. He may have been taken from this world, but the impact Remington has left on us all will endure for eternity."

Smiles and tears hopefully and longingly marked the faces of those at the ceremony. "Remington's coffin is covered in a checkered flag today and his race helmet is here as well. It could not be more fitting. I know we are grieving his loss, and that cannot be diminished, but may we all find hope and peace knowing that Remington has won. Victory is his. The checkered flag has waved for him in this life. He ran his difficult race well, and he was welcomed into eternity with the words, 'Well done, my good and faithful servant.' May we all aspire to live life like Remington Mason."

CHAPTER 28

The Mallard

SNOW SWIRLED INTO THE LIVING ROOM as Lionel paused long enough to glance toward Remington's room before he closed the front door. Pepper was already in the truck. Lionel rubbed his hands together to warm them, turned his headlights on, then put the truck in gear and began to drive. Snow drifted over the dark road before them.

The clock on the dash read 4:45 when he pulled up to the gate and shut off the truck. Pepper whined with excitement. Lionel consoled his gray Lab with a scratch behind the ear. "I know. I'm anxious too, bud." The frigid air pierced the truck cab as Lionel put on his heavy jacket. He took a deep breath, opened the door, and slowly lowered himself onto the fresh layer of snow. He used the side of the pickup as a handrail and limped his way to the back of the truck, where he sat on the tailgate and slipped into his chest waders. He filled his pockets with hand warmers and shot shells before grabbing a small bag of decoys and his shotgun from the bed. He made his way to the passenger side of the truck and lifted Pepper from the front seat. Lionel's hips were only slightly better than Pepper's, and he groaned as he lowered his beloved hunting partner to the ground. Pepper thanked him with a lick.

Lionel could hear the ducks cackling in the slough as he and Pepper worked their way around the cattle guard. Pepper limped along a few steps ahead of Lionel, occasionally pausing to check on his master. They stopped when they came to the edge of the lake. Lionel shined his head lamp onto the open-water side of the slough. The lake was rough, and it was nearly impossible to see anything in the snow flurries that were building to a tempest. They pushed on. Lionel gathered his breath before slowly easing his way into the thigh-deep water. Pepper whined at him from the bank, knowing the dangers lurking before them as they ventured to the end of the point.

"It's okay, boy."

Lionel scooted his feet along the bottom to locate the roots that snarled up at him, while Pepper eased his way through the thick cover on the bank. Lionel stopped again to catch his breath, then forged ahead. In an instant, one of the entangling roots latched to the boot of his waders as he tried to take his next step. It wrenched him to his knees in the frigid lake. Lionel instinctively plunged his gun into the depths to stop his fall and keep the water from gushing over the top of his waders. The stock of his 12 gauge found bottom, and Lionel freed himself with nothing worse than a wet arm and gun. Pepper's anxious whimpers sounded from the bushes.

"We're almost there, Pepper."

Lionel navigated the last fifty yards to the end of the peninsula. Too tired to plunge into the freezing water again, he took aim and hurled the decoys off the end of the point, trying to replicate the J-pattern he had used so many times before. He shuffled back through the cattails and placed his chair where he could best see the ducks as they set their wings and swooped in. He loaded his gun, pulled his scarf tight around his neck, and reached for the thermos of coffee clipped to his waders. It was gone.

Lionel did his best to clear his mind. The wind had died off and he could hear the snow landing on the hood of his hunting jacket and on the cattails around him. In the stillness, he could almost feel Remington sitting next to him, smiling as he loaded shells into his gun and turning to offer him coffee. Lionel grinned at the thought as he glanced at his watch. Sunrise was in thirty minutes. It was just him and Pepper on the point, but for now, just for now, Lionel felt his son's presence on the edge of the quiet slough they had hunted together for years. He was determined to absorb every moment. While Remington's memory would live forever on this point, both Lionel and Pepper knew this was their last visit, a final hunt.

The snow continued as the first promises of daylight arrived. The reeds swayed softly where Remington used to sit beside him. Lionel had always given his son that side so he could take the first shots as the ducks whistled by the point. Today, the first shot would be his alone, in honor of his son.

The morning passed, the only movement in the sky the swirling flakes of snow. Lionel tried to call in a few pairs flying high over the point, but they did not even consider the invitation. Snow had settled on the backs of his decoys, making them look unnatural, probably the reason no ducks flew in. He left them as they were. What strength he had left he would need to make it back to the truck.

"Don't worry, Pepper," Lionel said. "You'll get your chance."

Lionel had his eyes fixed on the toe of the bay when he heard the distinct whistling of wings somewhere in the swirling snow above him. His hands shook as he readied his gun and clicked off the safety. He searched the sky for any birds willing to land among the tufts of snow that used to be his decoys. Lionel panned in every direction, trying to catch a glimpse of the duck. It announced itself with a subtle garble as it emerged from the snow, hugging the surface of the water. His heart jumped. "Patience, patience, patience," he said under his breath. Pepper instinctively let out a youthful whimper from behind his gray muzzle. "Not yet."

All at once, the mallard turned directly at Lionel, arched its back, and cupped its wings. Just as its orange feet skimmed the surface of the water, Lionel jumped up and shouldered his gun. He had no recollection of the gun's report or feeling the kick of the 12 gauge against his shoulder, but he clearly heard the splash of the duck as it barreled into the water in front of him.

That was all it took. Lionel collapsed to the ground, tears melting the fresh snow on his face. Pepper emerged from the water, quietly crawled up to Lionel, and nuzzled the drake mallard into his arms. Its iridescent greens and purples glistened against the snow. Lionel examined the duck and pulled Pepper close.

"Remington would be proud, don't you think?"

The delivery truck beeped as it backed up the driveway toward the small manufactured home, making the first tracks in the fresh snow. The driver double-checked his clipboard before knocking on the door. A woman answered.

"Hello. I have a delivery for Ms. Kate and Ricky Coleman."

"I'm sorry sir, but I think you have the wrong house."

"Are you Kate Coleman?"

"Yes, but we didn't order anything."

"Well, this is the right address and it says your name right here." The courier scanned the shipping label. "Looks like it's from a Mr. Remington Mason." Tears welled up in Kate's eyes.

"Are you okay, Ms?" Kate nodded and signed for the delivery.

Kate went in to find Ricky reading a racing magazine. It was one of only a couple Christmas presents she had been able to afford, most of them necessities: new gloves, a stocking cap, and boots that were a little too big so he could grow into them. "Hey Ricky."

"Yeah, Mom?"

"I think you got one more Christmas present. You want to open it?"

"Are you serious? Who's it from?"

"You'll have to go find out. It's in the driveway."

The delivery truck was already gone by the time Ricky and Kate put on their winter clothes. Ricky sprinted out to examine the delivery. The crate was twice as tall as he was, a mass of plywood and two-by-fours with no indication of its contents, only a sticker that read "this side up." Kate grabbed a crowbar from the garage and began to peel away the corners of the crate. Ricky pitched in where he could, barely able to contain his excitement. Before long, they were able to slide the top off the wooden box.

"Why don't you climb in and see what it is, Ricky?" She gave him a boost to the top of the crate. He paused and stared as he swung his legs over the top. A smile spread across Ricky's face unlike any Kate had seen since before his father left.

"What is it, Ricky?" He disappeared without a word.

The metal was cold and smooth in his hands as he traced the shiny black roll cage and the straight, perfectly adjusted tie rods. He looked at his fingers: no grease or track grime. It was tight in the crate, but he slowly worked his way toward the rear of the car, examining every detail along the way. He removed the tail cone, unveiling a shiny new motor. Ricky sat on the right, rear tire and took note of the remaining contents of the crate: spare tie rods, gear sets, shock absorber combinations, and specialized tools. Finally, he worked his way to the cockpit of the small race car.

He stared at the seat. Neatly folded in the cockpit of the quarter midget was a brand new driver's suit, a helmet, and gloves. He slipped one of the gloves on and raised his fist in a triumphant salute to the thousands of snowflakes he imagined were roaring fans coming down to congratulate him in victory lane. He untied the helmet bag, slipped out a custom-painted helmet, and flipped open the visor.

He was about to pull the helmet over his head when an envelope fell from inside. It was simply addressed, "Ricky." He set the letter on the nose cone of the car, plunged his head into the new helmet and lowered himself into the driver's seat. He squeezed the cold, plastic steering wheel in his hands. Ricky imagined himself racing at full speed as the snow continued to pour down on the stationary car. He could hear the tires squealing, and smelled the Nomex in his new helmet. His heart fluttered at the thought of his competitors and soared at the thought of beating them. For a moment, Ricky was already a racing champion. He had never felt so alive.

Kate knocked on the door of the ranch house. Lionel Mason answered. "Well hello, Kate. Please, come in. It's freezing out there. Can I make you some coffee?"

"No, but thank you. I can't stay long. I just wanted to say I am so sorry for the loss of your son. Remington was an amazing person, an inspiration to my son."

"Thank you, Kate. He was an inspiration to me too."

"I brought you something I thought you should have. We received a package the other day from Remington and this was in it. I made a copy for Ricky, but we both wanted you to have this one." Kate handed Lionel the hand-written letter and hugged him goodbye.

Lionel sat in his recliner at the edge of the fireplace, Pepper curled at his feet. He pulled his Hudson Bay blanket a little tighter around his neck, took a sip of tea, and slowly opened the letter Kate had given him. It was in Remington's handwriting.

Dear Ricky,

It was such an honor to meet you earlier this fall. I loved getting to hear about your life and about your passion for car racing. Your knowledge of motorsports was incredible! It is refreshing to see someone who has such a zest for life. I am sorry about your father leaving you. I can't imagine how hard that must be, but I am proud of you for holding your head high and for not giving up on your dreams. You may not see it in your own life yet, but the perseverance you are showing at this crossroad will serve you well for years to come. If you found this letter, you must have dug through the delivery by now. This car is all yours. When I saw my first quarter midget, it lit a fire in my heart that burns on to this day. It shaped the entire course of my life, both the good and the bad.

This gift comes with great responsibility as well. I pray you win more races than you lose. But the seat of that car will take you far beyond the track. You will have many seats in life, and you can use each of them to make an impact in people's lives. Whatever seat you find yourself in, it will be up to you to choose how to use it. My prayer for you, Ricky, is that you will use each seat you have to show others the love of Christ. Some seats will feel good, some will hurt beyond what you think you can bear. What is important, is that you use them all for good. I wanted to provide you with your first seat. May it bring you victory on and off the track, and may the glory go to God.

Go get 'em, Ricky!
Remington Mason

Epilogue

"**Mr. Mason,** would you like me to put another pillow under your feet?"

"I think I am fine, Val." Lionel slipped off his glasses and set his book on the side table.

"Okay then, Mr. Mason, my shift is about over. I'm going to wrap up some charting and I will see you tomorrow. Mrs. Everleigh will be back soon. She'll take over until I return."

Lionel groaned as he repositioned in his chair and reached for the TV remote. "Val?"

"Yes, Mr. Mason?"

"I'm sorry. One more thing. Would you hand the remote to me? I want to make sure I have the race recorded."

The door opened, startling Lionel. He must have fallen asleep. His blood pressure medication always made him drowsy.

"Lionel?"

"Come in, Blake. I'm in the family room."

Blake set a vegetable platter and some soft drinks on the kitchen table before kneeling down beside Lionel. "How are you feeling, Lionel? You look great."

"Oh, you know, I'm all right. Things are pretty quiet around here these days, but I don't mind too much. I've got my books and my decoy restoration. I can do most of it from right here in my chair, and Val is great about helping out. I think I drive her a little crazy, but she is the nicest woman, and a great nurse. How was the business trip?"

Blake took a seat on the couch across from Lionel. "It was great. We had some successful promotional events, landed a couple corporate partnerships, and filled out the remaining spots on our roster for the season."

"That is just great, Blake. You're doing incredible work, worthwhile work." Lionel glanced at the picture of Remington next to his chair. "Are you excited for the 500 today?"

"Lionel, *it's the 500!* You know I'm excited. Speaking of the 500, I better help my wife carry in the rest of your groceries. Mrs. Everleigh is probably wondering where I went."

Lionel watched as Blake walked out the front door and grabbed a bag of groceries from the back of the BMW. His rugged, handsome appearance drew attention, and Lionel had come to learn that his calm, steadfast presence was the cornerstone to his business success. His empathy for people was what endeared him to his clients. But Lionel's favorite thing about Blake was his love for God. It was what drove him.

Jersey ran across the living room and wrapped Lionel in a hug as Blake looked on from the kitchen. "I missed you so much, Lionel," Jersey said as she straightened the collar on his flannel shirt and ran a finger through his white hair. "Is Val taking good care of you?"

"I missed you too, Jersey, and of course Val is taking good care of me. I really appreciate you and Blake finding her to help me. I just can't inconvenience you anymore than I already do, and she lightens your burden. You two need your space."

Jersey glanced lovingly at her husband. "You don't inconvenience us one bit, Lionel. I know that running Seat Time Ministries takes us on the road a lot, but Blake and I wouldn't have it any other way. We want to be close to you whenever we are able. Besides, Montana is home for us now. We love it here."

"Jersey is right, Lionel," Blake said. "We do love it here. It makes us feel good knowing we are close if you need anything. Plus, we get to celebrate days like this together." Blake finished arranging cheese and meat slices around the edge of a cutting board and placed it on the hearth. "I don't know about you two, but I'm pumped to watch this race. You have the recording pulled up, babe?"

Blake brought Lionel a plate of snacks and made sure he was comfortable in his recliner before cuddling up next to Jersey on the couch. The TV flickered to life, ushering the familiar voices of the Indianapolis 500 broadcast into the living room.

Lionel had watched the Indianapolis 500 with a childlike charm for seventy-five years, but this race day, his greatest happiness came from watching the joy Jersey had in her life once again. Blake had helped guide her through a dark time after Remington's passing. He had been good for both of them, but there was a lingering corner of Lionel's heart that yearned, that broke at the absence of his son. The ache, he knew, would be ever-present and could only be remedied when they met again in Heaven. But in the meantime, Jersey's smile, her new life, soothed the pain of his loss.

On Lionel's loneliest days, he would turn to his Bible for comfort. His bookmark was a letter, worn and creased, marking a verse in Joshua. It had weathered its share of tears, and some of the ink had run and dried along with them, but the words of his son shone from the tattered pages, undaunted and unmuted by the passing of time. They spoke as loudly as they had the day Kate Coleman delivered them to his front door. For this, Lionel thanked God.

He stood in the cockpit of his car breathless, drenched in five-hundred miles worth of sweat. The victor's wreath hung around his neck, the smell of its fresh flowers mingling with the expended ethanol still swirling in the air over the Speedway. Reporters shoved their way toward him, sticking their recorders and microphones as close as they could. He couldn't hear one of them or make out any of their faces. They were just a peripheral blur as he watched his mother crawl onto the side-pod of his race car. He embraced her as she repeatedly kissed his sweaty cheek. For a moment, it felt like just the two of them, eight years earlier, standing inside a wooden crate, his gloved fist raised in triumph to the snowflakes settling around them.

Her voice brought him back to the moment. "We did it Ricky. We did it!" Kate held her son, her forehead pressed against his as cameras captured the moment for the Memorial Day edition of the *Indy Star*. "We did it."

Pit reporter, Dr. Jerry Punch, wrestled his way to where Kate Coleman was unwilling to relinquish her son's embrace. Dr. Punch got Ricky's attention.

"Ricky, what a moment for you." Ricky straightened his Firestone hat and turned to face the cameras. "You are an Indianapolis 500 champion. Can you put into words what this means?"

Ricky shook his head, searching for something, anything to describe what he was feeling. "I never fathomed this moment was even possible, yet here we are. I'm not sure I could ever put into words what this means or what I am feeling right now." Ricky pulled his mother close. "Hey Mom, we're Indy 500 champs."

"I think that pretty much says it all, Ricky — Indy 500 champs." Dr. Punch gestured toward the Borg Warner trophy. "Your mother sacrificed a lot to get to where you are today, to get this ride with such a great IndyCar team." Punch acknowledged Ricky's crew. "You are an Indianapolis 500 champion at twenty-one. You could go on to win a few more of these things in you career. What do you attribute your rise, and almost instant success, in this sport to?"

"First of all, I hope I do win more, but I am going to bask in this one for the time being." Ricky slapped high-fives with his crew, anxiously waiting to celebrate with him. Jerry pushed his microphone closer. "This win is obviously for my mother, but also for everybody over there in the grandstands." Ricky pointed across the track. Not a seat was vacant. "Specifically, what those seats can mean. What *this* seat can mean." Ricky stared down at the cockpit of his IndyCar. "Sometimes, we may not feel that we are in the ideal seat, or that we are dealt an undeserving seat. But when we recognize that our seat, our story, can be used for good, we can live at our full potential. Our challenges become opportunities to grow and inspire others. Regardless of who you are, whether you are sitting in a grandstand, one of these cars, or in a seat you never would have chosen yourself, you matter. You are valuable in God's eyes."

Kate watched from behind the network TV cameras streaming her son's words to millions of viewers around the world. Ricky continued. "While I did not know him long, Remington Mason taught me that something as simple as a seat matters, even the seat of a wheelchair." Ricky put his hand on the Borg Warner trophy. "Without him, I would not be here in victory lane at the Indianapolis Motor Speedway." A wave of cheers erupted from the crowd at the mention of Remington's name. "Rem bought me my first real race car, but most importantly, he showed me how to live for God. I will never forget the lessons he modeled for me with the way he lived his life. So while I stand victorious today, I want to use this seat, this moment, to give all the glory to God."

Lionel's hand shook as he unfolded the letter and ran his weathered fingers over his son's words. He traced the frayed page as if reading it for the first time. Lionel could hear Remington's wisdom and passion resonating from Ricky's interview. It felt like Remington was reading the letter to him, letting him know that he had lived on, far past the confines of the earthly seats he had chosen, and those he was dealt. He was free. His race was run, and he was victorious. Blake and Jersey watched in silence as Lionel struggled to speak. "We did it Rem. We did it. We won."

THE END

Acknowledgments

Joshua 1:7 *"Only be thou strong and very courageous . . . "*

THIS SCRIPTURE HAS PROVIDED ME ENCOURAGEMENT for years. It was written in my college notebooks, highlighted in my Bible, and taped on a yellow sticky-note between the tachometer and fuel shut-off switch on the dash of my race car. I would give my race harness a final cinch, take a deep breath, and glance at the scripture before barreling down the front stretch under a waving, green flag. At times, my rumbling nerves and the vibration of the car would blur the words on the note, but just seeing its yellow glow behind my steering wheel was enough. I knew God was with me, and the strength I found in Him was sufficient in both victory and defeat. Writing this book was a lot like strapping into a race car. It often felt unpredictable and out of control. At times, I certainly questioned whether or not I would triumph. It was at those moments that I reminded myself of Joshua 1:7 and of the privilege I had of writing a story I believe in and pray God will use to encourage others. For the past five years, this book has been my *Seat*. But, like any successful race driver, I had a championship caliber team supporting me. They pushed, encouraged, coached, and prayed. For that, I am grateful. My beautiful wife, Nicole, endured my endless hours behind a computer after the time-clock was punched at my day job and encouraged me to push forward when sleep beckoned. My daughter, Sienna, seemed to know exactly when levity was needed and would bound into my office with a hug. My parents, Jan and Steve, (both writers themselves) inspired me to take this crazy journey to begin with and kept me on the right path with hours of proofreading and old-fashioned wisdom. My brother, Spencer, with his expertise in design, marketing, and web development was invaluable as we both desire to share the message of *The Seat* with as many people as possible. I'm also appreciative of how hard he pushed me during our early days racing Quarter Midgets together. He is one of the best competitors I have ever driven against. I am thankful for Russel Davis, and the team at Gray Dog Press, for guiding me through the publishing process and producing a stunning final product. Finally, I am indebted to Dennis Held for taking a chance on a rookie author and working with me to edit my manuscript. While I still have much to learn, Dennis coached me beyond what I thought possible. Not all of them were easy to swallow at the time, but Dennis's abundance of handwritten notes in the margins of my early manuscripts shaped my development as an author and will inspire and guide me for years to come. Not only did we develop a manuscript we are proud of, we developed a friendship.

Father God, thank you for the team you have surrounded me with, both on this project and in life. I pray that whoever chooses to read this book would be encouraged. Encouraged to overcome, to chase their dreams, to make the most of their Seat. Most importantly, I pray they choose your unconditional love. Amen

Find out more at TylerIrwinAuthor.com